the Uninvited

TIM WYNNE-JONES

WALKER
BOOKS

U·the·ninvited

TIM WYNNE-JONES has won numerous awards for his work, including an Edgar Award, the Governor General's Literary Award, and a *Boston Globe–Horn Book Award*. He is a faculty member at Vermont College, teaching courses in the MFA program in Writing for Children and Young Adults, as well as the author of more than twenty books for children and young adults, including the popular Rex Zero books. Tim Wynne-Jones lives in Ontario, Canada with his family.

First published in Great Britain 2010 by Walker Books Ltd
87 Vauxhall Walk, London SE11 5HJ

2 4 6 8 10 9 7 5 3 1

Text © 2009 Tim Wynne-Jones

Cover photograph (house) © Keith Levit/Photolibrary.com
Cover photograph (paddle) © Hugh Whitaker/Photolibrary.com

The right of Tim Wynne-Jones to be identified as author of
this work has been asserted by him in accordance with
the Copyright, Designs and Patents Act 1988

This book has been typeset in Meridien

Printed and bound in Great Britain by Clays Ltd, St Ives plc

British Library Cataloguing in Publication Data:
a catalogue record for this book is
available from the British Library

ISBN 978-1-4063-2598-0

www.walker.co.uk

This book is for
the wonderful Lunbergs,
my other family.

≽| PROLOGUE |≼

WAYLIN PITNEY WAS GONE. His white panel truck was no longer parked on the brow of the hill behind the old drive shed. *Good,* thought Cramer. Now maybe things would get back to normal.

He squinted in the light reflecting off the creek. He steadied his canoe, rubbed the back of his hands, torn with new scratches. He was tired from a long paddle upstream but in no hurry to disembark. He looked up again, up the dying hill, already in late-afternoon shadow. There'd been a frost that morning; the day had grown sunny and warm, but it would grow cold again. His mother didn't like the cold. She'd have hung on to Waylin, pleaded with him not to go. It would take Cramer a day or two to bring her down.

There were cockleburs on the sleeves of Cramer's shirt. He pulled them off, one by one, and threw them onto the water. He looked up again, half expecting the truck to still be there. Cramer had dreamed it away so many times, he didn't trust his eyes.

Waylin's "people" had come weeks ago, emptied the vehicle, left it high on its springs. Cramer had watched from his window. There'd been a moon out that night, and the side of the panel truck had shone like an empty movie screen. Two anonymous vans, four shadowy characters, with Waylin smoking, a beer in his hand, giving directions, laughing now and then, as box after box was transferred, money changed hands, and the vans rumbled off into the dark.

Waylin had stayed another week—longer than usual. Cramer had worried he might stay for good this time. But it wouldn't be good, no matter what his mother might like to think. Cramer let her believe what she needed to believe. That's the way you did it. Kept your thoughts to yourself, kept things steady. Kept the shaky boat from tipping.

The truck was gone. And Cramer was pleased but wary.

When Waylin came around, Mavis was happy—her sugar back from the mines, she liked to say. When Waylin came around, there was rock 'n' roll till all hours, cases of Molson Canadian piling up by the door, and that fool jacket of his hanging on the back of a chair. Red, white, and black, with the checkered-flag design and the Pennzoil logo on it as if he were some kind of race-car driver. When Waylin was around, he took over their old Taurus. Some race car.

Mavis would rub Cramer's shaved head and say things like, "Sonny boy, he thinks he can get you a job in the gold mines up there in Val-d'Or. What do you think of that?"

"Hell, yeah," Pitney would join in. "You'd do good in the mines." He'd look Cramer up and down out of the corner of his eye, with this sly smile, like he was checking out something he was planning to steal. "You been hitting the gym, kid? You pumping iron?"

Cramer had all the gym he needed in his bedroom. A bar fixed in his closet door frame, a bench, a few weights. Once, a couple years back, he'd taken a swing at Pitney. The man had grabbed his fist in midflight and whipped it behind his back so fast, Cramer lost his balance and fell over. Pitney hadn't stopped there. He'd pushed Cramer's arm up his back so high, Cramer had cried for mercy. He cried over and over before Pitney stopped. Yeah, Cramer had bulked up, big-time. And he was just dying for Pitney to try anything like that again. But he wasn't going down any mine shaft with him, all the same. He didn't trust the man. And besides, without Cramer looking after her, his mother would not survive. This was the only certainty he allowed himself. Men friends would come and go—there had been others before Waylin. But Cramer was steady as a rock.

Without Cramer, his mother would probably forget to eat. For sure she'd forget to sleep. She'd just paint all the time until her paints ran out. The thing was to keep her in paint and canvas. Keep the dream alive. Keep the Creativity

Pact with herself that she had signed and hung on the wall of her studio. It was something from the book *The Artist's Path*. "I am a creator. I am recovering my inner genius."

The recovery seemed to be taking a long, long time.

A breeze dimpled the water on Butchard's Creek, made the reeds by the bank quiver, bent the grasses on the hill. The canoe rocked gently under Cramer. He paddled into shore.

He stared up at the ramshackle cottage on the bluff, its yellow paint peeling, the roof sagging. His mother's studio window faced this way, the best view in the house. Now the window was full of sky and autumn clouds. He could not see her moving about inside.

He climbed from his canoe and hoisted her onto shore, lifting her by the thwarts and laying her carefully on the bank, his paddle tucked underneath. He took a deep breath and made his way up the hill on a path he had worn himself through the goldenrod and wild asters and spilling milkweed.

The screen door hung open.

He found Mavis on the floor of the studio slouched against a cabinet, her body limp, her left arm trailing on the floor, blood flowing from a deep and ragged cut across her palm.

"Framing a picture," she said. "Hand slipped. Honest. *Hon*est."

Beside her on the floor lay wicked shards of glass, the edge of one of them glistening red as his canoe.

Cramer cleared the space around her with his foot and gripped her forearm to try to stanch the flow. Her face contorted in agony.

"Where've you been?" she whimpered. "Where'd you go to?"

He didn't answer. Found an almost-clean rag on the counter amid her paint supplies.

She swore at him—called him heartless and a lot more—but he had a feeling the name-calling was meant for someone else. He went quietly about his business, made a bandage, pressing her thumb closed to hold it in place. He found another rag, tore it in two, and made a tourniquet.

"Can you stand?" he asked.

He helped her up. She was woozy, unsteady on her feet. He held her tight around the waist and elevated her injured left hand, resting it on his shoulder. She shook her head to get the blond-as-dead-daisies hair out of her face. She stared at him and managed a sad-eyed smile.

"My shining knight," she said.

He lowered his mother into the passenger seat of the Taurus, praying that the car would start, praying Waylin had left some gas in the tank. Mavis slumped against the door, her face pressed against the glass.

The driveway was treacherously steep, and the fall rains had eroded a grand canyon down the center of it. Gingerly he pulled out onto the Upper Valentine, cringing as the front bumper scraped the surface of the road.

Mavis started to sob. Cramer put his foot to the floor. There would be no cops. Not out here. He'd long since stopped hoping someone else would be around when you needed them.

"You hide things," she said after a while, her voice weak and shaky. "You hide things on me."

Cramer gripped the wheel tightly. *You bet I do*, he thought, but didn't dare say it.

"Now you're mad at me," she said. And when he glanced her way, she was leaning back against the head-rest, her eyes closed tightly, her cheeks wet with tears.

"Wasn't suppose to be like this," she said. He wasn't sure which *this* she was referring to.

The doctor in the ER had a round face, hair as short as a man's, and soft brown eyes. "Dr. Page," she said, intro-ducing herself, when they were curtained off from the main room. She carefully undid the tourniquet, tossing Cramer a quick smile. "Is this your handiwork?"

He nodded.

"You should think about a career in medicine," she said.

"Lou" was the name on the doctor's badge. Dr. Lou Page. She cleaned up the site with surgical swabs, mur-muring sympathetically as she doused the wound with antiseptic. Mavis swore under her breath. Over the doc-tor's shoulder, Cramer could see his mother's eyes smol-dering with something more than pain.

He watched as the gaping wound was revealed in all

its horror. It stretched from the fleshy part of the thumb up toward her wrist.

"You've sliced a palmar tributary vein, Ms. Lee," said the doctor. "There might be nerve damage. Can you wiggle your thumb?"

Cramer stared at his mother's thumb as if he might be able to make it move by the strength of his mind. It twitched.

"Well, that's good, then." Dr. Lou sighed. "You were that close to nicking the deep radial. How did it happen?"

Mavis glowered. "I already told the nurse," she said, looking away. Her face was indignant. "An accident. Occupational hazard."

Dr. Lou did not reply. But when Cramer looked closely into her brown eyes, he saw the same question there he had asked himself.

"She's an artist," he blurted out. "She was cutting glass for a picture frame."

Dr. Page looked at him and smiled. "Well, your mother is very lucky," she said. And it felt to him as if she was saying how lucky Mavis was that he had come along when he did. How lucky Mavis was to have a son with skill at bandages and emergency situations.

"I'll have to stitch this up," said Dr. Page. She passed through the pale green curtain, and Cramer heard her calling for a nurse to prep his mother.

"Cow," muttered Mavis, cradling her wounded hand in the other like a broken-winged bird.

Cramer smoothed back the hair from his mother's brow. She shook him off. "Lucky it's your left hand," he said. And his mother cast him a fierce expression.

"Did you hear her?" she whispered. "Did you hear what she was saying?" Mavis stared a hole in the curtain. "She accused me of attempted suicide."

"She didn't say that, Mom."

"She insinuated it."

Cramer sat back in his chair, folded his hands in his lap. He looked down at the linoleum floor, suddenly tired—so tired. When he looked up again, his mother was still staring at the curtain, but there was a sly kind of smile on her dried lips.

"Did you see her necklace, Cramer?" she whispered.

"Necklace?"

Mavis propped herself up on her right elbow and gestured for him to come closer. He leaned over until his ear was level with her mouth. "That big mother of an emerald," she said. "As big as a fingernail?"

For a moment he wondered if maybe his mother was hallucinating. "What about it?"

"Shhh!" His mother's eyes grew wide with alarm. When no one came, she laid her head back on the pillow. And there was that smile again, sneaky. Scheming.

"Did you notice how the green of it was the same as my eyes?" Mavis opened her eyes wide, the better for him to see.

He nodded, just to keep the peace. His mother looked pleased with herself, and he was glad for that.

"You wear a gem like that with a gown, Cramer, not hospital scrubs." She held her right hand to her breastbone as if she were holding a jewel between her fingers, feeling its sharp edges and cool greenness against her sallow skin.

Cramer stroked his mother's shoulder like you might stroke a child who'd had a fight in the school yard and come home with a black eye.

"When you wear a gem like that, people stare. People take notice. Do you think she measures up to a necklace like that, Cramer? I mean seriously?"

Her voice was getting an edge to it that he recognized. He wondered if he could sweet-talk Dr. Lou into some kind of downers. Painkillers.

"Does it do anything for her with her how-now-brown-cow eyes?"

Cramer remembered only the kindness in the doctor's eyes, but he shook his head, just to quiet his mother down. Then suddenly the fingers of her strong right hand grabbed him by the chin, steering him to look her in the eye.

"When she comes back, you take a good long look at that emerald," she whispered. "You tell me if it isn't the same color as my eyes. Like it was *made* for me. You hear me?"

He nodded. "Okay," he said. "Sure."

And he did. And as the nurse and doctor concentrated on their work, he nodded to his mother to let her know he had done what she'd asked.

Her eyes gleamed back at him, the winner of some victory in her head. Then as they left the ER together, Mavis all stitched up and a little container of painkillers tucked in Cramer's pocket, she leaned on him and whispered into his ear, her breath hot and heavy.

"I should have that necklace, honey," she said. Then she kissed him on the cheek. "You get it for me, okay?"

❧ PART ONE ❧

⋙ *Cramer listens. They're up there. Just above the darkness. Mimi is nearer; Jackson is a little way off. Her voice is clearer, though Cramer can't always tell what she's saying. Then Jackson comes near, too, and they don't say anything now, but Cramer can feel them hovering above him, just hanging there. It's as if they're waiting for him to say something, as if they could actually see him. Then they go away and he's alone again, and he tries to put things back together, tries to think how it all happened. There are so many beginnings, so he chooses just one: the summer day he first saw Mimi. The day she arrived at the house on the snye.*

≽| CHAPTER ONE |≼

Mimi missed her turn and screeched to a stop.

"Shit!"

She checked the map on the seat beside her, backed up, and squinted through her own dust at the signpost.

Uppe V lenti e Rd.

"Close enough."

A deep-throated bark seized her attention. A gargantuan dog was tearing toward her from the dilapidated house on the corner.

"Shit!"

The animal bounced up and down at her door, brindle and with far too many yellow teeth. She threw the Mini Cooper into reverse again and slewed to the left, almost hitting the ugly mutt.

"Take that, Hellhound!"

Then she thrust the stick shift forward and left the paved road, sending out a rooster tail of gravel.

Undaunted, the dog stayed on her tail—stayed with her for a hundred yards or so—then finally fell behind, his territory no longer in danger.

Mimi took a deep breath and patted the leather-upholstered steering wheel. "Ms. Cooper, we are now *officially* not in Kansas," she said. And the Mini's horn beeped twice in reply.

The little car was red with a black top, and Mimi had red shades and black hair. She wore a red T-back sports bra and black low-rise capris, as if the car were an accessory. Well, it was small, after all. Like Mimi—small and powerful.

Gripping the wheel tightly in her left hand, she picked up her digital camcorder from the passenger seat and held it at arm's length, aimed at her face.

"News update," she said. "This is Mimi Shapiro reporting from Nowhere!" She swiveled the wine-red JVC HDD around to take in the countryside: the empty dirt road stretching out before her, the overgrown borders and broken-down fences, the unkempt and empty fields, the desolate forest beyond them.

"Not a Starbucks in sight," she said, returning the camcorder to her face. "What do you think, Chet? Have we actually entered the Land that Time Forgot?"

"Well, Mimi," she replied in a low and amiable TV side-kick kind of voice, "you'd think the officials at the border might have warned us about this, wouldn't you? 'Welcome to Canada. Sorry we're out right now.'"

She put the camcorder down in order to negotiate a long S turn, and there up ahead—just to prove her wrong—two huge mud-stained trucks were pulled over onto the shoulder, nose to nose. Farmer One leaned on the driver's side door of Farmer Two. With both hands on the wheel, Mimi swerved around them, glad to be driving such a small and responsive vehicle. Both men wore ball caps, which they tipped as she flew by. They took her *all* in with their shaded eyes, and she wished she hadn't taken her shirt off back at the rest stop on 401.

"Oh, Ms. Cooper," she muttered. "What have we gotten ourselves into?"

She had left New York City yesterday morning and stayed overnight just outside Albany. Then bright and early this morning—way earlier than she was used to—she had set her compass due north, and here she was, though with every passing mile she wondered if maybe Marc had been lying to her. He was hardly the world's most reliable father.

"Almost there," she told herself, to calm her misgivings.

She glanced into her rearview mirror, half expecting Clem and Jed to be on her tail. She imagined them hopping into their trucks to follow the half-naked girl in the toy car. Yee-haw! But the road was empty behind her. She crested a hill. There was a house ahead, though it was hard to tell if anyone still lived in it.

She whooshed by the driveway, where an old woman with an even older dog was collecting the mail from her mailbox. The woman glanced Mimi's way, clutching a letter to her flat chest, glaring at the girl as she flew by. She was wearing a ball cap, too.

"Got to get me one of those," said Mimi.

The road was climbing now. On her right she caught the odd glimpse through the trees of a river—the Eden, she hoped, though it wasn't as impressive as Marc had led her to believe. She wouldn't put it past him to turn a creek into a river. She wouldn't put anything past him.

Lost Creek. She had seen a piece in the Tate Modern by the Irish artist Kathy Prendergast. It was called *Lost* and it was a map of the United States, but the places marked were all lost places: Lost Valley, Lost Hills, Lost Swamp, Lost Creek. All these lost places. She wondered if Prendergast had done a map of the lost places of Canada. She could use it about now. Or GPS.

A magical place, Marc had said. It wasn't the kind of word he used very often. A place to get your thoughts together.

Just then her cell phone started playing "Bohemian Rhapsody." She found it under the map, looked at the number, and threw the cell phone down. It stopped after a while but then started up a few minutes later.

"Fuck off, Lazar Cosic!" she shouted. "What part of 'leave me alone' don't you understand?"

Then she pulled the map out from under the cell

phone and laid it on top. Ontario was a big province—seven times bigger than the Empire State. Surely you could escape someone in a place this large? She pressed a little harder on the accelerator.

Now the road began a lazy decline, and soon she was in the bowl of a wooded valley. Towering maples made a tunnel of the road ahead, though she could see late-afternoon sunlight glinting through the canopy, tinting the leaves with gold as if she had traveled right through summer into fall. She shuddered at the thought. Shuddered at the coolness of this leafy tunnel. She tried to reach her shirt on the backseat but swerved dangerously and gave up. There wasn't a lot of road to work with. Then she was out in the open again, and there was a flurry of tilting and rusted-out mailboxes. And then nothing . . .

In all fairness, Marc had described much of this, but he had never really gotten across the isolation of the place. But that's what she had wanted, wasn't it?

She slowed down and picked up the tiny camcorder again. "Note to self," she said, glancing sideways at the camcorder's beady eye. "Listen to Dorothy next time you think you need to go off and find your heart's desire."

And then she saw it.

"Yes!" she shouted, putting down the camcorder and pounding the ceiling with her fist. "Woo-hoo!" Ms. Cooper beeped her approval.

She brought the car to a stop beside a long driveway, over which a sign read PARADISE.

A new definition of the word, she thought, for at the end of a long dirt driveway, through a field of waist-high grass, stood a handful of fall-down buildings, one of which she supposed must be the farmhouse, though she couldn't tell which one. But it didn't matter, because Paradise was just a marker, not her final destination.

From under the camcorder, iPod, cell phone, Doritos bags, sandwich wrappers, mints, and maps, she found the e-mail from her father. She skipped down to the mention of this sign, highlighted in yellow.

"The letters are two feet high, cleverly constructed out of lengths of cedar sapling cut just so to make the curves of the P, the R, the D, and the S. The driveway to McAdam's Snye will be your next turn on the right."

⋈ CHAPTER TWO ⋈

JACKSON PAGE PICKED UP the Gibson ES-175 gingerly, as if it might be trip-wired to some explosive device. He examined the pickups, the toggle switch, the controls. It wasn't even plugged in, but you couldn't be too careful. No, it was okay. Still in tune—well, close enough for rock 'n' roll. Right. And that was the problem.

"I am regressing," he said to no one. And then he listened to see if no one had any suggestions.

He closed his eyes to try to hear the music in his head. *Simple.* He had already laid down a bunch of tracks, knew the overall shape of the thing, the musical through line, but there was something missing in the final movement. Ha! Movement—as if it were a symphony. Maybe he should say there was something missing in the final stages, as if it were a disease.

The big old guitar was still new to him. He'd found it in a secondhand store in Toronto. The ES-175 was a work-horse in the jazz world, the kind of guitar someone like Pat Metheny played, not some twenty-two-year-old with concert-hall pretensions. Then again, what was he doing playing around with electric guitars at all?

He swiveled his chair westward and tilted the top of the Gibson toward the window of the loft. He watched the daylight glint off the sunburst finish. The light also picked up the dust. He grabbed some polish and a rag from his worktable and set to cleaning the guitar, lovingly, until the lacquer finish gleamed. Just because he was screwing up didn't mean the instruments should suffer.

Simple had started out spare and clean. And serious. He'd been listening to Arvo Pärt and Toru Takemitsu. To Hildegard von Bingen, for Christ's sake! He wanted an unadorned, almost mystical sound, off the top, with lots of space around every note. He'd always known that the piece was going to get weird and dissonant, that "simple" was not easy—that was the point. He just hadn't known *how* weird or dissonant *everything* was going to get. Then yesterday he'd lost it—strapped on the guitar, plugged it into the stomp box, and pretended he was Travis Stever of Coheed and Cambria. As if. He was no rock star. His garage-band days with Snye were far behind him.

Snye had packed the coffeehouse at Ladybank Colle-giate, rocked the legion hall, warmed up for Hammerhead in the city. Their musical influences were ancient: King

Crimson; Yes; Procul Harum; Emerson, Lake and Palmer. Big gaudy stuff. Jay had written all the band's tunes and was the only one who had stayed with music. Got himself a degree and now was taking a year off, courtesy of Mom, to consolidate, to write. Next year—graduate school. Next fall.

So what was *Simple*?

It was *supposed* to be a tone poem, not some emo-punk piece of shit. But right now, emo-punk shit seemed about all he could channel. He had to get serious back. He closed his eyes again. Listened. It was in there somewhere.

He let the quiet build up around him. He started playing the riff he'd recorded yesterday but at half the tempo. He played it sweet. It was an inversion of the first motif, and when you didn't distort the crap out of it, you could hear that.

He plugged the guitar into the amp. Switched it on. There were chorus dials on the Roland: he kept the rate low, cranked the depth up to six. There was that nice flangey sound. He added some reverb. Nice and wet. Pressed the distortion pedal for some crunch.

Right. Rock on, dude. What was he doing?

He dumped it all. Dumped the crunch, dumped the reverb. Everything. He closed his eyes and played the riff over and over, pure and simple, letting it worm into his ear and down into his bones. It was comforting and sad. A teen ballad. He was Linus, and the ES-175 was his electric blanket. A year out of the University of British Columbia and he was backsliding, big-time.

He clamped his hand over the strings, damping the sound. He cocked his head and listened: nothing but the amplifier's throaty hum. He leaned forward, turned the Roland off, and placed the Gibson on its stand beside the baby-blue Stratocaster and the old yellow Martin acoustic. Then he groaned a great long emo-punk-shit groan.

"I am losing my mind," he said.

But what he was really afraid of was that he was losing his sense of what it was he did. They'd crucify him at Indiana. The Jacobs School of Music was right up there with Juilliard and Eastman, for Christ's sake. He had gotten in on great marks and a crazy-good letter of recommendation from Gabriel Zouave, the composer in residence his last year at UBC. Zouave was the one who had recommended Indiana and advised Jay to include the composition *Gunk* in his application, scored for bass clarinet, button accordion, tabla, and street sounds. The people at Indiana had called the piece "cheeky and brave." His lighter side, now missing and presumed dead. Because serious didn't have to be dead serious, right? But it had to be more than jacking off. And here he was playing three-chord riffs on the guitar.

He crossed the loft to the dormer window that looked out over the ragged garden sloping gently down to the snye. He leaned on the sill, and his flash drive, on a string around his neck, tapped against the glass. His kayak was down there in the undergrowth by the stream. You couldn't see it from any approach, as far as he could tell.

There was a row of fist-size stones along the window-sill. He picked one up and rolled it around in his hands. It was blue-green, shot through with cream, and smoothed almost perfectly round by the sea. It was warm from sitting in the sun all day. He held it up to his cheek. Closed his eyes again. Which was when he heard the car.

≫| CHAPTER THREE |≪

It WAS MAGICAL.

The driveway meandered through a meadow alive with slender trees, their bright green leaves trembling. And so was Mimi — trembling with anticipation.

There were wildflowers, all kinds of them. She would get a book. Was there a bookstore in Ladybank? A library? But even without a book, she knew a black-eyed Susan when she met one, and there were hundreds of them, hundreds of Susans waving at her.

And there were buttercups, and pink things.

At a weeping willow, the driveway veered right and passed into a copse of slender who knows what and some other kind of tree, still in showy bloom, though it was already July. Dogwood? The name came to her, but her knowledge of flora and fauna came mostly from fiction. So all she could say with any authority was that it was beautiful. Something from a fairy tale.

"There's this tulloch—that's what they call it," Marc had told her. "In the meadow out back of the house. Back in Scotland, a tulloch is *usually* a fairy mound. Keep your eyes peeled!"

But it wasn't fairies Mimi was thinking of as she glided along the overgrown driveway. This was *Wind in the Willows* territory. And around the next turn, she would surely meet the Piper at the Gates of Dawn. Or Dusk, more likely, since it was getting on in the day.

She came at last to what she knew there would have to be, a tiny bridge to cross the snye. She pulled the car to a stop in a dappled grove and turned off the ignition.

"Snye," Marc had said, as if it were something sexy, a sly new four-letter word. "A side channel that bypasses a falls or rapids and rejoins the river downstream, creating an island. A narrow, meandering thing that sometimes comes to a dead end."

The quiet flooded into her, but it was a busy kind of quiet full of insect sounds and birdsong and the wind in the . . . well, the willows! She climbed out of the car, stretched and yawned, and looked around. It was half fairy tale, half impressionist painting, and half golden-age Disney. "Yeah, so I suck at math," she muttered to Ms. Cooper. Ms. Cooper wasn't listening anymore. "Good baby," said Mimi, patting the hot and dusty side of her car.

She shook her head in wonder and went to examine the bridge.

She was lucky she had stopped.

The bridge only covered a span of about twelve feet but was built over two stone arches, the second of which had crumbled into the stream. Mimi rested her hands on her hips and considered the problem. The narrow drive curved again up ahead, but she could see glimpses of the house between the foliage. It looked as if she would have to complete her journey on foot.

She headed back to the car and was just about to lock the doors when a squirrel chattered at her from a branch not far above her head. Mimi laughed.

"Thanks for reminding me," she said. And she deliberately did *not* lock her doors. This was why she was here, wasn't it? To stop locking things up . . .

The grass beside the driveway was damp. She slipped out of her black-and-red flip-flops and, oh, how cool the earth was under her tired feet. She made her way down the bank to the stream—the snye—a totally magical name. And because of it—this tiny gurgling stream—the other side was an island. Not a very adventurous island, hanging so close to home like this, but an island all the same.

There were water lilies. Of course.

"Snye," she said, "you are too picturesque for your own good. Do you realize that?"

The stream was clear and not very deep, no more than

a foot or so, she guessed. The bed was sandy. Minnows glinted. Jesus bugs flitted across the surface, an everyday miracle. All of it was a miracle. She didn't see anything down there that might nibble on her: no crawfish, suckers, crocodiles. She breathed in deeply and closed her eyes and let the sound of the stream enter her and calm her city brain. The sound of the stream also reminded her of how badly she needed to pee.

She could do it here, surely, she thought, looking around at a grove that was about as treacherous as a postcard. But, for all the traveling she had done in her nineteen years, she was a girl from the Upper East Side, and outside was outside wherever you were.

She needed to ford the snye, but her capris were too snug to roll up. So she headed back to the car and opened the back door. She looked around at the pretty vale— 360 degrees—and then, satisfied that she was alone, she shimmied out of her pants and stuffed them in the suitcase that was open on the backseat. She was wearing a thong, and the air felt silky on her naked backside. She found a pair of cutoffs and slipped her shirt back on, though she didn't bother to button it up.

The water came to just above her knees, deeper than she'd thought. Looks were deceptive, even in pretty vales. She climbed the other bank and slipped her wet feet into her flip-flops before taking to the road again.

And next thing she knew, she was standing in a beautiful wild garden, before a house that was truly something from a fantasy. Not that it was made from gingerbread. Not that it was grand. It wasn't the slightest bit grand. In fact, it was small in scale, like a toy house that had grown up but never really made it into full-blown adulthood. A Munchkin house. There was one gable above a tiny porch with a shed roof held up by pillars to either side of a door that had once been blue. The green roof was dappled with moss and patched here and there, the porch tilted drunkenly forward, and one of the three steps had rotted away. The clapboard was in serious need of paint. It was a dingy white, but it glowed in the west-leaning sun and the windows to either side of the front door gleamed like mirrors reflecting trees and sky. Despite its grungy hide, the house looked far from deserted. It looked loved and welcoming.

For maybe the first time in her life, she blessed her father. He'd finally come through. He had abandoned her when she was scarcely two, and she had hated him for years before bothering to get to know him. And, yes, she was hungry and road weary and she needed desperately to find a bathroom, but for one moment she forgave her father everything.

The plinth under the left-hand column contained a secret drawer in which she found a little tin key box. Yes! Her father had not been here in over twenty years, and the key was just where he said it would be.

She carefully climbed the steps—what was left of them—to the front porch, which was slippery with rot. The flooring bent under her weight.

"All those potato chips," she muttered. She'd work it all off. She imagined herself in a sky-blue do-rag and yellow Oshkosh overalls, with little Disney bluebirds circling her head as if she was some kind of Snow White, returning the cottage to its pristine comic-book self. She would whistle while she worked. Or not. She had never really gotten the hang of whistling.

She tried the key. It didn't fit.

She tried again. She pushed and pulled and jimmied without success. And then, when she looked closer, she realized that the key was a lot older than the lock. In fact, the lock looked new.

She stepped back from the door. She looked at the nearest window. She could not see inside, but she could see what she hadn't thought to notice at first. Marc had said the windows would be boarded up. None of these windows was boarded up. She felt cold all over. The wrong house?

She backed down the steps, slipping and falling to one knee.

Ridiculous! There couldn't be two enchanting little white gabled houses with keys hidden in secret drawers. Not unless she had entered a parallel universe. And Mimi *hated* parallel universes.

Then she remembered her contingency plan. The back door.

"Who knows what the weather will have done to the place," her father had said in his e-mail. "The back door exits into a little shed. There are shelves along the back wall of that shed, and on the top shelf there are old cans of paint. Behind the green can, you'll find the back-door key on a nail."

Mimi scurried around the house to the shed. The shelf along the back wall was still there and so were the cans of paint. She lowered the one whose label was stained green and behind it there was, in fact, a key.

She was just reaching for it, when she heard a noise behind her and glanced back to see a man standing at the entrance to the shed.

"Can I help you?" he said in a voice that did not sound as if he had help in mind.

She turned to face him, pulling her shirt closed. There was no escape. But his voice was young, and Mimi was not easily intimidated.

"I asked you a question!" He had lowered his voice, not in volume, but in pitch, and it made Mimi think of someone who was trying to sound more menacing than he really was. A skinny someone. There were, after all, some skills a girl learned living in the big bad city.

"Well, since you asked so nicely," she said, "I was look-ing for this can of paint."

"Bullshit," he said. "You were looking for the key."

"Got me," she said. "And, by the way, who the hell are you? No wait, hold that thought. I have been driving all day, and if I don't get to a bathroom pretty quick, we're both going to regret it. Me more than you, obviously, but you get my point."

He approached her, angrily, and she stepped out of his way, throwing up her hands, wondering if she had been mistaken about how harmless he was.

"I don't have a cent on me," she said.

He stopped directly in front of her, a head taller than she was but with eyes that while serious could hardly be called menacing. And what she saw hanging around his neck gave her hope.

"Well, actually I did dab on some Trouble by Boucheron, but I have no *money*. Honest!" He didn't seem amused. "Bad joke," she said, lowering her arms. "Sorry."

Meanwhile, he slipped a key into the lock and opened the door.

Indignation rapidly replaced fear, but it would have to wait, for a more pressing problem needed to be addressed first. He faced her from just inside the kitchen door. He pointed to the right.

"It's all yours," he said.

"You bet it is!" she said.

His frown hardened. "Be my guest."

She pushed by him. "We'll see about that," she said curtly. She slammed the bathroom door shut behind her and locked it. Then, as she pulled down her shorts, she looked around for a weapon. A toilet plunger? It would have to do.

≫| CHAPTER FOUR |≪

THE LOCK ON THE BATHROOM DOOR was just a hook and eye. The kind guys in movies break down with one good shove. But she didn't think her "host" looked beefy enough for that. Mimi steamed at the idea of it. She had thought squats were just a city thing. And what if he had been living here for years? Wasn't there some kind of law about squatters' rights?

She flushed the toilet and washed her hands. The tiny bathroom was spotless. A clean towel hung on a rack on the back of the door. Had *he* done this? Was he married? Was he gay?

She reentered the kitchen, without the plunger.

"Thanks," she said. "Now I'd like to know what the hell you're doing here!"

He was sitting at a little table by the window. In the light his hair appeared amber; his eyes looked amber, too, as she got closer. He was slim, all right. Not the breaking-down-the-door type at all. He sported a bit of fluff on his chin that didn't look as if it would ever get a diploma as a full-fledged beard. He was older than her but not by much, she guessed. He didn't look angry anymore, just clinically perturbed.

"Jackson Page," he said, "but I go by Jay. Not that you asked. But a name gives us something to work with."

She folded her arms across her chest. She had buttoned up her shirt in the bathroom. No need to inflame the locals. She noticed a kettle on the stove, a teapot waiting on the counter. The kitchen, like the bathroom, was Spartan, but in apple-pie order.

"Sorry," she said. "I'm Mimi. Nice to meet you, Jay. And now that we've got the intros out of the way, do you live here?" He shook his head. "Well, that's good," she said. "Because this is private property."

Jay pushed himself back from the table and stretched out his legs. He was wearing white jeans and an olive drab tee. And the memory stick around his neck. She didn't think the average redneck carried a memory stick, but she didn't know about the average psychopath. "So, you're the one who's been leaving the little messages?" he said.

Now it was her turn to look perplexed.

"Messages?"

"The bluebird. The snake skin. The cricket. The voice."

Mimi backed up a step. "What?" Jay looked more or less normal—handsome, even. But he was clearly nuts. *In which case, gently does it, Mimi, and stay as close to the door as you can.*

"Funny," she said. "I was thinking about bluebirds only ten minutes ago, but the animated ones, you know? In *Snow White*."

He didn't speak, just stared at her, frowning, waiting. The muscles along his jawbone twitched.

"Well, my bluebird was not animated," he said. "It was dead. It was lying right here on the table."

She stared at the table, at his hands resting there, making a nest for an invisible dead bird. His hands were long and slender but strong looking. He wore a yellow bangle around a slim but muscled wrist. *Stay on task,* she told herself.

"Could it have gotten in somehow—the bluebird, I mean—and then tried to escape through the window?"

He shrugged. "I have no idea," he said. "You tell me."

"Well, I just did. Except it was only a guess."

"And the snake skin?"

Mimi rolled her eyes. "Listen, the only snakeskin I've ever seen was on a really nice pair of boots at Bloomingdale's."

His frown lessened. Or at least his forehead uncreased a little.

"I couldn't afford the boots. And seriously, I have no idea what you are talking about."

"This snake skin was curled on the pillow on my bed," he said.

"Eeuw! But I thought you said you didn't live here."

"I don't. I crash sometimes. I have a mattress in case I end up working late."

"'Working late'?"

"We were talking about the snake skin," he said.

"Right." Mimi shuddered. "That is gross!"

"Yes, it is."

Her arms were still crossed, and she hugged herself a little tighter at the thought of what he was saying. Then the kettle whistled and he got up to attend to it.

She backed out of his way, but from the way his head was hanging, she didn't think he was much of a threat anymore. Kind of sweet, really.

"So, Jay," she said, her voice upbeat, "what is it you do here? Which is not the same as what are you *doing* here—a question you still haven't answered."

He grinned a little. He was still clearly pissed, but just maybe she could win him over. She had a habit of shooting first and asking later, but she did not want this to get messy.

"You want some tea?" he asked, good manners winning out over smoldering resentment.

"Thanks," she said. "Tea would be good."

"There's no milk," he said.

"And no lemon, I guess."

He shook his head. "No fridge." Then, with the tea

steeping in a Brown Betty teapot, he resumed his seat at the little table. She pulled out the chair across from him. It was a bright yellow chair that might have seemed cheery under different circumstances.

"I'm still waiting," she said.

But he stirred his tea and wouldn't look at her.

"Listen," she said, "whatever's been happening here, it wasn't me. I left New York yesterday and crossed the Peace Bridge at around two this afternoon, entering Canada for the first time in my life."

He looked at her candidly.

"And I hate snakes," she said. "Except in expensive boots."

He smiled. What a treat! Maybe she'd keep him around—as a maid. Then the smile wilted. He sighed and lowered his head. He knitted his fingers together.

Shit, she thought. *He's going to say grace.*

But he was just sad. Sad and drained.

"This stuff has really gotten to you, huh?"

He looked up at her and nodded. "You could say that. Somebody obviously doesn't love me being here."

It was the perfect segue. But some instinct made Mimi hold her fire. She knew she'd have to burst this guy's bubble sooner or later, but she was intrigued. And she wasn't stupid, either. If somebody didn't want Jay here, was that somebody going to take kindly to her?

"It's not what you'd call an all-out terror campaign," she said. "I mean you haven't found any dolls that look like you with pins stuck in them or pentagrams written in blood on the door, right?"

He chuckled. But then he looked hard at her, and his shiny brown-gold eyes glowed so strongly she had to look away. That wasn't something she did very often.

He poured their tea at the counter. "In a way, it's worse," he said, handing her a mug. "Come on."

He led her from the kitchen into a front room that was empty except for a vacuum cleaner standing guard in one corner and a beanbag chair by the east-side window with a few books and magazines strewn around it. Through a door she saw a mattress on a bare floor in the only other room. The bed was covered with a bright blue comforter.

There was a stairway with light cascading down it like a warm yellow carpet. She followed him up to the second level, and this was another story altogether. She had heard about this from her father, but he had been vague about the details, either because he'd forgotten or preferred to keep it a surprise. And what a surprise!

There had been interior walls up here, a bedroom or two, but they were gone now. The space was wide open — a loft — with posts and beams to take the weight of the missing walls. The room was naturally lit by a gable window in the front and one in the back. There was also a window at the east end and two smaller windows to either side of the chimney stack on the west wall. The floor was stained with colorful spots and dribbles, courtesy of her father. A large carpet of industrial gray twill covered most of the central space, and on the carpet sat a couple of Ikea-type trestle tables, upon one of which sat an impressive Mac connected by all sorts of cables and adapters and who knows what to a couple of synthesizers and an array of black boxes stacked in a rack behind what she guessed had to be some kind of mixing board. There was a ratty-looking Yamaha keyboard and several other electronic thingies strewn on the floor, their little LED lights glowing in readiness. Guitars were arrayed on stands around Action Central. So was what she thought must be an electronic drum kit. There were mikes on stands, speakers and headphones, and a music stand and . . .

"Shit!" she said. "It's a recording studio."

He laughed. "Well, sort of," he said modestly. Then once again his face fell and he looked sad, defeated. She carefully put down her mug of tea on the floor by the stairs.

"I have bad luck with liquids and computers," she said. "I fried my laptop with a double latte."

"Bummer," he said. But his mind was elsewhere. "I want you to hear something."

He cleared a space on the desk and put down his own teacup. Then he booted up the Mac. He sat, put on a pair of headphones, and started moving things around on the screen with a mouse, so quickly and expertly that she didn't have time to catch what he was doing. When he stopped, the screen was filled with blocks of color like a Mondrian painting on a gray background. He vacated his seat and the headphones.

She sat and he placed the headphones on her and tightened them for her. And when she nodded that she was comfortable, he punched the space bar.

Simple was written in the title band at the top of the screen. There were instrument names written in a list down the left-hand side of the screen. It was some kind of musical composition. Yes. There was a goofy-sounding riff played, she guessed, on the Yamaha. Her mother had bought her a similar keyboard when she was a kid, before her musical talents had been tested and found to be non-existent. But the goofy theme soon was undermined by a deep and resonant sound and a wind song that seemed to blow the melody out of the water, replacing it with a harmonically complex tune that she realized was a variation of the rinky-dink Yamaha melody. Meanwhile, a rhythm was beginning to pulse under the rich tapestry of sound, picking up momentum. She nodded in time with it, smiling.

"Can you hear it?" he asked.

She went to take off the headphones, but he stayed her hand. He wanted her to keep listening. "Hear what?" she said, too loud, because of the music pounding in her ears. The question was ridiculous.

"Listen closely," he shouted.

She concentrated but felt a little exasperated. This was nuts! And then suddenly she heard something unexpected. Unexpected because it was random—out of sync to the orchestration. A chirping sound.

She looked up at him. "The cricket?" she said. He nodded. Then he reached over her shoulder and paused the piece, and she leaned back in the chair and pulled off the headphones. She looked at him. "You didn't put it there?" He shook his head. "And you can't get rid of it?"

He shrugged. "I can. I mean it's on its own track. But it took me awhile to figure it out."

Mimi looked at the screen, at the charts and graphs there that indicated the paused music. There were tracks arrayed down the screen; each instrumental voice had its own. And sure enough, there was a track labeled "cricket." She pointed at it.

"Yeah, well, when I figured it out, I labeled it," he said. "I mean, at first I thought it must have just gotten in the house and I'd picked up the sound of it. You see there's an acoustic guitar track that isn't recorded direct."

"English, please."

"Sorry. I had to mike the guitar, and if there had been any ambient sound in the room, the mike would have picked it up. But when I listened to that track, it was fine. No cricket."

"And the other tracks?"

"Direct."

"And, like, there couldn't be a cricket actually *in* the computer . . . No. I guess that would be your classic really stupid question."

"So?"

Mimi wasn't sure if she got it, but when she looked

into Jay's face, she could see that he wanted her to try.

She twirled around slowly in the chair and stared out the eastern window. A rough meadow rose to a low hill. Was this the tulloch that Marc had told her about? A hundred yards beyond it, there was an impenetrable wall of conifer green, as if that was the end of the magic vale and the beginning of the proverbial deep, dark forest. The one your father took you out to get lost in if you didn't remember to bring your bread crumbs.

"You're saying someone sat here and actually recorded that sound onto your piece—into it?"

"Yes," said Jay.

"Weird," said Mimi.

"And now listen to this," he said.

"Now wait, enough already. We have to talk."

"Just one more thing," he said.

"Seriously, Jay—"

"Please," he said, interrupting her. "I haven't told anyone about this shit, and it's been driving me crazy."

She could see that. Okay. With one last glare, she put the headphones back on while he zipped around with the mouse, moving ahead in the score. Then he pushed the space bar again. The music had progressed into a driving rhythm with a wailing guitar over the top, and if it was Jay playing, he was pretty good. But she knew now that compliments were not what he was after. So she sank down below the sound, and this time there were no crickets. But there was something odd. Something that she didn't think was supposed to be there. She scanned the instrument tracks. No. Not listed.

Someone was breathing. Breathing hard. But not in the sexual sense—it didn't sound like that. It just sounded like someone breathing to be heard.

She took off the headphones and rolled her chair away from the table. She got up, wanting to be as far away from the computer and that breathing as she could get. "Okay, that is fucking weird," she said.

Jay nodded, his face grave, but softened by what she guessed must be gratitude.

"Let me get this straight. You've changed the locks?"

"Yeah," he said. He had taken the seat and was putting the computer to sleep.

"So this weirdo guy—does he come in through the window?"

"Who says it's a guy?"

"It's a guy," she said. "Trust me."

Jay threw up his hands. "Okay, whatever, Sherlock." She walked over to the gable window and felt around the frame. Painted shut. No sign of being opened in years.

"I already checked," said Jay. "They're all like that, except for the one on the eastern wall. I had opened it to air the place out."

"Ah!" said Mimi, turning and resting her butt against the sill. "In New York we have second-story men. Ever heard of those?"

Jay nodded. "Yeah," he said. "I was kind of slow on

the uptake. Then I remembered the ladder."

"A ladder? How convenient is that?"

He snorted. "It's an old rickety, handmade thing. I found it out in the meadow. I think it was used for picking apples. I used it myself to fix some broken glass. Then I stowed it in the rafters in the shed. When I went to look at it again, the feet were muddy. I hadn't put it back that way."

Mimi nodded and looked around. "No muddy-footed ladder for our Jackson," she said. "You're a pretty anal guy, right?"

"If you want to call it that." Jay stood up, shoved his hands in his pockets.

"All I mean is it's so *tidy*," she said. "That isn't exactly common among twenty-year-olds."

"Twenty-two," he said. "Twenty-three in September."

"Ah, well. There you go."

"People use the term *anal* as if it's some kind of disease," he said. "You know what it means to me? It means getting organized. Staying on track. Getting things done."

"But you're an artist," she said. "What about creative chaos and all that?"

"Art is the opposite of chaos," he said. Then he smiled. "And thanks for the compliment. If it was one."

"It was," said Mimi. "The music is dead cool. And hey, sorry about ribbing you. You've got like sixty million dollars' worth of electronics here, so dust and crud are probably not a *good* thing. Let alone heavy breathing."

"Thank you."

"So," she said, taking a deep breath. "You smashed the ladder to little bits with an ax and nailed all the windows shut and that was that, right?"

He shook his head. "No. But I did chain the ladder to the rafters and locked it with my titanium bike lock."

"Ha!"

"What?"

"Those things are so easy to break," said Mimi. "You just spray the thing with starter fluid—*pssssssssst!*—pop it with a hammer and—*poof!*—titanium dust."

"More wisdom from the city."

"Hey, I lost three bikes before a cop finally set me straight."

"Well, anyway," said Jay, "nobody's touched the ladder since." He leaned against a post. "And still this he or she or *it* manages to get in, access my computer, and leave behind some heavy breathing."

"Fairies?"

But Jay wasn't listening. "There has to be a way in that I haven't discovered," he said.

Mimi smacked her palm to her forehead.

"What?"

She took his hand. "Come on." She led him downstairs and into the bedroom.

Mimi got to her knees and started feeling the floor with her hands, fingers splayed. It was parquet, a pattern of squares of different-colored wood.

"Did you lose a contact?" he asked.

"Uh-uh," she said. She ran the edge of her thumb along an almost imperceptible groove. "Move your mattress."

"What?"

"Really. Just do it!"

He lifted the foam mattress and pushed it vertically against the wall. By then she'd found what she was looking for, a loose square of wood, which she lifted to reveal a circle of brass, laying flat on the underflooring. She lifted the ring and then pulled harder. A trapdoor opened.

"Voilà!"

"Holy shit!"

"No," said Mimi. "A hidey-hole. Kind of a nineteenth-century panic room."

He joined her and lifted the door completely open. It was heavy. Chains held it from folding all the way back. They peered down into a space about five feet deep, a tiny earthen room.

"I've been using this house for years," said Jay, "and I had no idea that was here."

"There's a tunnel to the outside," said Mimi. She was glowing with the sweat of lifting the heavy door.

"How did you know about it?" he asked.

She looked up at him, pushed a wing of hair back from her eyes.

"My father told me about it," she said. "He . . . Well, he owns this place."

Jay stared at her, his mouth hanging open. Then he closed it and swallowed. "That's really funny," he said at last. "Because *my* father owns this place."

≫| CHAPTER FIVE |≪

CRAMER LEE SAT IN HIS CANOE in a stand of bulrushes so dense and high it was like being in a small green room. A windowless room with a high blue ceiling and a browny-green shimmering carpet. A room laced together with the whirring of dragonflies.

A breeze picked up, and his hands gripped the gunwales steadying his craft, steadying himself. His breathing was ragged with excitement. He wiped the sweat off his face and then picked up the digital movie camera that he cradled in his lap. He flipped open the viewer screen and started it.

"*A Murder of Good-Byes*, a documentary by Mimi Shapiro," said a perky voice. It was her—the girl in the car. She was wearing a yellow summer dress with thin straps.

A flower-print little-girl dress revealing a lot of leg. She was standing in a living room in front of a modern-looking fireplace with a pale green marble front, veined in white. On the mantel were sculptures—African, he guessed.

"First of all, Dmitri," she said, and the eye of the camera swept around a lavishly appointed room to a golden-colored couch, where some kind of long-haired Siamese-type cat lounged, staring impassively toward her as she coaxed it to speak.

"Say, 'Good-bye, Mimi,'" she said. "'Meow, Mimi.'"

The cat looked away as if with disdain. But Cramer wasn't interested in the cat. The room seemed gilded with light, something from a movie or a fancy magazine.

"Good-bye, apartment," said Mimi. And then she took him on a tour of her home that ended in her bedroom, where she said good-bye to a stuffed monkey named Ray and every item of furniture.

"Good-bye, bed. Good-bye, closet. Good-bye, dresser. Good-bye, vanity," she said, and then she laughed as if she had made a joke. The camera grazed the floor strewn with clothing, CDs, magazines. From her window she aimed the camera down to a city street six or seven floors down. A yellow cab pulled up below, and she watched someone get out and disappear from view under the awning over the front doorway. Then her camera floated out toward a busy intersection and suddenly stopped. The girl swore and the camera faded to black.

New York, thought Cramer, but he already knew that

from the Mini Cooper's plates.

The movie continued. Now the camera focused on a faggy-looking Asian guy with his top button done up and yellow thick-rimmed glasses.

"Say good-bye, Rodney," said the voice behind the camera.

"Good-bye, Rodney," said the boy. "Oh, my God! Am I going, too?"

"Not this time, oh favorite rummage-sale friend. Mimi must make the trip to the Great White North alone."

"To find herself," said Rodney. "And lose you-know-who."

"Amen," she answered.

Then Rodney smiled and waved a faggy wave, which Mimi held on to in another long slow fade.

When she faded back in, the scene had changed and there were two girls in a park somewhere, one holding on tightly to the leash of a Doberman. "We want cheesy post-cards of Mounties," she said. "Right, Jamila?"

"Or real Mounties," said Jamila. "Bring back a real Mountie we can share."

Again the screen went to black, and Cramer wondered if the little show was over, until he heard the sound of low jazz and the hubbub of a restaurant: clinking plates and glasses, people talking, laughing, muffled traffic. The black was not really black anymore, but only a dark ceiling. The camera panned downward until the lens was full of a man's face, paunchy, nearly bald, but with wisps of sandy-colored hair fading to gray at the temples.

"Here's the father figure hiding shamefully behind dark glasses."

The man's smile was low-key but indulgent. "Good-bye, sweetheart," he said.

Then he lazily reached for a glass of red wine, from which he sipped while she trained the lens on him. He looked away, scratched at his unshaven cheek, waved at someone across the room, and then turned back toward Mimi, all without her moving the camera. He waved his hand as if shooing away a fly. She stayed on him and then zoomed in until his face became distorted and there was little on the screen but his nose, blue-veined—a drinker's nose.

"Is there anything I should say to Canada when I get there?"

As Mimi zoomed out again, the man sipped his wine and sniffed, but not because of any strong emotion that Cramer could see on his placid face. All Cramer could see where his eyes should have been were two Mimis reflected in his shades.

"You had the car checked?"

"Yes, Father dearest."

"And you phoned the insurance people?"

"Daddy—"

"Just checking," he said, downing his wine. "It's a parental prerogative."

"Like you'd know anything about parenting," she said.

Cramer gasped, half expecting the man to slap her. But Mimi's father only chuckled and put down his glass.

"You're supposed to say, 'drive sensibly and be careful,'" said Mimi.

Her father scratched his neck. "Yeah, well, I'll leave that to your mother. She's the expert on parenting, right?"

He called a waiter, and Mimi made the waiter say good-bye and wish her good luck. Her last shot was of a number of crisp dollar bills left on a white plate.

Cut.

And now, at last, the girl seemed to be sitting in the little red car with her camera aimed through the open passenger window at the front door of what Cramer guessed must be the apartment building in which she lived. THE SAXBOROUGH, it said on a brass plate. It was red brick and there were flower boxes bursting with blooms, under many mullioned windows, alive with sunny reflections, but with black bars on them to keep the world out. Dead center of the tiny screen was the awning he had seen earlier from above and standing under it, half in shadow, was a woman in a suit, with strong, shapely legs and high heels, her hand grasping a black leather briefcase.

"Action," shouted the camera-girl, and the woman, on cue, walked out from under the canopy into the light and down the short walkway to the sidewalk with an impatient smile on her expensive face. She had gold earrings, gold hair, and some kind of a huge scarf wrapped around her shoulders.

"This is high-powered tax attorney Grier Shapiro of Cavendish, Goldfarb, Shapiro, and Vik, saying good-bye to her only child. Say 'Good-bye, Mimi, dear,'" said Mimi.

The woman poked her head in the window, arched her stenciled eyebrows, but smiled and complied. "Good-bye Miriam," she said. Up close, Cramer could see the wrinkles on her turkey neck that her makeup couldn't hide.

"Did you remember your passport?" she asked.

"Oh, my goodness!" said Mimi. "Is Canada a separate country?"

Her mother smiled wryly. "Phone me tonight," she said. "On my cell. I'll be at a fund-raiser until about nine."

"Yes, Mommy dearest."

"And drive sensibly, darling," said the mother, her voice sounding more irritable than concerned.

"I will. And I promise I won't give any hitchhikers a lift unless they have a degree from an accredited university," said Mimi.

"You are insufferable," said the mother.

"And I promise never to drive over a hundred," said the camera-girl. And then before her mother could argue, she added, "*Kilometers* per hour."

Her mother looked vexed, but then her expression softened. "I'll miss you, you awful child," she said. "Be careful and *thoughtful.*"

"I will be careful, Mom," said the girl, with real affection. "Hey, nothing bad happened in London last summer or *Firenze*—ahhhh, *Firenze*! Well, nothing I couldn't handle. So what could happen in Canada? Aren't they mostly famous for being polite?"

"Not the moose or the bears," said her mother. "And there are Socialists up there. They've got their own political party, from what I hear."

"Well, I'll watch out for moose and bears and Socialists. Anything else?"

Her mother touched her fingers to her lips, kissed them, and reached out to touch her daughter's lips.

Mimi made an exaggerated kissy sound, and then Grier withdrew her hand.

"Phone!" she said, wagging her finger at the lens. She left, looking at her watch as she marched sharply to the corner, where she hailed a cab. One stopped immediately.

Cramer fast-forwarded through scenery and strangers in roadside diners and gas stations until he came to a close-up of Mimi's own face fringed in dark pixie hair and with her impossibly blue eyes. Cramer's heart rate speeded up.

"News update," she said. "This is Mimi Shapiro reporting from Nowhere!" She swiveled the camera around to take in the countryside.

"Not a Starbucks in sight," she said, returning the camera to her face. But for a second the lens took in her cleavage, too.

His arms went limp and he lowered them to his lap. He closed the viewer, resisting the urge to look at her again. He closed his strong hands around the camera. It was red, a

JVC HDD, with thirty gigabytes of drive. Laser-touch panel operation. He could guess what it was worth, a thousand bucks or so, and yet so small he could completely conceal it in his grip.

So many toys, he thought.

He took a deep breath. Closed his eyes tight. If only he'd had this camera when she had changed by the car. If he closed his eyes, he could see her, almost entirely naked, the cheeks of her butt paler than her tanned legs.

This changed things.

What happened now?

He would be patient. Patience was his greatest gift. He had read something about that in his mother's book *The Artist's Path.* "Above all else, be patient with yourself. The overzealous boater swamps his craft."

Cramer had felt the author was talking directly to him with that quote. But he knew she wasn't talking about canoes. He understood what she meant, all right.

Calmer now, he stared toward where the house on the snye stood, though he could not see it from here, anymore than they could see him. He tugged on his one gold earring. Tugged until it hurt.

He wondered what they were up to in there. Was she a new girlfriend?

He took a long deep breath.

The wind picked up again and rocked him. From the look of what she had in the car, Mimi was planning on more than an overnight visit. So she was going to be around for a while. The thought made Cramer's blood buzz in his veins.

⇒∣ CHAPTER SIX ∣⇐

JAY AND MIMI STARED at each other for one very long uncomprehending moment, standing in the middle of his bedroom by the gaping hole in the floor.

"Marc Soto, the artist," she said.

"Right."

Then Jay led her back to the kitchen to sit down.

"I feel numb," said Mimi. "Catatonic."

"Catatonia is characterized by rigidity of the muscles," said Jay. "You're as wobbly as Jell-O."

She stared at him. "I'm impressed," she said.

"Yeah, well, I'm not only anal; I'm a doctor's son."

They sat for long moments at the table not quite able to look straight at each other. Embarrassed—at least he was. He had been entertaining *thoughts* about her, for Christ's sake! Thoughts that now made him cringe, but only sort of. And that made it worse. Then a desperate idea occurred to him.

"Your birth father?" he said.

She nodded, frowning, as if she wished it weren't true. Then she looked down again, suddenly demure, though that seemed the last word he would ever use to describe her.

Then finally their eyes snagged, and he tried to say what neither of them had been actually able to articulate yet.

"So you're like . . . We're . . . I'm your . . ."

She laughed. "Nice try, Shakespeare," she said.

They looked hard at each other—looking for themselves in each other's faces. That was what he was doing, anyway, and assumed she was doing the same. "You've got Marc's forehead," she said.

"I wouldn't know."

"Trust me."

"I've never laid eyes on the man," he said.

"Not even photographs?"

He shrugged. "Yeah, I guess. When I was a kid. He left before I was born." The answer seemed inadequate to him, as if he should have cared more.

She was staring at his face again, her eyes taking him in with an intimacy that made him a little breathless. "You've got the line of his jaw, too," she added. "Or what it used to be like. Now his face has gone all kind of spongy."

Jay felt his jaw with his hand, realized how tightly clenched it was.

"Are you okay?"

She sounded so solicitous. And after a moment he was able to say yes, which was ridiculous, really, under the circumstances. Then his mind wandered back to the hidey-hole, and he must have glanced in the direction of the bedroom, because she stood up and reached for his hand again. He didn't take it this time.

Jay dropped down into the earthen room. The floor was compacted soil, as were the walls. The tunnel was only a meter high and only a couple of meters long. He crawled along it to another trapdoor. How could he not have seen the trapdoor outside? But when he pushed it up and open, he found himself directly behind the shed in a dense thicket of prickly ash, which shielded the doorway. Ducking his head, making himself as small as possible, he crawled through the thicket out to the scruffy patch of long grass and the wall of undergrowth and scrubby cedar that pressed up against the shed. He never came back here.

Mimi followed on her knees. She swore colorfully. He helped her up, pulled away a thorny twig tangled in her hair. She stared at him, her expression unguarded. His gaze slipped away. Her eyes were ultramarine, so vivid that he wondered if she was wearing special contacts.

Closed, the storm door looked like a stained and filthy piece of plywood left to rot, propped up against the back wall of the house, deep in a winterkill of leaves. Nothing more. In the shadow of the house, it was hardly visible.

Jay shuddered. He shoved his hands into his pockets and walked out into the sunlight. He walked halfway down the lawn to the snye, then stopped. There was a bit of wind out there in the open. He realized he had been holding his breath and let it out now.

Mimi followed him silently. It seemed she was out of things to say. Who could blame her? There was far too much to say to know where to start. She wandered past him down toward the snye. He didn't follow, just watched her, as if she were some exotic animal that might bolt if he moved.

Mimi . . . Mimi . . . Where had he heard that name before? Ah, right: the waif in Puccini's *La Bohème.* Mimi was no waif. She was thin, but only in the right places— not in any danger of wasting away. He allowed himself a good long look. His sister.

His cell phone rang.

He dug it out of his pocket, looked at the name on the screen. "Hi, Jo," he said.

Mimi leaned against a tree, down near the water's edge.

"Jackson, I have purchased the most wonderful salmon," came the voice on the phone.

"Uh . . . okay," said Jay hesitantly.

"Are you all right?"

No, he thought. *Not even close!* But he was not going to talk about this over the phone, not even to his mother's partner. "I'm fine, Jo," he said.

She paused for just a fraction of a second, seeing through him, no doubt. "Well, you will be more than fine when you see this fish. And that's why I'm phoning."

"You're phoning about a fish?"

"Uh-huh," said Jo. "I was hoping I could interest you in making your famous coriander-and-lemon-zest rub."

"Uh . . . I don't know."

"Don't say you're too busy. It's Friday night, for goodness' sake."

Jay was going to protest but checked himself. "Okay. Sure. Why not?"

"Great."

"Yeah. So I'll see you around . . . What time is it now?"

"It's sixish. Jay? You sound funny. What's up?"

Mimi had turned and was staring at him now.

"I'm out at the snye," he said, as if that answered Jo's question. Mimi looked tiny suddenly—a little bit frightened, even.

"The creativity battle not going so well?" asked Jo.

"Actually, no," he said, his voice now pitched loud enough for Mimi to hear. "The battle is not going well at all."

Mimi smiled a terrible smile.

"Well, like I said, it's Friday night. Lighten up. Lou says she'll break out one or two of those New Zealand sauvignon blancs she's been hoarding."

"Cool."

"Maybe you have other plans?"

"No," he said. Then he realized that this was not entirely true. "Well, I might. Have other plans, I mean. Except . . ." Mimi was already shaking her head. "Jo, mind if I bring someone?"

Mimi started up the lawn toward him, frantically waving her hands back and forth, nixing the idea.

"Is it Iris? Is she home?"

"No, it's not. Actually, Jo, it's another woman," he said, glancing Mimi's way. She looked horrified, and it brought out the devil in him. "You should meet her," he said.

"Is she pretty?"

"Naaah, not really pretty. But amusing."

Mimi was standing right in front of him now, giving him the finger. She made as if to grab the phone, but he turned away, holding his elbow up to block her.

"Amusing is good," said Jo. "And the salmon is huge. And the girl . . . is this serious?"

Jay stared straight at Mimi. "No, nothing serious," said Jay. "Just some girl." Mimi rolled her eyes and walked away. "Uh, Jo, it'll take me a while to get home."

"I'm all wrapped up at the office. Won't be home myself until after seven."

"No problem," he said. Then they said good-byes, and he flipped the cell phone closed and shoved it in his pocket.

"That was so sweet, Jay," said Mimi, giving him a look that could turn titanium to dust. "But I really don't want to party tonight."

He nodded. "I know what you mean. But I think this may be good."

She slapped her hands against her thighs. "Seriously, I am not into an evening with Joe and the boys."

Jay threw back his head and laughed.

"This is not a laughing matter!"

"Sorry," he said. "It's just that Jo is *Joanne*, and, believe me, she is *not* one of the boys."

"Your girlfriend?"

"Guess again."

"Oh, shit, your mother. And you've got to start the macaroni and cheese because she's going to be late getting home from the office."

"I *do* have to start dinner, yes. But Joanne was asking if I'd make my coriander-and-lemon-zest rub for the salmon she's bringing home. And Joanne, by the way, is my mother's partner."

He watched her closely. She looked surprised, not shocked. Good. Then she just looked amused. "Can this day get any stranger?"

Jay shrugged. "I don't see how."

Mimi shook her head, but he didn't think she was saying no.

"So you'll come?"

She nibbled on her bottom lip. "I guess. I mean, how can I turn down salmon with a coriander rub?" Then she looked thoughtful. "Just as long as your mom and her girlfriend aren't Socialists. My mother warned me there are lots of those up here."

He grinned. "Lou's a lefty," he said. "Jo's a fiscal Conservative. They sort of balance each other out. But do not talk politics if you can avoid it."

Mimi looked at him with a sheepish grin. He guessed it was an expression she didn't use very often.

"So, as you've probably noticed, you've got an idiot for a sister."

He reached out and touched her arm. Made her look at him.

"Are you sure you want to take an idiot home to meet the folks?" she asked.

"Yes. Absolutely. And we should probably get going."

Mimi nodded but her shoulders drooped. He put his arms around her, and the next minute she was sobbing and swearing and smacking her palms against his chest and then holding him close. They rocked back and forth, and neither of them could think of anything to say for a very long time.

⇒| CHAPTER SEVEN |⇐

IT WAS ONLY a twenty-minute paddle by kayak down-stream to Jay's place, but he would ride with Mimi in her car. Before they left, she helped him move the table from the kitchen to the bedroom. It was surprisingly heavy. They laid it upside down on the trapdoor and piled the vacuum cleaner and a couple of chairs on top. It was the best they could do. Then they carried his kayak up to the enchanted little house. He wasn't going to leave it outside.

"Sorry for the mess," she said as she moved all the debris from the passenger seat to the back. She almost cried with relief when she saw everything was still there: her cell phone, iPod, and the new camcorder. Not because of the value of these things—well, not *just* because of the value—but because seeing them there restored something of the golden feeling she had felt when she first arrived at the place so little time ago.

"You look a little freaked," he said.

She tried to shrug it off. "It's just my stuff," she said. "I love my stuff."

Her little red-and-black car, her colorful tangle of clothing strewn all over the backseat—her room away from home. And she felt very far from home now. She phoned her mother right away, at the office. She was tied up in a meeting, so Mimi left a message with the secretary. "Tell her I'm here. Tell her everything is fine." There was nothing else she could say. Not yet. Jay raised an eyebrow. "Yeah, well . . ." Then she sat in the driver's seat for a moment, dazed.

"Not phoning Dad?"

"Screw him," she said.

Another long moment passed.

"What's the matter?" said Jay.

She meant to laugh, because it was a pretty crazy thing to say. But before she knew it, she was crying again, surprising herself probably more than Jay. Then she swore a bit, pushed her hair back off her face, and got herself together. He patted her shoulder, saying stupid, gentle things, until she pushed him away and finally managed to laugh.

"Jesus!" she said. "Enough with the big-brother routine!"

She wiped her eyes and spun the Mini around, heading back out toward the road. She glanced at him as she turned onto the Upper Valentine.

Her brother. Jesus!

🐟 🐟 🐟

They were quiet for a long time on the ride before she said, "I can't believe he never told me about you."

And Jay laughed. "Yeah, a bit of a kick to the ego," he said.

"I didn't mean that!"

"I know, I know. Take it easy. But like I said, I've never met my father, let alone talked to him. No birthday cards, nothing."

They drove a fair bit farther still before Mimi said, "That's something he's good at," she said. "Leaving people."

There was a tall cedar hedge bordering the front of the Pages' half-acre lot on the north bank of the Eden River a few minutes out of town. The driveway curved leisurely to a turnabout in front of a modern house of floor-to-ceiling glass and honey-colored stone, one story high, with a roof of cedar shakes and set on a well-tended lawn, splendid with maple, willow, and butternut trees.

The path to the front door wound through a flower garden of irises and poppies, the borders brimming with blossoms Mimi didn't know the name of but that were pink and purple and lavender and cream. A tilting stone Saint Francis looked down in a saintly way at a stone toad sitting in a patch of white alyssum, which held the saint's gaze with amphibian reverence. Jay unlocked the door and turned off the security system.

"Ah, the tranquillity of country living," said Mimi.

Jay shrugged. "We never even used to lock the doors until last fall. We had a break-in. My mom lost some jewelry."

Mimi shook her head. "What is this, the crime capital of Canada?" It was meant to be a joke, but from the expression on Jay's face, it hit a little too close to home.

Inside was deliciously cool, a cool blond house. It was open and airy. There were maple floors and creamy yellow walls, butterscotch trim, and everywhere was light. The same honey-colored stone as outside formed a wide and impressive fireplace. It was comfortable, lived in. Mimi's mother had hired an interior designer to make their apartment look lived in. Tastefully lived in. This was the real thing. As tired and freaked out as she was, Mimi was instantly happy to be here and slightly jealous.

She sat across a kitchen island from Jay while he started grinding up coriander seeds with a mortar and pestle. By turning, she could look out the front windows, which she did regularly.

"This is going to be worse than my interview at NYU."

"Take it easy," said Jay. "They'll like you."

So she stopped looking over her shoulder, but after a moment she sagged on the maple countertop and rested her head in her arms.

"Why don't you take a shower?" he said.

"Do I smell that bad?"

"Uh-huh."

She retrieved some clothes from the car, and he showed her to the guest room, where there was an en suite bathroom. She emerged fifteen minutes later in a sparkly silver halter top and a denim skirt and resumed her seat across the counter. Jay was rubbing a lemon against a zester. The smell made her feel cleaner still.

"How are we going to handle this?" she asked.

"How about I tell them you're my muse?"

"Ha-ha."

Then Jay got some salad things out of the fridge and put her to work.

Finally, a boxy, black SUV pulled up beside the Mini, and a slim woman in her mid-forties got out, gathered some groceries from the back, and came inside, singing "Hello" from the front door.

Joanne McAllister was wiry, probably a runner, Mimi guessed. She was wearing a dark gray pinstriped suit over an oxblood-colored blouse. Her chestnut-colored hair was shoulder length, her eyes bright and inquisitive, her smile puckish.

"Jo," she said. "I'd shake your hand, but—"

"Let me help," said Mimi, taking a bag of groceries from her. "I'm Mimi."

"Thank you," said Jo. She dumped the salmon in the sink and leaned on the counter facing them. "Well," she said, "you two got everything under control?"

Jay glanced at Mimi and they shared a look. "We're okay," he said.

For a moment Jo held Mimi's eye, then she smiled as if to say, *Something is going on here, but I guess you'll tell me when you're good and ready*. Then she turned back to the sink and washed her hands to get the fish smell off them.

"If you'll excuse me," she said, "until I am out of these clothes, I will not truly be able to get into a festive spirit."

"Yeah, like we're so festive," said Jay.

When Jo had gone, Mimi asked, "What does she do?"

"She runs the town," he said.

"She's the mayor?"

"No. She hates the mayor. She's an administrator. She says her job is to follow the mayor around with a trash bag, cleaning up after him."

Jo joined them in the kitchen in mauve sweats, and soon everyone was busy.

Then Lou arrived in a vintage green Mustang, though when she emerged, she looked to Mimi like the last person who would ever tool around in a sports car. She was big. She wore a sharply pressed pale-blue button-down shirt with the tails out, pressed blue jeans, and Birkenstocks. Her one concession to femininity was a pair of dangly ear-rings. The giveaway was the stethoscope around her neck and the little black bag. *A house call*, thought Mimi. *And who knows, a doctor might be needed.*

Lou didn't seem like Marc's type, Mimi thought, apart from the fact that she was a doctor and he was always attracted to money. But when she met Lou up close, she saw a face as perfectly round as some doyenne from a Renaissance paint-ing, with creamy-colored skin, chocolate-brown eyes, thick eyelashes, and a smile worthy of La Gioconda herself.

Lou took Mimi's hand warmly and looked so frankly into her eyes that Mimi felt nervous as a kitten for a moment. Then, strangely, she felt all her nervousness fall away. She was afraid, suddenly, that she might cry again. Did the Canadian border guards mysteriously strip you of your chutzpah once you crossed over?

"I have the oddest feeling about you," said Dr. Lou, standing back appraisingly. There was nothing discourteous in the comment. Her voice was friendly, but it was alarming nonetheless.

The three housemates stood around the kitchen island staring at Mimi in silence for a good few heartbeats. Her eyes darted from one to the other of them but always came back to Lou. She seemed just like a doctor coaxing a reluctant patient to elucidate her symptoms, explain more fully about the ailment that had brought her here.

"I hope that doesn't sound rude," said Lou.

"No, it's okay," said Mimi. Then she swallowed hard and asked, "What do you see, Doc?"

And Lou looked closer still. "It's your eyes," she said. Then she smiled. "And maybe something about your license plate?"

"What's this all about?" asked Jo, but nobody paid her any attention.

Mimi clutched at her skirt, a little frantically. "Did you . . . did you know about me?"

Lou shook her head very slowly. Then she reached out and gently smoothed a wet fringe of hair back from Mimi's forehead. "No, honey, I didn't know about you. But I'd know those eyes anywhere."

≫| CHAPTER EIGHT |≪

THEY ATE ON THE SCREENED-IN PORCH overlooking the Eden. Salmon grilled on the barbeque, mango salsa, a salad with goat cheese and dried cranberries, washed down with cool glasses of white wine.

Mimi caught them up-to-date on her infamous father.

"They just bought something of his for MOMA," said Mimi.

Jay didn't say anything, but he was impressed and a little weirded out, as if somehow he should know this.

Then Mimi told them what she knew of Marc Soto's marriage to her mother, which had lasted less than four years. She had been two when he moved out and didn't connect up with him again until she was eleven and became curious about this man whose name cropped up now and then in the Sunday *Times*.

"And you read the *New York Times* when you were a eleven?" Jay asked.

"Not cover to cover," she said without missing a beat. "Just the parts about my father." She was very smooth.

"Mom and I were squabbling a lot in those days," she said. "Marc became my go-to downtown connection. Not 'go-to' in the sense that he would actually solve things."

She laughed and glanced at Jay. She looked tired to him, a little nervous, as if she was hungry for acceptance. Big-city girl to waif in a New York minute.

"I mean it was easy to tell he wasn't good for much but painting pictures," she said. "That and finding rich patrons to pick up his bar tab."

"He had the beginning of a drinking problem way back when," said Lou.

"Well, he's been working on it," said Mimi. She screwed up her nose. "Not that he's a drunk. I mean he's real disciplined when he's painting. But . . ." She shrugged and sipped her wine. Put down her glass. She'd barely drunk any. Barely touched her food.

The conversation stalled in the cooling night air. Jay watched her—couldn't take his eyes off her. Such an exotic creature. She was looking out at the lawn as if it were an exhibit. He followed her gaze to the lively shadows. A breeze rustled the leaves.

"I don't know why I do that," she said.

"Do what?" he asked.

"Bad-mouth Marc like that."

"Maybe you thought it was what we'd want to hear?" said Lou.

A bullfrog croaked down by the river.

"It's really hard to imagine him ever living here," said Mimi.

Lou laughed. "That's what he used to say."

Mimi stared at her, her head cocked to one side. "Didn't it bother you?"

"Do I look bothered?" said Lou.

Mimi shook her head. "No, you look like the least-bothered person I ever met. So how did you and Marc end up in Ladybank?"

Lou leaned back in her chair. "We met in Toronto when I was a med student. Marc was . . . well, he was dazzling. Hotshot artist — you just knew he was going to make it. It was fun." She dragged her finger slowly around the edge of her plate like a phonograph needle looking for music. She smiled. "But it got old pretty quickly," she said. "The openings, the hangers-on. I never took a course in small talk."

"I'm majoring in it," said Mimi, and everyone laughed. She looked pleased. But Jay saw something else in her eyes. *She's a little intimidated,* he thought, though the idea surprised him.

"You must be so tired," said Jo. She didn't miss much.

"Thanks," said Mimi. "I am. But this is really good — really helping." She looked at Jay. "You're so lucky."

"I know, the two best mothers in the world."

"My mother and I eat together about once a month," she said. "She is a walking appointment book."

"There you go again," said Jay.

"Hell," said Mimi. "Now I'm bad-mouthing my mom. What's with that?" She looked down, picked up a piece of mango in her fingers, then put it back on her plate. "She's pretty great. Really. I mean she puts up with me."

"Must be a saint," said Jay, grinning.

Mimi made as if to throw her napkin at him. Then she turned to Lou. "Marc is so downtown, so SoHo. I just can't believe he ever lived here. Like, hello?"

Lou laughed. "You're right. A recipe for disaster. I wanted a family. I wanted my own medical practice. And so when Marc was set up with a gallery and all, we decided on a trial period here in Ladybank. He could paint anywhere, right? That was the plan. I got a yearlong job as a temp for a doctor at the clinic who was going on maternity leave."

"And you caught the bug," said Jo.

Lou smiled and sipped her wine.

"Did he, like, hate it?" asked Mimi.

Lou considered the question. "Actually, you've nailed it," she said. "He like-hated it. He missed the city, but he had that boyish enthusiasm about things."

"Still does. Well, sort of."

"He taught some night classes at the college, enjoyed being a big fish in a little pond. He took up kayaking. We both did. Then he found the old place on the snye, and he was just as happy as a clam. For a while. Which is when I made a very serious mistake."

"Uh-oh," said Mimi, glancing at Jo.

Jo laughed. "Not me! I was the mistake she made later."

"It was me," said Jay. "Right?"

Lou nodded and smiled across the table. "You bet. The best mistake I ever made," she said. Then she raised her glass to Jo. "Sorry, darling," she added.

Jo chortled, not at all offended. It was getting dark and she went for candles. The others waited for her to return, each of them lost in thought.

Then Jo was back, and in the new flickering light, the story continued.

"Marc started spending more and more time upriver," said Lou. She chuckled, as if "upriver" was a euphemism. It was funny, thought Jay. This story was for Mimi, and yet it was news to him as well. He'd never really asked about his father. His mother was smiling at him as if she had just realized the same thing. "The fatter I got with child, the less time he was around. It was as if my growing body was pushing him out the door. I'm not stupid. I could see what was happening. But you know something? I didn't really care."

"No?" said Mimi.

"No. I think I already knew by then that Marc was a biological necessity, little more. Cute and entertaining but, well . . ." She smiled again at Jay. "It was clear to me," she said, "that whoever the child I was carrying turned out to be, it would probably not end up with Marc's last name."

Jay looked at Mimi. "You don't have his name, either."

"I used to," she said. "But when I was ten, Mom got it legally changed to hers."

"He didn't care?"

"He didn't dare! He'd have been crazy to take her on! Anyway, he never spent a dime on support. And, to tell you the truth, I don't think my mom would have accepted his money."

"But he's part of your life?" asked Jay. "Now, I mean?"

"Yeah. Well, sort of. It's not exactly a typical father-daughter relationship."

She looked down. How strange it would be, thought Jay, to feel as if you always had to distance yourself from someone. But stranger still, that the someone Mimi was distancing herself from was his father, too. Someone he didn't even know.

"He was never a part of my life," said Jay.

"Well, don't be too sad," said Mimi.

"I'm not really sad."

"Wistful?" asked Jo.

"I guess."

Jay looked at Mimi. "It's weird—I don't even know what he looks like."

Mimi has been slouching, tired, fading. Suddenly she sat bolt upright. "I can fix that," she said. "I've got footage of him on my camcorder."

And so Mimi went out to the car for her camcorder. And when she came in, everyone was clearing the table, but they stopped as she opened the JVC.

"Nice unit," said Jay.

"Lots of memory," she said, and found the documentary she had made. *"A Murder of Good-Byes,"* said her recorded voice.

Mimi scrolled to the restaurant scene.

"Well, I never," said Lou. "Even the glorious Marc Soto is getting old."

Jay stared at the screen. Jack Nicholson came to mind, but it was probably just the dark glasses and the what-me-worry grin. He glanced at Mimi; she seemed to be waiting for him to say something. But what could he say? He took the camera from her and looked at the stranger who was not a stranger and saw in him . . . what?

"You've got his forehead," said Lou.

"That's what I thought," said Mimi. "And his long tapered fingers, too. See?"

Jay saw fingers wrapped around a wineglass.

"I've got way more hair," said Jay.

"He's pretty self-conscious about hair loss. He had this jet-black rug for a long time."

"He was going prematurely bald when he was in his twenties," said Lou.

"Well, he's now pretty much bald," said Mimi. "I'm not sure how mature he is."

"I'll make coffee," said Jo. "Or should I break out the Scotch?"

Apparently, she was only kidding. She drifted back to cleaning up.

Jay just stared at the moving image before him, as if in a spell. "This is so freaking weird," he said.

His mother slipped her arm around his waist. "You okay?"

"Sure," he said, his eyes never leaving the screen. He rewound the bit and watched it again. Lou joined Jo at the counter and started loading the dishwasher. It seemed to Jay as if they had tacitly agreed to give him some space—some privacy.

He looked at Mimi. "Chill," he said.

She shrugged. "I think I'm nervous because I want you to like him. And I'm trying to figure out why."

Jay reached out and touched her arm. It was maybe the nicest thing she'd said all evening. But her eyes wouldn't hold his gaze. This was hard for her, too, he realized. As if her life was somehow under scrutiny. He examined the camera. "Very cool," he said.

Mimi looked relieved. She showed him the features of the HDD. She showed him the rest of the film, too.

"Who is that?"

"Jamila. Hot, huh? Well, stand in line," said Mimi. She fast-forwarded.

"This is my mother," she said. She tilted her chin up and did an impression of her mother raising an eyebrow. Jay laughed.

The women came over to look and said how intelligent Grier Shapiro looked and what a beautiful color her pashmina was, and Lou marveled that anyone could walk with such style in high heels. "I never mastered that," she said. Then they went back to cleaning up and Mimi joined them, but Jay didn't. He'd made dinner, and anyway he was distracted. He sat on a stool at the kitchen island, playing with the camera. "Hey," he said. "Here's the house at the snye."

Mimi was carrying stuff in from the porch. "What?"

He held up the camera for her to see. She put down the plates and bowls and took the camera from him. She frowned.

"I don't remember shooting the house," she said. The camera zoomed in on the upper gable. Someone was standing in the window, looking out at the garden.

It was Mimi.

≥∣ CHAPTER NINE ∣≤

HALF A MILE UPSTREAM from McAdam's Snye, the mouth of Butchard's Creek opened onto the Eden. But you had to know it was there to find the creek's mouth. Passing by on the river, you'd see nothing but swamp, dense with soft rushes, water lettuce and arum, arrowhead, loosestrife. Cramer knew where the seam of water ran deep. He had an eye for the creek's current and a craft responsive to his every demand. She was a fifteen-footer, cedar covered with red canvas, modeled on the old prospector trapper, the Bunny model. Bunny was a good name for her, too, the way she leaped to his response.

The creek opened out about fifty or sixty yards up from the river—too far away for any casual boater to discover it by chance. There were too many mosquitoes, anyway, and the fetid smell of rotting vegetation turned back even the most intrepid explorer. The result was that Cramer had never seen a soul on the creek. It was his private highway. He was its lord and master.

The sun was behind the trees by the time he passed under the Upper Valentine Road Bridge. Just ten minutes from home. The road continued for another couple of kilometers where it used to cross the Eden, but that bridge had been washed away years ago and never been replaced. The road beyond their place had gotten tired of waiting to be repaired. It petered out to a rutted and overgrown trail. The Lees' box was the mail lady's last stop. Cramer would watch her drive on up the road to a better turnaround spot to avoid using their steep and pitted driveway. The oil truck wouldn't deliver to them, either, so they'd had to stick with wood heat. Mavis wanted to convert to electric, but that wasn't going to happen any time soon, not with the money Cramer made. He was supporting the two of them.

The last house on the road, the last place up the creek; that's where Cramer Lee was heading, filled with emotions he couldn't put a name to. There was jealousy in there, resentment, too, but something else—something deeper. A shifting.

There was a quiet and deep pool just past the bridge, where he could pause for a moment without having to fight the current, where he could catch his breath, though his final destination was hardly any distance now. He stopped and laid his paddle across the gunwales. He closed his eyes and could feel the calm of the water rise up through the canoe's hull. He breathed deeply, tried to block from his mind Mimi Shapiro's *Cracker Jack* voice—a voice like some comedian on *Saturday Night Live*. He tried to block the vision of her naked bottom, her cleavage, her shiny eyes and defiant smile. And he tried to get out of his head the thought that she might be Jackson Page's girlfriend. What had happened to Iris? Was he two-timing her? Cramer shook his head at the unfairness of it all.

The worst thing was that it would be awhile before he would see Mimi again. God, what if she left! What if she was only there for the weekend? No, there had been things in the back of the car—a box of dishes, kitchen stuff. *She has to stay until I'm free again.* He worked the nightshift, eight out of twelve days at the 3M plant just outside of town. That started up again tomorrow. He might sneak in an early afternoon trip to the snye, but he also worked part-time at PDQ Electronics, and Hank Pretty had extra work for him. Cramer couldn't turn down extra work.

It was more unfair than anything.

He opened his eyes and stared down at his hands gripping the paddle. The veins stood out in high relief. He breathed deeply again but couldn't get the calmness back. He imagined himself in Mimi's documentary. "This is Cramer," he could hear her say it. "My good friend Cramer." And in the film he smiled at her and winked. Then he said something clever like her clever friends to make her laugh. Yeah, right.

He dug his paddle deep into the creek's dark water, and the canoe shot forward, rounding the last bend.

Up ahead, to his surprise, he saw his mother down by the shore. She was sitting on a granite boulder that poked out into the creek. She had her bare arms wrapped around her knees, and her head was tipped back to catch the very last of the sun. She saw him and waved.

He waved his paddle at her, tentatively, wondering what had happened to bring her down here. She didn't venture outside all that often. Hardly went to town anymore, had a friend or two she seldom saw. She didn't look agitated, as far as he could tell.

Cramer's eyes scanned the hill for a white panel truck. Nothing. Thank God.

She stood as he neared his docking place. She was in a white T-shirt and her torn-up work jeans, stained with paint. Her hair was tied back in a red ribbon. She was wearing the emerald necklace. She looked beautiful. Happy.

"Isn't this some kind of day?" she said, bending to catch the nose of his canoe.

"Yeah," he said. "Are you good?"

She reached out her hand to him, and when he took it, she pulled him and the canoe toward the shore as if he hadn't done this a thousand times by himself. Still, it was a nice thing for her to do.

"Is Bunny behaving?" she asked, patting the curvy side of the canoe, the tumblehome, as if it was the neck of a faithful horse.

Cramer climbed out onto the grassy bank, nodding.

"Remember that old canoe you found in the barn?" she said. "I was scared shitless of you going out in that thing, but there was no stopping you. No, sir."

"It's still around," said Cramer, pointing toward the drive shed. "Still seaworthy."

"Yeah, right!" she said. "Seaworthy. That's a good one. Hey, maybe I should haul her down here? Get out on the creek myself?"

Cramer smiled encouragingly, but he couldn't quite imagine his mother doing anything like that. They had canoed together in Bunny, when it was new, and she'd been good at it, as if maybe there had been canoes in her life, when she was young. Her arms were strong enough, but still. He couldn't see it.

He hauled the canoe out of the water.

"We love Bunny, don't we, Cramer? Remember when I got you Bunny?" she asked, her voice as excited as a kid's.

"I do," he said.

"And it was the best birthday present ever, wasn't it?"

He balled his fists on his hips, arching his back to stretch after the upstream voyage. "It sure was, Mom," he said. In truth, it was the *only* birthday present he could remember receiving. The last few years there would be a card—handmade. He kept them all. They were works of art. But Bunny was the only actual present. She was every birthday present rolled into one.

He gave his mother a smile. She had been right about

the emerald. It was exactly the color of her eyes, and those eyes were gleaming now, with sharp glints of yellow sunshine in them. He knew what was going to happen. She was going to tell him the story about when Bunny arrived in their lives, how surprised he was.

"You were just bowled right over," she said.

How she had led him, blindfolded, out to the drive shed—

"Made you open that big old door yourself to show me how strong you were getting."

And there was the canoe sitting on two sawhorses, brand-new and glistening red. *Red as—*

"Scarlet lake," she said.

I was only ten—

"You were only ten," said his mother, shaking her head back and forth at the bright happiness of this memory.

And it was a good memory. She'd been painting well—painting up a storm! And somehow she'd attracted the interest of a gallery in Ottawa.

"I hightailed it down there in the Taurus one day, when the Taurus was new, and damned if Simon Whiteside didn't offer me a show."

A one-woman show—

"A one-woman show."

And every piece sold—

"Every damn piece sold, Cramer. Can you believe it?"

He looked at her, her face shining, as if the show had happened that very week instead of half his lifetime ago.

She never knew—he'd never told her—how terrified he had been arriving home on the school bus that day to find the house empty, no note—no nothing.

But it was all water under the bridge now. He didn't mind. She could tell him this story every day, if it made her happy. Her contentment helped to ease his mind, distract him from the other things he was thinking, feeling.

She reached out for him, wrapped her arms around his neck, and held him tight. She only came up to his chest. He rested his chin on her head.

She sniffed. Sniffed again. "What's that pretty smell?" she asked.

Cramer gently pushed her away. "Must be some new flower come up," he said, looking all around, hiding his face from her scrutiny.

She grinned at him, one eyebrow raised. "Smells like a girl to me," she said, in a teasing kind of voice. "What are you getting up to on these jaunts of yours?"

Cramer dug his hand deep into his pocket, trying to keep what was there out of sight. He looked down at his bare feet. He never wore shoes in the canoe.

"I do believe you're blushing," said his mother.

"I am not blushing," he said.

"Yes, you are. Why, maybe I *should* get that old canoe down from the shed and follow you one of these days. See what kind of trouble you're getting into." He looked out toward the creek. Saw a kingfisher skim the surface. Mavis poked him in the ribs. "I hope whoever she is, you won't be bashful about bringing her home."

"Mom."

"Or too proud," she said, her voice teetering a bit now. It didn't take much to deflate her.

Cramer wished there was something he could do to drive her demons away. "I promise *when* there's a girl, you'll be the first to know."

She gave him a hug. "'You are my sunshine, my only sunshine,'" she started to sing, her voice muffled in his shirt. She swayed back and forth, trying to lug him around with her on a dance on the uneven shore. He held on to her lest she slip off the bank into the water. Something was up.

She must have sensed what he was thinking, because she pulled away and held him at arm's length. She was still smiling to beat the band.

"You think your mother's gone cuckoo on you?" she said.

"No, Mom—"

"It's okay, Cramer, honey," she said, and then she tipped her head back and laughed out loud. "It's okay, it's okay, it's okay!" She looked into his face, her own suddenly composed and sober. "I know how difficult I can be," she said. "I'm not famous for being levelheaded."

"Mom—"

"And I know that if it weren't for you, I'd've been toast a long time ago."

"Ah, Mom, it's not like—"

"Shhh! Yes, it is!" she said, gently pounding his chest

with her fists. "You really are my knight in shining armor."

He swallowed hard, proud and self-conscious.

Then she smirked and said, "Come on. I want to show you something."

The painting stood on the easel, still wet in patches but remarkable in its energy. His mother didn't speak. She just let him gaze upon her work.

It was an abstract piece, all in lavenders and ochers and blue-veined greens, so that it looked like a garden seen in a cracked but bright mirror. Cramer didn't know much about art, but he knew this: the painting before him contained all of the excitement and enthusiasm and sparkly-eyed optimism that his mother had revealed to him down by the stream.

"It's so good," he said.

"Do you think?"

"I know!"

"Oh, honey," she said. "I do, too. 'I have found the key to my courage locker,'" she said. He recognized it as a saying from *The Artist's Path*, and he had to admit it was true. This painting *was* courageous—it seemed to shout at him across the room.

"Now I know why you're so happy," he said. And she squeezed him tightly and pressed her head against his chest as if trying to smother a scream or stop herself from bursting into tears.

"It's back," she whispered. "I am recovered."

"I'm so proud of you, Mom," he said, drinking in her excitement.

Then she pushed him away again, though she held on to his hands tightly. Unconsciously, he rubbed his thumb along the scar on her left hand. Then he stopped himself, lest it set her off. But she seemed happily oblivious of her painful past. She gazed at the painting, the way he'd seen people in movies gaze through the window at a baby in a maternity room. Then she looked up into his eyes. "There's more where that comes from," she said confidently. "I mean it."

"That's good news," he said.

She turned around to give the painting her complete attention. "We'll be rich again," she said, and laughed because they had never been rich, but they had once been happy, for a while.

"I know it," he said.

"There's just one thing," she said.

He could hear the hesitation in her voice. He braced himself.

"I'm going to need more paint and more canvas," she said hurriedly. "A lot more paint, a lot more canvas."

He didn't speak for a moment. Hardly breathed. She felt the change in him. She turned. "It will be worth it," she said.

"I know."

"I've made a list," she said. "I phoned the supply place in Ottawa."

"Good," he said, not wanting to lose her.

"Five hundred dollars ought to cover everything," she said. "For now." She held his eyes for a moment longer, then her gaze skittered away.

"Okay," he said quickly, not wanting to let her down. "I'll handle it."

"Of course you will," she said. Now she looked up at him again, and her eyes went all coquettish, the way she'd get with Waylin when she wanted something from him. She rubbed Cramer's upper arms, squeezing his biceps. "God, when did you ever get to be so strong?" she asked.

He didn't answer. His mind was reeling. *Five hundred bucks*, he thought. Where would he ever get five hundred bucks? It didn't matter. What mattered was that he would.

"You can count on me," he said.

Her smile softened. She shook her head in amazement and respect. "Whoever that girl is I smell on you, she is one lucky lady."

He didn't bother to argue with her. Kind of liked the idea that there could be a girl—a lucky girl—who was his alone.

≽∣ CHAPTER TEN ∣≼

JAY SAT IN BED LISTENING to Gabriel Zouave's *Sang-Froid* on his iPod, reading the score along with the music. The oversize manuscript was propped against his knees. He had seen the premiere, heard Zouave talk about it. Jay dreamed of writing something this good—this big. But right now all he wanted was for the music to take him away. He did not want his mind to wander. Did not want to think of Mimi down the hall.

There was a knock on his door. He paused the iPod, instantly felt a panic attack coming on. He waited. The knock came again, softly. He glanced at his alarm clock: 11:45. It would be her. She'd want to talk about what happened. About the video footage: her own image on her own camera captured by an unknown watcher. *His* unknown watcher. Had to be. It seemed fatherhood wasn't the only thing he and Mimi shared.

He wasn't sure he could face this right now. But it surprised him, bothered him that only half an hour after saying good night, how much he wanted to see her again.

"Jay?"

He let out his breath. It was only Mom. He wasn't sure if he was relieved.

"Enter."

The door opened and there was his kind mother in her terry-cloth robe and sheepskin slippers.

"Am I disturbing you?" she said. He had to laugh.

She gently closed the door behind her, crossed the room, and sat on his bed. She patted his foot, under the comforter.

"That a good read?" she asked.

"Yeah, a real thriller," he said. He held up the score so she could see the cover. She took it, looked at the open spread, and shook her head. "I can't imagine how you do it," she said.

He shrugged. "I can't imagine how you take out somebody's tonsils."

"Tonsils are a piece of cake. But reading all these parts. And you actually hear it in your head, don't you?"

Jay pointed to his earphones.

"I know, but you do read scores. I've seen you."

Jay placed his iPod on the bedside table. "Zouave told me the only time music was ever perfect for him was when he read it. No one's flat; no one plays too loud. Perfect balance. Perfect harmony."

His mother nodded in an abstract way, as if perfect harmony was something she didn't see a lot of at the clinic. She handed him back the score. There was a shift in the expression on her face. He closed the score and dropped it to the floor beside his bed.

"Pretty weird night, huh?" he said.

Lou nodded. "You might say." She brought her hands together in her lap. "I thought I should tell you I phoned Marc."

Jay wasn't sure what he had been expecting her to say—something about Mimi, no doubt. "Really?" She nodded. "You know how to reach him?"

She nodded but with her chin pulled in as if this wasn't quite the response she had expected. "He's at the same number I reached him at when you wanted to use the house on the snye for band practice, back in high school. He still pays property taxes on the place, which means he's on the township roll. Jo found his address and phone number easily enough."

Jay thought about the balding man in the shades. He imagined him in the same café, as if that was where he lived, with a glass of wine in one hand and a phone in the other, talking to Lou.

"What'd he say?"

Lou folded her bathrobe over her knee. "Well, he was a bit surprised."

"That makes a whole bunch of us."

"He remembered that he had given you permission to

use the house but that it was a long time ago. Seven years, I told him. He also knew you'd gone out west to school."

"How'd he know that?"

"I wrote him," said Lou.

"Jesus! So you two are like buddy-buddy and I don't even know about it?"

"What do you think, Jay?"

That was the sixty-four-million-dollar question. What was he *supposed* to think? "My father suddenly crash-lands right in the middle of my life via this pretty much grown-up daughter—aka my half-sister—and now I find out my mother is all palsy with the guy."

"Nonsense," she said.

"Mom!"

"Keep your voice down, honey. There is one very tired, equally discombobulated young woman down the hall trying to sleep."

Jay didn't need reminding.

"Marc and I are anything but palsy-walsy. I have communicated with him precisely twice in the last ump-teen years—three times, counting tonight: once, back in . . . whatever it was . . . 2000?—when you were in tenth grade—to ask if you could use the house on the snye for the band; then once again to let him know you'd graduated from high school, summa cum laude and vale-dictorian of your class. Bragging rights. And tonight to let him know our present situation."

Jay didn't dare speak. He could feel words as sharp

and belligerent as sticks and rocks piling up behind his teeth. He wasn't exactly sure what he was so angry about; he just was.

"He's fine about you being there, if that's what's bothering you."

That helped a little. But not much. It had been a very long time since Jay had thought of the house on the snye as belonging to anyone else but himself. Now it was as if his hold on the place was being threatened from every side.

"What about her?" he said, nodding toward the spare bedroom.

"That's for you two to decide—you and Miriam."

"Who?"

"That's what Marc called her. He thinks it's up to you guys how you deal with this. And I agree."

Jay crossed his arms, leaned back, and banged his head a couple of times against the backboard. "I dunno, Mom. I can just barely wrap my head around *having* a sister. But sharing a place with her?"

His mother smiled sympathetically. "Marc thinks there might be something she's running away from."

"What? She rob a bank?"

Lou shrugged. "More personal, I'm guessing. He wouldn't say. Or didn't know."

"Or didn't care," said Jay.

He looked away, knowing his mother would be regarding him attentively and wishing she wouldn't. Her hand was still on the comforter, stroking his foot. He slid it out of her reach. She didn't speak and eventually he glanced her way again.

"What is it?" she asked.

"What do you think?"

She shook her head. "It's not *just* Mimi. Something's up. Something's been bothering you for a while."

Jay rolled his eyes. "Like my life, for instance?"

Lou smiled.

"You think that's funny?"

"No," she said. "I would say your life was pretty good."

"I didn't mean that."

"You're going away in just a couple of months. Back to school. You're going to love that."

"I know. Of course I will. And I am a fortunate child. Believe me, I do realize that. You know I do."

"But?"

"But . . ." He couldn't tell her what was going on up at the snye. He could talk to Lou about almost anything, but not this. Not something she might see as threatening. And it was threatening, though he didn't want to see it that way.

"You take life very seriously, Jay," she said. "It will always be a bit of a burden for you. But I wouldn't be much of a mother—let alone a doctor—if I didn't know that something's been on your mind for a while now."

Jay looked at her frank expression. Nothing really ruffled her. Hell, she worked in the ER: crash victims, heart attacks, mortally wounded children. Why couldn't he talk to her?

"Are things okay with Iris?"

"Sure. Of course. Why shouldn't they be?"

Lou shrugged. "Just probing," she said.

Jay glowered, without having any noticeable effect on her attentive smile.

"Is she still coming home this summer?"

Jay nodded. "In a week or so."

"Good." Lou grinned. "What a surprise this is going to be for her."

Jay didn't bother to comment. Right now Iris just seemed like one more thing to have to try to juggle, and he had run clean out of hands. He slid a little down in his bed, hoping his mother would get the hint and leave. She didn't move. She was staring across the room at nothing.

"She's very pretty, isn't she?" said his mother.

"Who? Iris?"

"No." Lou shook her head. "Iris *is* pretty. I adore Iris, as you know. But I was talking about Mimi." His mother smiled at him in a way that made him think that she could see clear inside him, all the way down to thoughts he was trying very hard to hide from himself.

PART TWO

The room was quiet, but Mimi was there, up there, just beyond seeing. She wasn't talking, but he could sense her, hovering nearby, like an angel. Maybe she was an angel. Maybe he had died without knowing it and this black hole was hell with her only an arm's length away. So close, if he could only move his arms.

"I know you're there," she said, her voice quiet. "I think you can hear me."

She had found him.

She had found him, but he couldn't do a thing about it, couldn't say anything, couldn't move. She would go and he wouldn't be able to stop her, or follow, or call after her.

"I want you to come out from there," she said. "I think you're hiding, Cramer, and I want to talk to you, okay?"

And this was the hardest thing of all, he thought. Because all he wanted in the whole world was to talk to her and it was beyond him. She was beyond him. And maybe it would be that way forever.

≫ CHAPTER ELEVEN ≪

DESPITE THE AVALANCHE of shocks and surprises, or maybe because of them, Mimi slept like a baby. The revelation that capped the evening—that someone had used her own camera to shoot footage of her—had stunned her speechless. Luckily Jay had been right beside her. She had grabbed on to his arm for support, and he had taken the camera away from her, gently, before she dropped it, as if it were a grenade with a loose firing pin. It was his serious eyes as much as his strong grip that held her up. And his eyes seemed to say, *Let's keep this our secret.*

"Good of him not to steal the JVC," Jay said when they were alone. But the look in his eyes said what Mimi was thinking. It *wasn't* good. It was intimidating.

They were in the guest room; he'd gone out to get her fresh towels, and just as he returned, her cell phone rang.

She didn't answer it, and, luckily, Jay got the hint and left her alone, pulling the door shut behind him.

She had gone to bed, missing the comforting sound of traffic, of car horns and sirens. Of cabbies arguing with drunk passengers.

The next thing she knew she was waking to birdsong and a radio playing classical music softly somewhere off in the blond house.

She pulled up the blinds and looked out at the garden. Jay came into view, walking from around the corner of the house in jeans and a ratty denim jacket, heading down toward the river with a carpenter's tool belt hanging around his hips, the hammer tapping against his thigh.

"Very Village People," she murmured.

Jay was also lugging an orange-colored case, which she supposed contained some kind of power tool. He loaded it into the forward hatch of the kayak. Then he undid his tool belt and lowered it into the hatch as well. He was going to do some carpentry work up at the snye, she gathered, and as soon as she realized this, she recalled the secret entrance, the storm door hidden behind the shed, and the phantom who had been using it to gain entrance to the little house. The same phantom, presumably, that had borrowed her camera. Her shoulders sagged.

Jay looked as if he were about to leave. She grabbed her NYU hoodie from the muddle of clothes she had thrown on a rocker and raced for the back door, pulling on the sweatshirt as she went. She called him from the step as he was about to launch the kayak. He stopped, looked back at her. His expression wasn't quite impatience. It was the expression of someone too polite to be impatient.

She wondered how he had gotten the kayak back from the snye and then realized that it was not the same one he had left up there. The one they had hauled into the house had been completely yellow. This one was yellow on top but the hull was white.

Jay looked up at the sky. It was overcast. There was a bit of chop on the river caused by a stiff breeze. Mimi breathed in; the air was fresh, and the grass was wet with dew or maybe it had rained. She didn't often get to go outside in just her nightclothes and a hoodie. The garden was closed off, private. It felt liberating.

She joined him at the riverside. He didn't look like he'd had much sleep. She kicked the kayak lightly with her bare toe. "You buy these things by the six-pack?" she asked.

He didn't smile. "It's my mom's," he said.

"You're going to have a marina up there at this rate."

"I can tow the other one back. I want to get a lock on that door as soon as possible."

"Figured. I can drive you, if you give me two minutes."

He looked her up and down and frowned as if to say it would take more than two minutes for her to get ready.

"I didn't know you wore specs," he said.

She held out her arms and twirled around, present-ing herself for inspection. "This is your new sibling in the morning: bed-head, sarcastic glasses, and bad plaid pajamas."

Jay tried not to smile, mostly succeeded.

"You have a bad night?" she asked.

He looked out at the river and took a deep breath. "I'm not much of a morning person," he said.

"Sorry."

He looked out at the river, pinched the bridge of his nose. "Didn't mean to be rude," he said. "It's just that I want to get up to the place and deal with this thing."

"I understand. I want to help. Could I drive up and meet you there?" His eyes got shifty-looking. She spoke slowly to him, as if language was the problem. "Jay, I know you need to go batten down the hatches, but we need to talk. And, anyway, I could help. Maybe not with the hatches, but with . . . you know. Stuff."

He puckered his brow. "Stuff?" he said.

Mimi rolled her eyes. "I'm smart and resourceful and . . . something else. Oh, right—fearless!"

"You looked pretty scared when you saw yourself on the camera."

"Yeah, well, you've got to admit, that was special, wasn't it? Give me a break."

Jay raised an eyebrow.

"I've been around, Jay. I'm not some bimbo. Besides, I've got an idea."

"An idea?"

"Yeah. It involves motion detectors, infrared cameras,

and land mines, but we can improvise." She coaxed a grin out of him, but she was working overtime.

He sighed. "So we'll talk," he said, "when I get back." He looked at his watch, showed it to her. It was nearly ten. "I should be back by one."

"Great! We'll do lunch," she said, all perky-eyed. "I'll head into town and find something. Is there a sushi bar? Just kidding."

Now Jay just looked worn-out.

"Okay?" she asked.

"Okay."

"Good. I'll make lunch for everyone."

"It'll just be us. Mom and Jo went to Ottawa, won't be back until dinner."

"Lunch for two, then."

"Cool."

Then he started to push the kayak into the water.

"Oops!" said Mimi.

He stopped and turned around with a what-is-it-this-time look on his face.

"The security system," she said, pointing back toward the house. "How do you work it?"

Jay showed her how to arm the system and then took off.

Mimi explored the house, which she finally had all to herself, just her and the radio. Then she took a shower and went back to her room to get dressed. There were a series of framed drawings on the wall above the low dresser. They were lively Conté crayon sketches of rocks. She knew those rocks. She leaned close to see her father's scrawl of a signature in the lower right-hand corner with the year '82 after it. Six years before she was born. These rocks had gone on to big things. Literally. Mark's first major show in New York featured these very same rocks, nine of them in all, but painted huge—boulder size—and ganged up in diptychs and triptychs. She had read about it in an article in *Artforum:* "Soto—The Stone Age." Part of her father's long history.

She sat on the bed, her hands in her lap. She felt good. Rested. Seeing these sketches made her feel as if she belonged here somehow. She would ask Jay if they could share the house at the snye. It wasn't his fault—or hers—that they were both here. She'd stay out of his hair. And it would be good to have two people there, really.

She got up and started sorting through her clothes. She had understood Jay's caginess with her. It was kind of a weird variant of waking up after a one-night stand. Now there was a thought! He'd get over it. So would she. Had to.

But then what about her need to be alone? She had a lot of thinking to do, in somewhere other than New York. Somewhere Lazar Cosic wasn't.

Decisions. Oh, well. For now she would be this useful sister who went out and found something nutritious for lunch. She turned to her suitcases.

What to wear? Something serious. Something that said, *This girl is not a freak. This girl means business. This girl is reliable.* She started sorting things out. Did she own anything like that? But after another moment of sorting, the idea of what to wear to impress her brand-new brother had gone clear from her mind.

She was missing something. A silver-framed photograph of Jamila and her at the Hassanalis' summer place on Long Island. They were goofing around on the beach, mugging for the camera. She hadn't forgotten to pack it. She remembered wrapping it in her pink polka-dotted top. The top was still there. But the picture was gone.

≍| CHAPTER TWELVE |≍

It WAS LIKE A BLOW to the solar plexus. Mimi sat, weak-kneed, without anyone to hold her up this time. She felt as if she had wandered into the middle of a battlefield. It wasn't her war, so why was somebody taking potshots at her?

She had lied to Jay; she wasn't exactly fearless. But by the time she had dressed, set the security alarm, and climbed into the Mini, she could already feel her anger start to nip away at the big lump of fear and resentment in her gut. Jack Russell terrier takes on the Blob.

She squealed out of the Pages' driveway onto Riverside Drive. And the Mini Cooper beeped twice, surprising a bicyclist off the road.

She found a nice-looking organic grocery store in town. She found a bakery where they made bagels.

"Bagels," she said, and sighed, clutching the bag to her chest. "All is not lost!"

She found a bookstore and the library and a street of charming shops. A village with a river running through it.

Jay was home by 12:45, and they sat down at a table of warm bagels, aged local cheddar, kosher dill pickles, sliced-up veggies, and freshly whipped mayonnaise.

"Listen," said Jay, "I'm sorry about the Grinch act this morning. I was worried about the house."

"It's cool. Everything okay?"

"As far as I could tell. I took the padlock off the ladder and put it on the storm door. I hope that'll do the trick." He frowned. "Hope he doesn't know the starter fluid trick."

She nibbled at a piece of celery, trying to decide whether to tell him her latest news, figured she'd better. "There was this photograph of me and a friend," she said. "Jamila, the one you thought was hot?"

He nodded, but from the expression on his face, he was already guessing the worst. "What about it?"

"I brought it with me," she said. "I remember packing it. But it's gone."

He stared at his sandwich. "You're saying this guy went through your stuff?"

She shrugged—didn't want to admit that Mr. X had pawed through her clothes, her underwear. She shuddered.

"I'm sorry."

"It's hardly your fault."

Jay shrugged and looked forlorn as if somehow it was.

"Jay, I don't know what's going on up there, but it doesn't change my mind. I mean I've come this far." She took a deep breath. "I want to ask if we could share the house. For a while, anyway."

He stared hard at her a moment. "Did you talk to Marc?"

She shook her head. "I'm too angry." She broke off a piece of bagel, crumbled it in her fingers. "He's such a jerk! I can't believe he didn't say anything about you." She shook her head. "All these jerks! What am I, a jerk magnet?"

"Thanks."

"Oh, stop with the hurt routine. You know what I mean."

Jay blundered into a bagel sandwich that was too thick. She shook her head in disgust. He stopped. "Kidding!" she said. She made an open-face, took a bite. Swallowed.

"Actually, I'm not being entirely honest," she said. "About Marc, I mean. I *can* believe him not telling me about you. He's . . . Oh, I don't know. It's like he's a socio-path or something." She glanced at Jay, whose mouth was open, his sandwich raised halfway there but stopped in midair. "Not in the Anthony Perkins–slash–Norman Bates way, but in the seriously irresponsible conduct way."

Jay was frowning now, and Mimi realized she was freaking him out. "Forget it," she said. "I have taken precisely one psych course. All I meant was that Marc doesn't seem to get it about caring, about family, about giving a shit."

She took another bite of bagel. She glanced at Jay again and felt guilty at the bewildered look in his eyes. She reached across the table and was about to give his hand a squeeze but then thought better of it; she wasn't sure why. "He's not a murderer or anything. I don't want you to think that. It just wouldn't occur to him to bother saying anything. That having relatives somewhere would be a big deal—that, like, I might *care*." Jay summoned up a smile. "Believe me, Marc won't see this as his problem," she said. "You and I wanting the place. He won't care what we do."

Jay nodded. "Well, you're right about that."

He had a weird look on his face. "How do you mean?" she asked.

"My mother phoned him."

"Get out of town."

"Last night. If it makes you feel any better about him, he probably didn't warn you because he thought I was still in school. So he didn't expect you'd run into me."

Mimi was almost pleased. It was sort of like an excuse. But when she thought about it, not much of one.

"He said pretty well what you said. It was up to us."

Mimi drank a sip of water. Didn't want to look at Jay. Didn't want to see *no* written on his face.

"What is it you want to do up there?" he asked.

"I want to write." She glanced up. Was he silently howling with scornful laughter? No. He looked impressed.

"Like a book? A novel?"

She shook her head. "A screenplay. I just finished my first year at NYU. Dramatic writing."

"Very cool," he said. "What's it about?"

Ah. She dropped her eyes. Then glanced at him, a little furtively. "It's about a girl who gets herself in a big mess in her first year at college and runs away to another country."

There. It was out. She picked up her sandwich and took a bite. When she looked, Jay was regarding her with what . . . concern? Affection?

"Boy-type trouble?"

"Worse," she said. "Professor-type trouble."

Jay picked up his own sandwich and took a bite. It was as if they were building a little wall of sandwiches between them. The kitchen was filled with the sound of two people not talking. A motorboat went by out on the river. Jay swallowed, took a drink of water.

"The phone call you didn't answer last night?" he said.

"Right. That was him."

"Why don't you block his number?"

"I did, so he's started calling from pay phones. Different ones."

Jay looked concerned, and it annoyed her because it only proved what she was worried about—that there was reason for concern. "So get a new cell phone from this area code," he said. "It'll be cheaper."

"I just got here, remember?"

"Sorry," he said. "It's none of my business."

You're right, she thought. But she needed Jay on her side and bickering didn't help.

"Hey," he said. "I really am sorry. I'm just, you know, anxious."

She nodded and thought that he was always low-grade anxious, as far as she could tell. "Thanks. It's a sore point," she said. Then she thought of something else and shook her head.

"What?"

"Oh, nothing. Just a random little memory that came to mind." She pointed at her head. "Sometimes it's like bumper cars up there!"

"Tell me," he said. "I like bumper cars." He grinned and she couldn't help grinning back.

Then she had to look away. The intimacy quotient was climbing way too fast.

Still, he might as well know what kind of a crackpot he was dealing with. "Lazar Cosic—he's the prof—he even accompanied me to one of Marc's openings."

Jay's head jerked, as if he'd been sucker-punched. "An opening? So, like, Marc was there?"

"Of course. That was the point."

He looked perplexed. "You wanted Marc to see you with—"

"A man almost his age? Yeah. Don't ask why."

"And?"

"And nothing." She laughed, a sad little laugh. "If Marc noticed, he didn't say a thing." Then she shook her head. "And that is the end of the amusing part of this broadcast. Lazar confused going to the opening with taking him home to meet the folks, which is when he started talking about leaving his wife."

"Yikes."

"And I freaked."

Jay chewed on his sandwich and looked to be chewing on what she had told him. "And so now you're going to turn the whole thing into a movie," he said.

"Well, you've got to admit there is some dramatic potential."

"I guess."

She leaned her elbows on the table. "I'm thinking maybe in the screenplay, the professor turns out to be a psychotic killer—the real kind."

"That sounds like fun."

"Uh-huh. Luckily my part is played by Angelina Jolie. And she's got great weapons."

He smiled wryly. "She's a little old for a freshman, isn't she?"

Mimi shrugged. "Yeah, maybe. So who do you suggest?"

But Jay was finished playing. He looked as if he had eaten something sour. "Men are such assholes," he said.

Mimi gawked at him.

"Well, it's true. Not all men, obviously. But really! A professor?"

"That's sweet of you. Thing is, it wasn't entirely his fault. I mean it was consensual."

"No way," said Jay. "He's in this position of power. It's harassment. Did you go to the dean?"

She shook her head. "No," she said. "I went to Canada."

Jay sat back in his chair and sighed. "So what happens next year?"

She shrugged. "I'm thinking of UCLA or maybe the University of Singapore, if they have a film studies program. Anywhere that's about a gazillion miles away."

"That is such bullshit. He's the one who should have to leave."

She thought about that for a moment. "I dunno. He started getting serious and I got seriously cold feet and it sort of went south from there. *Bam!* Suddenly I'm in the middle of a midlife crisis."

"A quarter-life crisis," said Jay.

"Hey, cool. Like the John Mayer song, right? But what I mean is I was in the middle of *his* midlife crisis."

The scene of their last meeting, unwished for, bullied its way into Mimi's mind: Lazar's face like something from a horror movie, his raised fist, his voice all ragged and out of control.

"Was he scary?"

She realized the scene in her head must have been playing itself out on her face.

She glanced at Jay and nodded. "Really scary," she said. Then she flung herself back in her seat, swore a bit, and crossed her arms. "Listen. I don't want to talk about this right now, okay? You asked me what I was doing here, and I said I wanted to work on a screenplay. Can we leave it at that?"

"Okay," he said. "I hear you. But I still think this guy sucks."

My big brother, she thought.

"Thanks, Jay. The thing is, right now what I want—what I *need*—is to be here. To be far away from the whole mess. Not to mention far away from him!"

She looked Jay squarely in the eye. "I am totally capable of staying out of your way. Seriously. I won't be coming up asking if you want coffee. I won't ask you to read scenes. I won't sing or tap dance or put up a lot of shelves. I won't distract you. Honest."

"It's not that," he said. He looked down at his plate. His hands rested lightly on the table. He flexed his fingers as if he were about to play the piano.

"There's still this other problem," he said.

"The creep?"

He nodded. And she could see the concern in his face. "I guess I was hoping whoever was doing this shit would get tired and go away. I mean sometimes there's nothing for weeks. I figured maybe I was winning the waiting game. But when I realized he'd taken the movie camera right out of your car, taken that footage, and then put it back, well . . ."

"And now the framed picture," she added.

He nodded again, combed his fingers through his hair, left it standing in a softly spiky heap. Then he looked at her with such considerate eyes, she thought she might fall in love with him, anyway, despite all the taboos about that kind of thing.

"I'm worried," he said.

"I'm not afraid."

"Yeah, but I can't be there all the time. What if you were alone at night . . . ?"

She favored him with a really big smile. "Wait here," she said. She went off to the guest room and came back with her purse. She sat down and rooted around. "There are two reasons why I don't want you to be worried for me," she said. "First of all, this," she said, and held up her cell phone. "I'll put the local cops on speed dial, if that'll help."

"It would take them twenty minutes," he said. "Assuming they didn't get lost."

"Which is where this'll come in handy," she said. She held up a miniature spray canister, with a red plastic top.

"What is that?"

"Mace," she said. "One spray and the creep is blinded. Temporarily. Just long enough for me to hit him with something large and get the hell away."

Jay shook his head, but he was smiling—a ghost of a smile. He was giving in.

"Listen, Jay," she said, grabbing his wrist. "This has been the strangest couple of days in my whole frigging life. And I'm not going to pretend I'm not a little freaked by what's going on. But it's good to be in the know, you know? And assuming there's only one of him—if it is a him—well, it's got to be better if there's two of us."

"Except for the nights when there's not two of us."

"Except for the nights when there's not two of us. Agreed. But those nights it'll be me and my friend Mr. Mace."

Slowly, reluctantly, he nodded.

"Shake?" she said.

"I already am," he said. And they both laughed, a little hysterically, as if they'd been holding way too much inside.

≥| CHAPTER THIRTEEN |≤

IT WAS WEDNESDAY before Cramer saw Mimi again. Just a glimpse, and it wasn't up at the snye but at the Page place on Riverside Drive.

The Taurus was not a car people noticed. It wasn't old enough to be antique or rusted enough to be an eyesore. Cramer himself wasn't sure what color it was: gray, green—he had no idea. The car, as large and ugly as it might be, was invisible. Which was just as well, when Mimi and Jay suddenly pulled out of the driveway in her Mini Cooper. There were high hedges to either side of the entrance, and so Cramer didn't see them until the last second, even though he was parked pretty well right across the road. He had a map open on the steering wheel as an excuse, a lost traveler. But neither of them so much as glanced his way. They were talking up a storm, oblivious. It wasn't just his car that was invisible.

A boxy black Honda Element pulled out of the driveway a moment later, a large old desk strapped to the roof rack, its legs sticking up in the air like some dead animal. The back of the Honda looked to be jam-packed with furniture. Dr. Lou was sitting in the passenger seat, the other woman driving. They didn't notice Cramer, either.

It was 7:00 PM. He was on his way to work. For the last couple days, he had taken the time to drive out of his way past the Page house. He was scoping the place out. He had done it before, after all. And tonight it looked as if he had caught a break. It wasn't hard to guess where they were all heading. The round-trip to the snye would take them an hour at least and who knows how long to unload all the furniture. Plenty of time. Now all he needed was to talk himself into it.

Cramer looked ahead and behind him. Riverside Drive was deserted in both directions. It was a stretch of road with farmland to the north and large riverside properties to the south, properties that were wooded and landscaped, hedged and fenced. Private. Some of them even had gates. But not the Pages'. A lawn mower was making a racket nearby, but Cramer couldn't see where. He skipped across the pavement and down the long, shaded drive without anyone seeing him.

ADVANCED ALARM. The little sticker in the corner of the glass-fronted door didn't come as a complete surprise. Clearly, he wasn't going to just walk in the door the way he had last fall.

He walked around the side of the house to the floor-length windows of the master bedroom. This was where he had found the emerald necklace. The curtains weren't fully drawn. Pressing his nose up to the screen, he could dimly make out the dresser where Dr. Lou had kept her jewelry case. He had a penknife, never went anywhere without it; the mesh of the screen would be easy to slit. And then what? Break the glass? He quickly glanced behind him. He was alone. He turned his attention back to the window. It all depended on how the alarm system was activated: motion detector, pressure detector, or metal contacts on the window frames. Yes, there they were. But how long was this going to take? Would the siren be louder than the lawn mower? The alarm company would contact the local cops, but not before they phoned the residence to see if it was a false alarm. He sure didn't plan on dawdling and he wasn't greedy. Shit! He hated this—just wanted it to be over!

He looked around for a rock, a stick. Nothing, just lawn. He backed off.

He'd had a plan. He'd seen other stuff when he stole the necklace: pearls, some silver earrings, whatever. Not much, but he was guessing it was good stuff. He didn't know any fences to get rid of stolen merchandise; that was Waylin Pitney's territory. But he figured Mavis could help him out. It was for her, after all. So she could dress up in something nice. She could still do that, when she took a mind to it. They would drive into Ottawa, go to a jewelry store or a pawnshop or something. She could pretend she was selling off a few family heirlooms. She could pull it off—he knew she could—if he could convince her. It was a big *if*, but then it was for her—for her art! And there was something else that might win her over. She hated Louise Page.

The lawn mower drew nearer. Cramer was standing a few yards away from a tall cedar fence. The lawn mower, by the sound of it, was right on the other side. The noise made him nervous. He wouldn't hear a car arrive over that racket. What if they doubled back? What if they had forgotten something?

He folded up his knife. He pressed his nose up to the screen one last time, trying to make out the shine or glitter of something of value.

But then he saw Mavis in his mind's eye—saw her face as he tried to explain his plan. He imagined her green eyes shifting away from the jewels he was holding out to her. *Think of all the paint, think of all the canvas*, he would say, trying not to raise his voice. He imagined her rubbing her hands together nervously, shaking her head. No.

Who was he kidding? He would have to sell the stuff himself, and there was no way he could do that. Stealing it was going to be way hard enough.

He glanced at his watch. He had twenty minutes to get to work, and only if he hightailed it. He took off across the lawn, angry now. He had three jobs: the plant, the store, and keeping his mother happy. It was one job too many.

The night-shift job was contract work. Cramer didn't get benefits, but the pay was good. Sometimes he'd get laid off without any notice for a week or two, but he'd always get hired back. He was a good worker. Reliable.

Usually, he worked at PDQ Electronics two afternoons a week, but lately business had been booming. He had been an intern there in high school, and Hank Pretty, who owned the place, kept him on as an apprentice. Cramer was good with his hands and was computer savvy, but there had been no thought of going away to school, even though Hank urged him to go. Who'd look after Mavis?

She was on her feet again now, and that made things better. Cramer would get home from the plant around five in the morning, and sometimes she'd be up already, hard at work. The other morning she had even stopped and made him breakfast, sat and had coffee with him. Then he'd gone to bed, and the last thing he'd heard as he fell asleep was her humming along with cheery morning music on the radio as she painted away.

Right now she was painting over old canvases. She wasn't complaining, not much, but he felt in his heart how hard it must be for her.

He was not a thief. He was not going to break into just anybody's house. The Pages were different, the way he saw it. He had not stolen the emerald necklace; he had recovered it to its rightful owner.

"It was meant to be mine. Just look at it, Cramer, for heaven's sake."

And when he had finally held it in his hands, looked at it, up close, he had known that Mavis was right. The jewel was exactly the color of her eyes.

He had staked out the Page place for days before entering the house that crisp October afternoon. He had watched from the water, from the deep shade on the south shore of the Eden. Watched the comings and goings of Dr. Lou and her friend, when the cleaning lady came, the postman. That was when he had learned that Jay was back from out west. He followed him upriver and discovered the little house on McAdam's Snye.

When he finally brought the necklace home and snapped the clasp of it at the nape of his mother's neck and saw how happy she was, he ventured to tell her about the house on the snye. She had smiled the saddest smile he had ever seen, and tears had gathered in the corner of her eyes. She didn't need to tell him why. The little house was where she and Marc Soto used to meet.

He knew the story. A love story. The story of an artist and his young and talented student—the most talented student he had ever come across. Mavis had turned the artist's life upside down, made him leave his wife. But she had given him the courage, the inspiration to paint as he had never painted before. That's what the artist had told her and that's what she told Cramer. The story never changed, every time she told him. Sometimes he wanted to say to her, *I'm a little old for fairy tales,* but he didn't dare.

The artist and his brilliant student would move to New York, according to the love story. He would go first and find them a place. She would follow. Except there was a glitch: by then she was pregnant. How proud Marc was, she told Cramer. How happy. But she mustn't tell anyone who the father was, Marc warned her. It might get back to Louise, and there would be big trouble. Legal trouble. It could ruin everything. Oh, she understood. The last thing Mavis wanted was trouble, when she was this close to a dream come true.

And so she waited.

At first Marc could only find a tiny one-roomed place; the prices in New York were outrageous. It was a wonder he could find anywhere at all. And this place was definitely not big enough for two people, let alone a new baby. But things were going well. He would get a bigger place.

And so she waited.

She didn't talk—didn't tell a soul. Grew fat with child. Kept the child's father her special secret. Not that she was often in Ladybank, anyway. She was living up in Chester's Corner back then. Didn't need to go to town hardly at all. Had the baby at the hospital in Smiths Falls. No birth announcement in the *Ladybank Expositor,* though she was dying to share her joy with the world.

And she waited.

And waited. And he stopped calling. And he never came for her. But still she waited, until the day when she didn't even know where he lived anymore.

A love story.

Cramer had Googled Soto a few times, back in high school. It had shocked him to find the man. He had half expected the artist was imaginary. But there he was, a big shot, just as Mavis had claimed. Mostly there were pictures of his paintings, articles from newspapers and magazines. But there were a few photographs of the man himself, too, the best one appearing in a profile on his gallery's website. He was a smooth man with glossy black hair. His eyes were as blue as Cramer's own eyes. It was eerie. Cramer didn't like him, didn't like his chiseled, smug face, his liar's smile. He wondered whether he should download any of this stuff to show Mavis. They didn't have a hookup out at the house. He decided not to. She had spent so long a time forgetting the bastard, it would be cruel. Cramer didn't check up on Marc Soto after that. By then Waylin Pitney had started coming around, and that was more than enough to deal with.

Until he saw Mimi heading out to the snye with Jay, it had been four days since Cramer had seen her; it might be four days before he saw her again. But he thought about her all the time, especially when he was working out. Four sets, fifteen reps. Upright rows, lateral raises, flies and pullovers, curls and squats. Chin-ups to bulk up his lats, bench presses for his pecs, bent-over raises for the deltoids.

Lunges, hack squats, triceps curls, wrist curls, reverse wrist curls. He piled on the weight, expanded his circuit. But he wasn't bulking up for Waylin Pitney anymore.

Cramer woke up. Thursday morning, 11:00 AM. He'd managed five hours sleep after getting back from the plant, but Mr. Pretty expected him at the store by one. Despite the lack of sleep, his mind felt wonderfully clear. He wasn't angry anymore—didn't want to be—pushed it aside. For one thing, she was staying. Mimi was obviously moving in. There was a bad side to that—namely, Jay—but at least she was still near. He lay there, his hands folded behind his head. Last night the shift manager had talked about getting him on full-time at the plant. Full-time meant security, and maybe he could parlay that into a loan. He'd talk to Hank Pretty about it. This money-for-Mavis thing would work out fine, without stealing stuff.

He listened. There was no sound downstairs. His mother must have gone out. That was another encouraging sign. She was getting out more, getting some air, going for walks up the road or down to the creek. One day she walked all the way to the old bridge at the very end of the Upper Valentine, or so she said. Quite a hike. But she looked better for it, stronger. He wouldn't tell her about getting full-time just yet. He'd surprise her.

He listened again. Then he dug the silver-framed picture of Mimi out from under his mattress. She and her friend on a beach somewhere, their arms around each other, their sandy cheeks pressed together, smiling at the camera. "Jamila and Mimi, summer '06" was written in gold across the bottom of the picture. He groaned softly, closed his eyes, and pressed the picture to his heart.

≋| CHAPTER FOURTEEN |≋

YOU CAN HAVE the bedroom," said Jay.

"Are you sure?"

"Absolutely. That way if I decide to stay over, I can work at all hours of the night and not bother you."

She nodded. "Thanks." She had thought the same thing herself.

"And you've got your desk in the front room," he added.

"Right." She grinned at him, felt awkward about him making all the decisions. She had never had to negotiate about who had what when and where. She was a spoiled brat and she knew it, but then so was he. This was so strange. She was moving in with a guy, and yet she wasn't really. Not a *guy*-guy.

"I'll help you with the mattress," she said. And so they hefted his bedding upstairs and flopped it in a corner. That was when she saw the stones. They were lined up on the windowsill of the gable, but she hadn't noticed them that first day up here; there had been too much else going on.

"These rocks are famous," she said, picking one up and turning it over in her hands.

"You recognize them?"

She nodded. "The sketches in the guest room?"

Jay looked impressed. "You don't miss much."

"Actually, they're even more famous than your guest room. There are paintings, too," she said. "Humongous paintings."

Jay looked skeptical.

"Utterly humongous," she said, proud of her father, despite herself. "Twelve feet square. Seriously!"

Jay took one of the stones from her and looked it over.

"The paintings are pretty abstract," she said. "More color-field stuff than really representational. But you'll recognize them when you see them."

"When I see them?"

She made a face. "Well, you're going to visit me, aren't you?"

"Hadn't gotten that far," he said. "But yeah, of course."

"There was a retrospective at the Whitney a couple years back," she said, putting the stone she was holding back down again. "There was this stupid column in the *Herald:* 'Soto Gets His Rocks Off!'"

"Ugh."

Then Jay's attention had drifted to the windowsill, and he looked concerned all of a sudden.

"There's supposed to be nine," he said.

Mimi counted. Eight. There *were* supposed to be nine; she knew that. Then they looked at each other, and she stroked his arm because his face had gotten sad again, bent out of shape over a missing stone.

"It could have been gone for a while," she said.

"Oh, that makes me feel much better."

Mimi set up the desk right where her father's desk must have been. It was in the big room, under the left front window, with a view of the snye, looking as pretty as a picture on a corny calendar. She could tell a desk had been in this spot — that her father had looked out at this same view — because the paint was faded above a certain line on the wall. Even though no one had lived in the place for over twenty years, it was as if there was still a shadow of him, his presence in this house. But that wasn't all. Scrawled on the wall beside the window, above where his desktop must have been, there were phone numbers, written in ballpoint pen or pencil or Conté or charcoal — some numbers with names or initials, some without. Some retraced and darker than others — the hand busy while the ear listened. There was no phone line any longer.

It amazed Mimi how energetic her father's writing was, even in such a mundane endeavor as scribbling down a phone number. But then, any mark making was serious to her father. There were also flurries of his very recogniz-able doodles. She stared at the wall—almost a piece of art itself. An art supplier in Ottawa, a framer in Richmond, a gallery in Montreal. There was even a 212 area code. She phoned it on her cell to see who it was. Caprice! So he had already made the connection with his present gallery way back then. It was a mini history—a connect-the-dots bio. The writing on the wall!

Tuesday and raining.

Eleven days since she arrived; almost a week since they took up residency. Except that only Mimi was in residence right now. Jay had stayed at the snye for the first three nights. Nothing had happened. Nothing *bad* had happened! Well, a famous rock went missing, but some-how she was sure that must have happened before. Jay had been back and forth since then, and she'd stayed in town at the Pages' on the weekend. And nothing bad had happened. Whoever had been stalking the place and leav-ing mementos of his visits had made no appearance, as far as they could tell.

"Guess I scared him away, huh?"

"You are pretty scary," he said.

They were old friends. Week-old friends.

But Jay wasn't here now, and he wouldn't be back until Thursday. He'd come by that rainy morning in Jo's Honda to tell her he was driving to Toronto to pick up his girlfriend.

"Your what?"

"Iris. Iris Xu. She's at school in Toronto."

"And when were you going to tell me about Iris?" Mimi had said, her arms crossed like some jealous high-school coed.

A crack appeared in the edge of his smile. "You're kidding, right?"

She wasn't kidding. She couldn't believe this hadn't come up. A girlfriend?

But getting her wits together, she said, "Of course I'm kidding. It's just the little-sister thing. You know. 'Uh-oh, what's he up to now, la-de-da.' That kind of thing, you know."

But of course he didn't know what kind of thing. Neither of them did. They were only children.

Only children.

That's what they had grown up thinking, anyway.

She would meet Jay and Iris at Conchita's in town Thursday evening for drinks. He'd phone when he was back to confirm. So now she was really alone.

"How far away is Toronto?"

"Just beyond the edge of the world where everything falls off into the Great Turtle's mouth."

She wished she hadn't asked.

Mimi stared at the screen of her computer. She was using Final Draft, screenwriting software that took all the work out of formatting—almost wrote the screenplay for you. Almost. You're in a scene with two people? The software knows it; as soon as you push the Return key after writing a bit of dialogue, it automatically centers the name of the other person in the scene. You type Z—it knows who you mean.

ZORBA

```
INT. OFFICE AT UNIVERSITY—DAY
```

ZORBA

```
    For Christ's sake, pick up the
    phone! Little bitch.
```

Her cell phone rang again. "Let me go, let me go, let me go!" She was beginning to hate "Bohemian Rhapsody." She checked the caller, didn't recognize the number; she didn't answer. If it was Lazar calling from some booth, she had to shudder at his uncanny timing.

```
EXT. PASTORAL SETTING—DAY
SASHA steps into the stream, bends down, and
lowers her screaming cell phone below the
water. She holds it there until it stops.
```

She pushed the laptop out of the way and flopped her head onto the desk. She closed her eyes and listened to the rain. There was a drip somewhere inside she didn't have the energy to deal with. She checked that it wasn't directly over her bed. Then she went upstairs and checked on Jay's computer, his instruments. Everything was fine. She sat for a moment and picked up the fat electric guitar. She had learned a song once, from Jamila. She tried to recall the chords. But then the cell phone rang. Again. *Shit.*

Jay was right. She should get a new one. She'd been here long enough; there was a place in town, but she kept putting it off. Why? Because she *expected* Lazar to stop. She *expected* him to get the message—to give up. To do the right thing. To act his age! That was part of it. Why should she be turning her life upside down because this supposedly mature—*way* mature—man couldn't take no for an answer? But it was more than that. She knew at some point she would have to pick up; she would have to have it out with him. But not until she was good and ready. And she wasn't ready yet. She was frightened of Lazar Cosic, and she didn't want him to know that, didn't want her voice to betray her.

She had brought with her a box of dishes and silverware, for one. And she had planned on buying a microwave or toaster oven if necessary. But the stove worked, and so she had purchased a tiny little beer fridge at the Canadian Tire store in Ladybank. A beer fridge from a tire store. Go figure. She kept soy milk and veggies in her little blue beer fridge. And wine.

She had settled in.

The first few days had been fun, a chance to get to know each other. A brother. She had a brother. The idea still seemed impossible. She had yet to phone her father to confront him with the news, which, apparently, wasn't news to him. She was still too angry, and yet she wasn't really sure why. And what was the point of being angry with him, anyway? Anger slid off his hide like water off a duck.

INT. SOHO STUDIO—NIGHT

> HENRI
>
> So, you've met him. Hell, I'd forgotten all about the boy. What do you think?

HENRI sips from a glass of wine. Dabs a Venetian blue smear across his canvas.

> SASHA
>
> Has it ever occurred to you that you are a first-class schmuck?

> HENRI
>
> So I'm told. But seriously, what's he like?

SASHA pours herself a large refill of the wine, then hurls the contents all over the canvas.

She hadn't told her mother about Jay, either. Not yet. She had fished to see if Grier knew anything about other siblings. She didn't seem to. So the only person back home who knew was Jamila. And when Jamila had gotten over the shock, she had said, "Oh, my God, welcome to the club!" Because Jamila had four brothers, and she had promised to get Mimi up to speed on the whole thing. They had chatted furiously back and forth by e-mail while Mimi was still staying at the Pages', but there was no Internet connection out here. And, for that matter, the connection at the Pages' had been dial-up, so not exactly a furious rate. They were too far out of town for the local tower to get high-speed, although there were rumors of a new tower going up soon. So Mimi had felt very far from home. She was welcome to use the dial-up at the Page house anytime — welcome to stay there whenever she wanted. Lou had given her a key. There was also a great little Internet café in town right on the park. But Mimi was trying very hard to do what she had set out to do, which was to be on her own, sorting things out, digging deep. Trying, in one way or another, to figure out who the sap was who had gotten herself in so deep with an almost forty-year-old professor who just might be mentally unstable.

She had been so happy to see Jay arrive that morning. But he was only stopping by to give her the news about his trip to Toronto. The news about Iris.

"Oh, and these," he said, heading back to the SUV.

He returned with a neat pile of sunshine-yellow folded material. Curtains. "Lou figured it might be good on the downstairs windows, anyway."

Mimi opened one out. "Lou made these?"

"Yeah, I know. A woman of many talents."

When she and Jo had carted out a "few sticks of furniture," as Jo called it, Lou had measured the five downstairs windows. Mimi hadn't even noticed. Jay had picked up curtain rods on his way out. Mimi was surprised at how happy she was. Curtains!

Jay had dragged his mother's kayak upstream a few days earlier so that they could both go down to the big house whenever they wanted without the long roundabout drive. Mimi laughed herself silly her first time out. "Hey, New York!" she shouted. "Look at me—Mimi Shapiro in a *boat*!" She imagined herself going back to the city buff and tanned. Yeah, right. Sore and drenched was more like it! She flipped three times the first day. She never felt really comfortable that first trip, though she was okay as long as she hugged the shore and moved at about five strokes per hour.

"You go ahead, for God's sake!" she said as Jay circled back to give helpful advice. "You're making me nervous."

But he stayed close.

"And to think the Eskimos hunt whales in these things," she shouted.

"Inuit," he said.

She looked at him, thinking maybe he was giving advice.

"They're not Eskimos; they're Inuit."

Well, she certainly wasn't Inuit.

"Don't worry, Ms. Cooper," she said to no one. "You will always be my favorite mode of transportation."

He had first left her alone on Friday night. He was meeting up with some friend who was in town.

"Are you sure you're okay?"

"I'm fine. Get! Scoot!"

She had waved him off down the snye, standing barefoot in the shallow water as he glided off into the gloaming. He had to lie back on the kayak to pass under the arch of the bridge.

"Have a good trip, honey," she called after him. It was meant to be a joke. Jay laughed. Good.

But the truth was she did feel like some hausfrau waving her hubby off to work. Then, as soon as he was out of sight, she returned to the little house, locked the doors, and checked the panic room. She hoisted up her mattress, opened the trapdoor, and dropped down to the earthen room, then shimmied along the tunnel with her flashlight in her teeth until she came to the door that led to the outside. Jay had put a good hefty hasp on it and padlocked it. So there were just the windows to worry about. She had gone to sleep the first couple of nights to the imagined tinkling of broken glass.

But there was no broken glass and there were no dead

birds or snake skins or messages of any kind.

She had worried about the car, too, wished she could bring it closer, in sight of the house. Jay had suggested laying some boards down over the broken expanse of bridge—only a few feet, after all. But she couldn't quite imagine driving on such a makeshift overpass. Worse still was the thought of having to escape the house and finding the planks gone! So she checked the car first thing every morning when she went out for her run. She checked the ground around it for signs of footsteps. For a week now, there had been nothing more serious than dew to contend with. Dew and the odd petal of a flowering tree.

And once deer tracks.

She imagined some deer peering into the Mini looking for whatever it was deer ate. Jelly beans? Cedar-flavored jelly beans.

And so, bit by bit, she let the magic place settle down around her. She got into a kind of rhythm that was comforting and stimulating at the same time in ways she had never imagined possible. Up at seven, a jog down the Upper Valentine Road to where it ended at the river, a shower, breakfast, and sitting at her laptop by eight or so. Lunch at noon, like any working Joe. A little nap just for the luxury of it, a little reading, work until five, and treat yourself to a glass of wine. She found a video store in town and rented DVDs to play on her computer. What more could a girl want?

EXT. TULLOCH—NIGHT

> FAIRY LIEUTENANT
> So what do you think, sir? Do we
> take her tonight?

KING OF THE FAIRIES sips from a glass of mead. Stares at the little moonlit house.

> KING
> (Nodding)
> Alert the voles, the moths, the
> bats. Tonight we move in.

Yikes! Maybe the aloneness was getting to her. Her script would not behave. She stared out the window at the hill in the meadow. No sign of fairy troops. Still, she wished Jay were here.

It had been great to have him around. He had worked on his music a lot. Compared to him, she felt like a fraud. Writing a film script, yeah, right! *He's four years older than you,* she told herself. But it was more than that. There was this commitment toward his art she didn't feel, not in the same way. Then again, she wasn't sure if he was always this conscientious or whether he was making some kind of a point.

He worked with headphones, so it was almost as if no one was there except for the squeaking of his chair. Then he'd come down and ask if it was all right if he played or listened to something out loud. So polite. And what could she say? If she was writing, she'd close the door to her bedroom and work with her laptop on her lap and her iPod playing music she could tune out. She couldn't tune out Jay's music. Couldn't tune him out, either.

Apart from her morning run along the road, she explored the island, her mace in her pocket, though it seemed absurd in the light of day. She explored but not too far. Never into the Dark Forest. And never to the end of the snye, where the wetlands took over. The land down where the snye met the river was owned by mosquitoes that seemed to have a thing for her virgin New York flesh.

It had been strange to watch Jay from her "office window," arriving at the little house, pulling his kayak up onto the bank. She had felt like a voyeur watching him strip off his flotation device. Odd the feeling she felt to look at him, the fluttering inside. *Don't go there, girl,* she warned herself.

And now there was Iris. This would help to settle things down—batten down the hatches on any unwarranted flights of fantasy. She would have to decide to like Iris.

≫ CHAPTER FIFTEEN ≪

Distance was a funny thing.

Cramer was twelve when Mavis found the little yellow house overlooking Butchard's Creek. It was so near to Chester's Corner, she didn't even have to change her phone number when they moved there. The school bus that picked him up at the foot of the drive took under fifteen minutes to get him to the school in the village, Eden Elementary. The bus trundled west along the Upper Valentine over the old bridge, and they were there, just like that.

Then in '96, the bridge was closed down.

The county seemed to take forever settling on what to do with it, deciding, at last, that it was underused and too expensive to rebuild. So it was condemned. And because it was unsafe to leave standing, it was torn down. All that was left now were two sets of crumbling concrete pylons in the middle of the river and the yellow-and-black barricades with DANGER written all over them, where the Upper Valentine Road ended. From the barricade, you could see the township works garage on the edge of the village. In winter when the foliage was off the trees, you could even see his old middle school. You didn't have to have much of an arm to hurl a stone most of the way across the Eden from where the road ended. But the bus that picked Cramer up after they tore down the bridge took over forty-five minutes to get him to school each morning. Chester's Corner, where he and his mother had lived since his birth—with its little wooden-floored grocery store and post office and the garage where she had bought the Taurus, second-hand—might as well have been the moon.

Distance was a funny thing.

His second year at Ladybank Collegiate, Cramer realized he could get to town quicker by river than road. It took him just over half an hour if he put some muscle into it. He didn't know back then who lived in the striking low house of window and yellow stone on the outskirts of town, the house with the sweeping lawns and the little jetty out onto the Eden. He passed it every good-weather morning and again as he returned in the afternoon without knowing that Marc Soto had lived there. And he didn't know about the snye, farther upriver, the secret stream that led to the little house that had been Soto's studio.

When he had followed Jay there last fall, it was the first time he had laid eyes upon the place, but he guessed right off what it was—what it had been—and he took it all in, in its every detail. This, he knew, was the house in which he must have been conceived. The little bridge leading to it was crumbling. He noticed that as well. All these bridges that used to lead somewhere and no longer did.

Distance was a funny thing.

It was not until he was in high school that Cramer found himself walking the same hallways as his half-brother, Jackson Page. He had known of his existence since he was a kid. Once or twice on trips to town, Mavis had pointed Jay out to him, a boy the same age as he was, shopping with his mother, skateboarding with a friend. Now here he was every day.

He was a month and a bit older, a big brother to Cramer. He was Jay to everyone who knew him, and everyone did—everybody, it seemed, but Cramer himself. How strange was that? They might have shared the same halls, but they were never in the same class. Jay read announcements on the school intercom, played piano at assemblies, served on the student council. He was valedictorian. They went through four years of school together but not really together, because the currents in a high school were not ones that Cramer could negotiate. He had no Bunny to handle school. He had no quick, responsive craft to find his way through those waters. But he watched Jay all the same, like he was some exotic animal or a movie star. Never talked to him, though.

Well, once.

He was in a line for something, and turning around he found to his surprise that Jay was standing right behind him with Iris Xu.

"Hi," said Cramer before he knew what he was doing.

Jay smiled. "Hi," he said. "Long line, eh?"

"Yeah," said Cramer, already regretting his impulsiveness. What was he supposed to say now?

"Hi," said Iris. Cramer nodded, words abandoning him. Then Iris remembered something she had been meaning to show Jay, and as she dug into her backpack to find it, the line moved on. Just like that.

And just like that they graduated. Jay went west and Iris went to University of Toronto and Cramer stayed in Ladybank, never really expecting to see any of that crowd again, the college crowd—the ones that got away. And he didn't, until last fall, when Jay returned and started hanging out at the house on the snye. Didn't have a job, as far as Cramer could tell. Didn't have to work. That stuck in Cramer's craw. Not working. He could hardly imagine such a luxury. But that first day he saw him on the river, Cramer didn't feel anything like anger. On the contrary! He had been sitting in the shade of a huge willow on the south shore of the Eden, looking through binoculars at the Page house across the way, and then suddenly there was Jay, climbing into his kayak, heading upstream. For one crazy moment, Cramer wanted to call to him. To paddle out of the shadows toward him—

"Hey, Jay. Hi! It's me, remember?"

Like they were soul mates or something. Princes of the river.

Jay became a project, something to do on his days off. The house on the snye became somewhere to go. Then he started leaving him things. It happened almost by accident. A bluebird crashed into his mother's studio window and broke its neck. She'd heard the crash and it had startled her. Cramer found the bird in the uncut grass, cradled it in his hands. It scarcely weighed a thing. But the iridescence of its wings was something. It was exactly the kind of thing you would run to show your big brother. And so he did.

Then there was the snake skin he'd found in the wood-pile. Cramer was no poet, but he looked hard at things and saw what was there. And when he looked hard at their two lives—his and Jackson Page's—he decided that a snake skin might also be a good thing for Jay to think about. The thing you had to crawl out of if you were to grow. Anyway, a little reminder to the golden boy that he was not alone in the world.

Then Jay fixed the upstairs window and Cramer was locked out, until he discovered the trapdoor. It was something he knew that Jay didn't. Something he had over him.

Cramer had never taken anything from him. The stone, but that was worthless. It was just to play with his head. Nothing truly nasty. He didn't want to scare him away. He wanted to be noticed, and he had no idea how—no other idea how. And yes, he wanted to disturb Jay's comfort. Comfort was what Jay had a whole lot of. A *world* of comfort! He wanted Jay to know what it felt like to never really be able to relax, to never really feel at ease, to never have any time off. In a way, though he couldn't exactly explain it, he was just trying to make smaller the distance—the gulf—between them.

⋙ CHAPTER SIXTEEN ⋘

CONCHITA'S WAS DOWN a flight of wooden stairs to a deck suspended only a foot or two above the river, shallow at this point, offering little risk of drowning if one happened to fall drunk over the railing. Or if you accidentally pushed someone. *Now, now, Mimi,* she muttered to herself. *I'm sure Iris will be lovely.*

The restaurant was tucked into what was once the basement of a building constructed by Scottish stonemasons a hundred and fifty years ago, never knowing that the building would one day serve quesadillas and killer margaritas.

Blue-and-yellow Corona umbrellas were open above every table on the crowded deck but served no real purpose, for the setting sun was blocked from the patrons' eyes by the massive old place that housed the restaurant, a craft store, and bookstore as well.

Jay and Iris had already ordered a pitcher of margaritas when Mimi arrived, Thursday evening. She arrived late, on purpose, determined not to be the one sitting there alone and waiting. She had only packed a couple of dresses for her trip, and she dressed in the flirtiest of them before remembering that it was hardly a date. So she changed, a little reluctantly, back into her black capris and a black V-neck. She wore a lime-green plastic belt and a button that read IMPEACH NIXON. A girl had to show some style.

Jay actually stood to introduce the two women. Could he be more chivalrous? Iris Xu was petite, but her handshake was firm. Her smile dissolved her face into a glinting array of smooth and burnished plains. Her long hair shimmered; her eyes were warm. Mimi laughed with relief. Liking her was not going to be hard at all.

"Are you beat from the drive?"

"No, it's just three and a half hours," said Iris. "Except that Jay drives exactly at the speed limit!"

"How boring is that."

"I know," said Iris, and patted Jay's hand affectionately. High-school sweethearts now old-marrieds. Mimi wasn't sure if she felt very young or very grown up in their company.

Then a waitress arrived, smiling—mostly at Jay. And Mimi got carded.

"I can vouch for her, Nikki," said Jay while Mimi fumbled for her ID.

"Okay, Jay," said Nikki, blinking and winking at him and stumbling away with her tray clasped to her chest.

Iris leaned forward, with her hand to the side of her mouth. "Nikki's been in love with Jay since third grade."

"Poor thing," said Mimi. "What does she see in him?"

Iris shrugged. "Back then I think it was his Han Solo action figure. But now I think she's after his kayak."

"Well, it is a really long kayak," said Mimi, and Iris cracked up.

"All right, ladies," said Jay. "Let's keep it down."

Nikki soon returned with the beer and a plate of nachos with jalapeños, sour cream—the works.

"Restraint is *so* last year," said Iris, who was as thin as a rail. And then leaning against the table, she whispered, wide-eyed, "So how weird is it to find you have a brother you never knew about?"

Mimi poured herself a drink. "Oh, it's right up there with getting arrested in the Uffizi," she said. And she told them all about it.

They talked about travel misadventures and then history, which was Iris's major, and art and music and New York. Spent napkins piled up around them.

"Sour cream alert," said Iris, and taking Mimi's face in her hand, she removed a smear from her cheek. They exchanged smiles and, unless Mimi was imagining it, blessings.

"Jay was telling me you left New York in a bit of a hurry."

Mimi frowned. "What exactly did he tell you?"

"A predatory prof?"

Mimi glared at Jay.

He threw up his hands. "She forced it out of me," he said.

"Yeah, right."

"Dish!" said Iris.

Note to self, thought Mimi. *Keep secrets from Jay.* But Iris was not about to be put off and so Mimi dished. She didn't mind. In fact, she was a little amazed at how crazy hungry she was to talk about it. So she told them about the exhilaration in the early days of the affair, the clandestine dates, the off-the-beaten-track venues, the surprising places one could find to be totally alone together even in an academic establishment. Then she told them how it all came undone, as Lazar got more and more infatuated.

"It got kind of surreal," she said.

"Like melty?" said Iris.

"Huh?"

"You know, that picture by Salvador Dalí with the melting clocks hanging from dead trees or whatever."

"Ah, melty," said Mimi. "I guess." But what she guessed was that Iris was getting pretty drunk. Come to think of it, so was she. Nikki had come back with a second pitcher of margaritas. Mimi had tried to decline, but Jay guessed her only real concern.

"Nobody's driving," he said. "Transportation is under control."

She didn't bother to ask what that meant, mostly because she wanted to keep drinking. Wanted to let go. And she had let go. Except that letting go had led to this discussion about her love life.

"Is he dangerous, this Lazar Coatrack?"

"Cosic," said Mimi. She shrugged and shook her head. Then thought a moment and nodded. Iris stared at her a little cross-eyed.

"Could you be slightly more definitive?"

"I'm here, aren't I?" said Mimi. And what she meant was she had run away, but they already knew that. Hell, half the people at Conchita's probably knew it by now, she realized. Her voice had gotten quite loud. It did that.

Jay looked serious, and she was about to apologize when he said something that stunned her. "He was stalking you, wasn't he?"

She felt panicky as if Jay must have been stalking her himself. "How did you know that?"

"Your documentary. There was some dude standing outside the apartment, on the corner."

Mimi stared at Jay and nodded slightly, a little unnerved. "Good eye," she said.

Jay shook his head. "Not really. You zeroed right in on him, swore, and then went into this dissolve. If I was writing the score, there'd be cellos."

"Cellos?"

He nodded. "Playing a lot of sharps."

Mimi was a little lost.

Luckily Iris was there to move things along.

"So tell us about the film treatment."

Mimi poured herself another margarita. "The script is so-so," she said, waggling her hand as if she was screwing in a lightbulb that didn't quite fit. "Actually, I'm thinking of turning it into a sci-fi thriller, set on one of the moons of Venus."

"Odd choice," said Iris.

"Does Venus have moons?" said Jay.

"Dunno. Could be a space station, I guess. Anyway, instead of an aging professor having a fling with a beautiful freshman, I'm thinking of an aging Gangroid with three heads, huge talons, and . . . well, you know. The rest."

"Eeuw, kinky," said Iris.

"And the beautiful freshman?" said Jay.

"Natalie Portman," said Mimi.

It was just then that a rowdy customer arrived, already three sheets to the wind, and it turned out to be good old Rudy Slater. Mimi shook hands, did the intro thing, smiled nicely, and then sank back into her chair, talked out—out of practice—and glad to be saved from any more dishing. Rudy, Jay, and Iris caught each other up—she wasn't listening. He left a few hearty moments later, but he had done the job of putting the Lazar Cosic Horror Show out of her dinner mates' minds. *Good! And,* she thought, *a great ploy to remember for screenwriting. Noisy guy arrives. Wipe.*

"Oh, I love being home," said Iris, leaning back in

her chair and staring out at the water. It was dark now, rippling with reflected light. Then she smiled at Mimi and made her feel as if she, somehow, was part of what Iris meant about being home.

"You love it for about three weeks," said Jay. "Then you go, 'Wait a second—there is absolutely nothing happening here.'"

"Harsh," said Mimi. "And not true. I saw a poster for a hoedown, somewhere. The Oompah something."

"The *Ompah* Stomp," said Jay, "and don't knock it."

"I wasn't knocking it. I want to go, just as soon as I get a ball cap."

"True," said Iris. "There's the Ompah Stomp; the Blue Skies music festival; the amateur theatrical production of Gilbert and Sullivan every fall; hockey, of course; and . . . what was that other thing, Jay?"

"Monster car rallies at the fairgrounds?"

"Right. Oh, and golf. Everybody golfs."

"My mother doesn't golf."

"Oh, right. *All* the lesbian doctors in Ladybank abstain from golf, but everybody else plays."

"I like it here," said Mimi. "It's so . . ."

"Pretty?" said Jay.

"Pretty," said Mimi, curling up in her chair and cradling her drink. Her sixth? Her hundredth? There was a lull in the conversation, and she listened to the voices around her, happy vacation voices. Except the accent was all wrong. And her thoughts drifted, inevitably to New

York and humid evenings, sun filtered through dust and crowded sidewalk cafés. Suddenly she felt an intense stab of homesickness.

Had she really let herself be driven out of the city by a professor? No, there was more to it than that. Getting away was a good thing. And look what she had found! She glanced at Jay chatting with Iris. This . . . this was something she had never experienced. Something to hang on to. And yet . . .

"You okay?" Jay asked.

"Homesick," she said. "But I'll survive."

Iris poured the rest of her drink into Jay's glass. "Ladybank is a wonderful place to be *from*," she said. And made a toast with her empty glass. "Here's to being from somewhere and getting away!"

"And visiting," said Jay. Mimi caught his glance and wondered if he was telling her something. That this was just a visit and she shouldn't get any ideas about staying. *Great,* she thought, *homesick* and *paranoid, a winning combination.*

"Hey," he said, leaning across the table to rest his hand on hers, "what's up?"

Mimi shrugged. "I'm rethinking Natalie Portman. Maybe Keira Knightley is more the coed-from-Venus type."

And on the conversation wobbled, veering away from anything serious and punctuated by laughter. Liberating laughter, thought Mimi, when she allowed herself to be liberated from her feelings of being out of place. There was something else bothering her . . . What was it? Ah, yes. They had left the house unguarded. Christ! She shook it off. She had locked the place up. It would be safe. Except that they wouldn't be going back there tonight. Couldn't. Whatever transportation Jay had planned, he was in no better shape to drive than she was. It really was time to go.

Jay picked up the tab. Mimi left the tip. She found a five-euro note in her purse left over from Italy, hiding like a secret in the detritus at the bottom of her purse. She was drunk enough to leave it—a *very* big tip. But Iris wouldn't let her.

"Nikki will think it's play money and throw it away," she whispered.

The three of them wound their way up the staircase from the river, hanging on to the railings. The happily reunited lovers had their heads together nattering about how well Rudy Slater's skin had cleared up but how his love life sucked, and Mimi looked up into the night sky for a friend of her own, like the moon, for instance. This was something she was only just learning how to do—look for heavenly light of one kind or another. Apparently, there were stars and planets, too, and you could actually see them sometimes. Who knew?

So she looked up and . . . Ta-da! There it was—well three-quarters of it, anyway.

"Hello, moon," she said.

Then she felt Jay slip his arm around her waist. "You're

staying at Mom's house tonight," he said. This was his plan. A taxi.

"What about Ms. Cooper?"

"Leave Ms. Cooper to me," he said. She looked into his brown eyes, suddenly flashing golden in the head-lights of a passing car. She started to protest, but then Iris slipped an arm around her, too, so that she was a Mimi sandwich.

"We can all have breakfast together," said Iris, "and I can tell you about the Intermarium, and Romanian-Hungarian politics prior to World War Two." She cackled in a most indelicate way, then burped. Mimi was pretty much in love with her by now.

"I've always had a thing about Romania," said Mimi. "It's, like, right next to Beatlemania, isn't it?"

Maybe it was the alcohol, but she wondered if she was going to cry. How maudlin. She *hated* maudlin. She hadn't simply scored a delightful brother; she'd scored his delight-ful girlfriend, too. And eventually? Delightful nieces and nephews!

"Okay," said Mimi, stopping to look around for her car. "So, Mr. Transportation-is-under-control person. What *do* we do about my vehicle?"

"We'll leave a note for the traffic guy."

"Is it still Bob the traffic guy?" asked Iris. Jay nodded, and Iris turned to Mimi. "He's been around so long, he used to ticket horses."

They found the Mini and Jay wrote a note.

Dear Bob,
Inebriated. Took a cab.
Back in the morning.
Yours respectfully,
A responsible driver

"God!" said Mimi. "In New York that would be an invitation to trash the car!"

Meanwhile, Iris pulled a cell phone from her purse and called a cab. She seemed to know the number by heart. Then they all sat on a bench at the corner of Forster and Kane, arm in arm, and waited.

Mimi was rapidly losing the pleasure of being a Mimi sandwich. She had the feeling that the two lovebirds would rather be in each other's arms than in hers. She got up, saying she needed to stretch.

There weren't many traffic lights in Ladybank, but there was one at Forster and Kane, and a moment later it turned red to the traffic on the main drag. Only one car pulled up at the intersection, a cherry-red Chevy with its back end up like a dog in heat and a muffler that needed serious attention.

There was a lone driver in the car, a greasy-looking guy with a mullet who leered at Mimi and then revved the motor to make his point.

"For me?" cried Mimi, clasping her hands to her breast. "That is *so* sexy. Can you do it again?"

She watched the driver's eyes grow wide with

expectation. But even as he revved the motor, the laughter broke from her, seeping and sputtering out like water over a dam. The driver's euphoria turned sour.

"Bitch!" he shouted.

"Damn straight!" yelled Mimi.

Mullet rolled up his window. He squealed away from the corner as the light turned green, and Mimi headed back toward the bench, not in a completely straight line but with her fist raised, triumphantly. She dragged her canister of mace out of her purse and turned toward the Chevy, now a block away, holding it up, ready to fire.

"Bite me!" she shouted.

"Whoa," said Iris when Mimi rejoined them. She reached over and took the canister to look it over. She'd obviously never seen one before.

"Jay told me about the creep," she said. "The other one, I mean. Up at the snye."

"He's gone," said Mimi. "We scared him off. Right, partner?"

Jay shoved his own fist in the air. "Woo-hoo," he said with as much energy as he could muster.

Mimi plumped herself down on the bench. "I leave one stalker creepoid behind in New York and—*bam!*—walk right into another. Well, kind of. "

Then they sat, waiting, until suddenly Iris sat up straight.

"Oh," she said. "It's like that kid at school, remember?"

"Huh?"

"The guy who used to follow you around."

Jay looked puzzled. He glanced at Mimi and shrugged. "She's a history major, what can I say?"

"No, really!" said Iris. "I can't remember his name. But he was always around."

"See?" said Mimi, poking Jay in the shoulder. "You had a stalker, too."

"Well, it wasn't really like that," said Iris. "I mean it wasn't truly creepy."

"It wasn't truly anything," said Jay. "I don't know what you're talking about."

Iris's forehead bunched up in deep thought. "What was his name? He was one of those totally forgettable people, you know?" Then she covered her mouth. "That was shitty, what I said."

"What do you mean?"

"About him being a totally forgettable person."

"Well, it must be true," said Jay. "I don't remember him."

"We talked about this," said Iris.

"I don't remember that, either."

Iris turned to Mimi. "You know the kind of guy I mean?"

Mimi nodded. A nobody. Sure. But one who had a thing for Jay? She turned to him, a question on her face.

He held up his hands in surrender. "She's on crack. I swear to God, I don't remember any of this."

The cab turned onto Forster and slowed down. Jay waved and it pulled a U-turn, stopping at the curb. They were all snug in the backseat heading out toward Riverside Drive when Iris said, "I remember why he freaked me out."

"Who?" said Jay.

"The stalker," said Mimi impatiently, and turned her attention back to Iris. "Go on."

Iris leaned back in the seat, looking straight ahead and talking quietly as if not wanting to jar the memory. "There was this time I was trying to catch up with Jay. I don't remember why—I mean why I was behind him, but I was. Anyway, my *point* is, there I was and I didn't feel like running, so I just followed. And that's when I realized that he—this kid—was following Jay, too. He was between us."

"And he didn't just live out that way?" said Mimi.

Iris shook her head again. "I don't think so. I know it sounds lame, but I felt sure he was following Jay."

"Get out of town," said Jay.

"Actually, the guy looked like he had been bused in from Hick Holler, if you want to know the truth. Oops! I'm being a snob again. But really . . ."

"And?" said Mimi.

"And . . . nothing," said Iris. "I mean he didn't *do* anything. He was just always there, a little way off. Wherever our boy Jackson Page was so was the Fan."

Jay chuckled. "Are you sure it wasn't you he had the hots for?"

Mimi turned to Iris. She was gorgeous. It would be easy for some lonely guy to have a big-time crush on her. But Iris just kept shaking her head. "Uh-uh," she said. "It was you, honey-bunch."

≫ CHAPTER SEVENTEEN ≪

SHE WAS ALONE. It was what Cramer had hoped for, dreamed of. In the four days he had off from Sunday through Wednesday, he saw Jay come and go but never stay the night. Who knows what had gone on the last eight days, but Cramer was full of hope. Mimi and Jay never held hands or kissed, as far as he could see. They were friends, just friends, he told himself, and almost managed to believe it. Cramer loved to listen to them talk — so quick and funny. He wished he could talk to a girl that way. He'd had girlfriends, sure, but no one like Mimi.

She would go for a run in the morning up the Valentine. She was gone forty minutes or so. *She is running right by my place,* he thought. And he was glad she wouldn't see the little yellow house up on its knoll above the creek. He had told his mother he would bring a girl home to meet her, but he would never take Mimi there.

One morning there was a heavy dew, and Cramer boldly drew a message on the windshield of the Mini Cooper:

I ♥ MIMI

She was late getting started that morning, and by the time she waded across the snye and put her Nikes on, the sun had more or less obliterated the message he had left her. She patted the car as she passed by and spoke to it—called it Ms. Cooper.

Look closer, he said under his breath, knowing that his message would not be entirely gone, would still be there, if she would only look.

The next morning he broke in.

The lock on the storm door surprised him at first but didn't hold him back. The wood was punk; the screws in the hinges pulled away without too much effort. He needed to get inside. He needed to be sure about something. And, yes—yes! Mimi seemed to have taken over the bedroom downstairs; Jay's mattress was up in the loft. Cramer wanted to shout his joy out loud but held it in.

He opened her laptop, a Mac PowerBook G4. There was no password. The desktop on the G4 was some picture from an old black-and-white movie: a guy with ridiculously curly hair and a funny face, wearing a baggy suit and playing the harp. There were too many icons on the screen. Cramer wanted to clean it up for her—such a waste of memory. He opened a folder called Screenplay.

He opened something called Ideas. He checked her e-mail: a lot of messages from Jamila, the girl in the photograph. There wasn't time to read anything now—he couldn't concentrate. And anyway, all he was looking for were boys' names, some boy's name repeated too many times. There were two or three guys she chatted with, but nothing in the contents of those e-mails to indicate they were anything more than friends.

He checked iPhoto. There was a large library but no boys there, either, except the Asian guy in the documentary. Cramer didn't think there was anything between them.

He checked iTunes, scrolled down a list of band names he had never heard of. He glanced out the window. He would see her coming from here; the way was clear. He clicked on a couple of tunes. He wanted to hear what she heard, like what she liked. He sat there for a few moments listening, noting the name of a group that was okay, though it wasn't the kind of stuff he listened to. He would Google the band at the shop—get to know their stuff. He didn't listen to much music, but he could learn. He toyed with the idea of leaving her a note on the screen, then he reeled himself in. *Get serious, Cramer!* This was *not* the same as leaving surprises for Jay. He closed down the computer, made sure it was sitting exactly as he had found it, then rubbed the brushed silver top clean with the tail of his T-shirt to remove his fingerprints. He was sweating like a pig.

He checked the window again, checked his watch.

There was still time and he didn't want to leave. He didn't ever want to leave.

He wanted to leave something for her, a gift! There was a place he knew where there were wildflowers. He would leave her a bouquet on the little table in the kitchen.

No. Get a grip.

He checked out the bathroom, lovingly picked up her toothbrush, her hairbrush, a tube of lip gloss. He held everything to his nose, breathing her in. With his eyes closed, he could smell the same spicy scent that was on everything in her suitcase. It was so beautiful it made him swear under his breath and then bite down hard on his tongue for letting such a word escape him, here of all places. As if the swear word might linger in the air like a bad smell.

Tonight he started work again. There might be an afternoon or two he could get out here, but his nights were not his own for another eight days. How could he stand it?

He opened his eyes suddenly. Why hadn't he thought of this before! He looked through all the clutter of cosmetics on the little shelf below the mirror and arrayed across the water tank of the toilet, but there was no bottle of perfume. He hurried back to her bedroom again and on his knees searched through her suitcase. And there it was. A squat brown bottle of perfume with beveled shoulders and an elaborate bronze-colored stopper. It was called Trouble. He opened the top and breathed in so deeply that the potency made him cough, made him dizzy. He wiped his eyes. He took the tail of his T-shirt and dabbed some of her perfume on it, then put the stopper back in the bottle. He was putting the bottle back in her suitcase when he heard the kitchen door open and close.

He dove for the hidey-hole, reaching up and pulling the top down as quietly as he could. There had been no time to put the perfume exactly where he had found it. Would she notice? He didn't think so. She wasn't very tidy.

He heard her enter the room and realized that the scent of the perfume would be strong. Would she notice it? He crawled up the tunnel to be safe. If she opened the trapdoor, she wouldn't see him, unless she actually jumped down inside. The thought of her doing that made his heart beat so hard against his chest he was sure she would hear. He crouched there, scarcely breathing. He couldn't leave through the storm door without making too much noise, so he waited, listening. He heard a thump and another thump. Her running shoes. She was stripping after her run. He closed his eyes tightly, seeing her in his mind's eye. And he felt as though he might not be strong enough to hold himself together at all. She was humming, out of tune. Then he heard her leave the room, and in a moment he heard the sound of the shower. He turned to leave, and as he crawled up the tunnel to the door, he was shaking like a leaf.

Mavis was outside when he arrived home, out in the bedraggled patch of weeds near the kitchen, which had once been a vegetable garden. As he crossed the yard toward the house, he wondered if she was going to do something with it.

"Want a hand?" he asked.

She turned and he saw that she was smoking. She didn't usually smoke except when Waylin was around. He looked but there was no truck.

"I was thinking of cooking up some of this madder," she said, kicking lazily at a knee-high weed that had over-run the garden where she was standing. "You can make a good dye from it, I hear."

Her meaning was not lost on Cramer.

"Course, I'd need some medium to actually make it into paint," she said. She was going to go on, but she suddenly screwed up her nose. "What the heck is that?"

Cramer backed off. He stunk of Trouble. "I've got to change," he said.

"What are you up to?" she called after him, but he headed into the house and up the stairs. He shoved the reeking T-shirt in the back of his closet. Then he headed to the shower, where he scrubbed himself so hard he was sure he was losing a layer of skin.

He dried himself off, wrapped a towel around his waist, and opened the bathroom door. Mavis was there, leaning against the wall across from the bathroom door.

"My, my, what an odor," she said.

He headed toward his room, with her marching right behind him.

"Who is she, Cramer? Come on." Her voice was teasing. "Don't keep me in the dark, sunshine."

"There isn't anyone," he said. And he closed his door on her. She knocked. Christ, why wouldn't she leave him alone!

"I'm getting dressed!" he said.

"Well, when you get dressed, come on downstairs. I want to talk."

"Mom, it's not—"

But she cut him off. "I want to *show* you something," she said. "If you're not too busy."

He took his time. Tried to think of what he was going to say, how he could explain away the scent. What was it she wanted him to see? Shit. He checked under his mattress. The picture of Mimi was still there, so it wasn't that.

The first floor of the house was just the one room really, with the wide, deep porch converted into Mavis's studio. Mavis was waiting for him at the foot of the stairs when he finally emerged from his lair. She turned toward the room, expectantly awaiting his attention. She glanced back at him and then again at the room.

Her paintings. She had put her paintings on display around the place. There were nine or ten of them, sitting on chairs, leaning against the window jamb, the latest— he supposed—sitting on the easel. He relaxed. She just wanted his opinion.

"Oh," he said. "Wow. Great."

"Really?" she said. "Are they *really* great?"

He looked again. Sometimes she needed more encouragement. He understood that. He had learned how to talk to her — learned from *The Artist's Path*. There was a quote there about the spark of uniqueness that is carried through you into action, and under no circumstances must one ever try to block it. This was called the quickening. It was scary sometimes. When Mavis was painting, her eyes flashed with a different kind of energy — good energy, like a car running clean, like a computer humming. And when she was happily tired, the light in her eyes was a soft thing you could come close to. But when the quickening arose, you paid attention and responded to every need, every whim.

"Well?"

He looked hard at the paintings, feeling her agitation growing — almost smelling it. Made it hard to think straight. There was that first one, which was so rich — writhing with energy. There were a couple more like that — bursting with colors, the line work strong. But as he scanned the little show, it was as if the lights were dimmer everywhere else in the room. Each canvas was duller, as if its battery was running low. There were more shades than tints. Less pure color. He could see that, but could he afford to say it?

There was a quote in *The Artist's Path*. "My vanity wants your lies but they are poison to my soul."

"Well?" said Mavis. She was rubbing her hands together nervously. They were spotted with paint. Blotched with paint she had not bothered to clean away.

"Some of them are real good," he said, reluctant to limit his praise but afraid of lying to her.

"Oh," she said, her voice tense. "But just some of them?"

He could feel himself being drawn into the trap. But there was no way to avoid it. He swallowed hard. "Some are . . . darker?"

"Darker? And what else?"

He hated it when she did this. She was like the worst teacher in the world, fishing for an answer he didn't have, an answer she wasn't going to like if he found it.

"There just seems to be more, you know, like, spirit in the . . . in those . . ." He pointed weakly toward the first painting and the other two that shared its intensity.

"Ahhh," she said. "Very perceptive." Then she grabbed his arm and dragged him toward the picture on the easel. The paint was still wet in patches. Just finished—if it was finished. He had no idea. It wasn't anything. Just a mass of conflicting patches of color, subdued color: browns mainly and grays. A yellow seam livened up the canvas, but it was thin; he could see the canvas through it. Looked as if someone had pissed on it. He sure wasn't going to tell her that. He glanced at the worktable and saw the wreckage of paint tubes and plastic jars, empty, lying on their sides.

Her point was pretty obvious.

"What about this one?" she said, her voice as thin as the stream of yellow on the canvas.

"You're out of paint," he said, tired of the game she was playing.

"Very good!" she said, and started clapping. "Three cheers for the art critic."

"Mom," he said softly, but it was no use.

"Congratulations to the boy too busy with his little smelly *games* to help his mother when she needs him the most."

"I've been trying—"

"His mother who is working her fingers to the bone to find her way back to the good place where the art happens and the *success* happens and the *happiness* happens."

"I will get you the money, honest, I—"

"Oh, good. When? When I'm dead?"

"Don't say that."

"Dead? You don't want me to say 'dead'?"

He tried to leave but she held on to him, dug her fingernails into the flesh of his forearm until he winced.

"I *will* die, you know," she said, her voice tremulous. "Cramer—*this* is what makes it possible to live." She threw out her arm to indicate the meager handful of paintings displayed around the room. "Without it, I'll just rot away. That what you want?"

"No."

"Because I'm this close," she said. *"This close!"*

He peeled her hand away from his arm. "Stop it," he said.

"Oh, I'll stop, all right," she said. "I *have* stopped, thanks to you. You want some ordinary mommy who drives into work at the Wal-Mart. Is that it? Is this your way of making me pay?"

"Shut up!" he said.

And the force of his voice stopped her, frightened her. It frightened him, too. He'd never yelled at her.

"I do have a plan," he said. "*I have a plan.* It's hard to do anything while I'm working, but I've . . ." How was he supposed to put it? "I've talked to someone," he said.

"Someone?" she said. "Is she the one who stinks like a whorehouse?"

Cramer's hands curled involuntarily into fists at his side. And his face must have looked fierce, because Mavis backed off, lowered her eyes.

"I'm sorry," she mumbled. "I . . . I didn't mean . . ."

She walked over to the easy chair and sat on the arm, her back to him, looking out at the sunshine. Very slowly, he regained his composure, but his voice was shaky now.

"I'll get your money. I don't want to discuss it till I know more. Okay?"

She could have given him something then: a thankful smile, a little slack. She could have acknowledged what he said in some small way. Was it so much to ask for? But there was nothing. When she looked at him, her eyes got kind of lost, as if she wasn't seeing straight.

"I should . . . find out in the next few days," he said. "Believe me, you'll be the first to know."

Her eyes found his, but there was nothing in her gaze but disappointment. No. It was worse than that. There was nothing in her eyes but disenchantment.

He turned to go. Stopped when he heard her clear her throat but didn't turn around.

"You've changed," she said. "Yelling at your mother like that. I don't hardly know you anymore."

≫ CHAPTER EIGHTEEN ≪

Mᵢᵢ SLEPT IN LATE. It was eleven before she stumbled into the kitchen, where Jay and Iris were sitting with the remains of toast and orange juice and a school yearbook open in front of them.

"Iris is trying to find my stalker," said Jay.

Mimi leaned over Iris's shoulder as she flipped the pages. She got to the end with no luck.

"Told you," said Jay. "He was a figment of your imagination."

Iris shook her head. "No, it's what I said last night. He wasn't remarkable in any way. I thought maybe the yearbook would jog my memory."

Mimi helped herself to coffee, which was all she could face. She had a headache, a serious one. She didn't drink much normally, and last night had not been good for her.

She wandered out to the screened-in porch and stared out at a gentle rain, felt the cool of it on her face. It helped a little.

Rain without exhaust fumes. Strange.

What was she supposed to do? She needed to get Ms. Cooper—that much was certain. But then what? Her laptop was out at the snye. Clean clothes were out at the snye. She would have to go and yet she didn't want to. She leaned her head lightly against the screen. She didn't want to do anything. She heard Iris giggle about something Jay has said. She wanted to go home. No. Yes. Hell.

Der ungebetene Dritte, thought Mimi. That's what I am. It was something her German grandmother used to say: the uninvited third.

Then Jay came out on the porch. "You okay?" he asked.

"I wouldn't go that far," she said.

"Do you want me to rescue the car?"

"I guess," said Mimi. "We don't want Bob the traffic guy to have a conniption fit."

Jay chuckled. He had a good-sounding chuckle. He seemed more relaxed. *Self-satisfied,* she thought. *Lucky man.* "Come on," he said. "I'll drive you."

She turned to go, then stopped and shook her head. "You know, a walk might do me good."

So she walked into town in the rain, with a borrowed black raincoat of Jo's and a very large black umbrella. It took half an hour, and by the time she got there, the rain had stopped. The sky was moving again; clouds were scudding—wasn't that the word for it?

Ms. Cooper looked shiny and new, as if maybe Bob had taken her to the car wash. The note, however, was still on the windshield, bleeding ink, indecipherable.

By the time she had driven home, there were even blips of sunshine, which helped to revive her spirits. But when she pulled into the driveway, Jay and Iris were on their way out. Iris was just about to phone her. They were going over to somebody's—did she want to come? But she didn't feel like it. It would probably be someone else who was happy, and she wasn't sure she could take that.

When they were gone, she realized that she didn't feel like hanging out at the big house, either, or driving forty minutes to the snye. So she decided to take the kayak and head upstream. That would clear her head, she thought. And even though the wind was high, it wasn't cold and looked to be going her way, even if the current wasn't. Battling the elements seemed a good choice for the afternoon. It would take her mind off her headache, if not her mind-ache.

She didn't want to take her purse in case she flipped the kayak. She was halfway up the river before she remembered her precious canister of mace.

The trip upstream wasn't bad, under the circumstances. She hugged the southern shore and took her time. Soon enough she reached the reedy place just beyond which there was the slightest hint of a bay, though you'd never know there was a sly small stream at its mouth. Tentatively, she nosed her craft into the tall weeds. And they parted before her.

"I'm the New Age Moses," she muttered. "In a flashy Kevlar basket."

She ducked, felt the soft willow tendrils trail across her back. Then she was in the open again, and there was a channel here, deep enough to navigate, as long as she stayed in the very center. It *was* magical, even with a hangover. She stopped to look down, saw tiny fish darting in the dappled light. She sat up again and glided on the still green water. Trees dripped on her. She looked up and felt tiny cold splashes on her face.

There was no wind back here, only a distant whisper of the weather out there in the real world. She had passed over into a dream of stillness, of filtered, green light, glossy with a night's worth of rain.

She rounded a bend and sniffed. There was a stench in the air. She remembered it from before, but it was worse this time, possibly because of the rain. And now she remembered what Jay had told her. All along the shore were tangled thickets of carrion flower. Thorny, green-stemmed, with heart-shaped leaves and beautiful blue berries. The stink attracted flies, apparently, which acted as pollinators.

Just what perfume's supposed to do, she thought.

She dug her paddle in deep and scooted through the thicket. Rounding the next bend, she saw the bridge up ahead; there was a black half-ton parked right in front of it.

She dug the blade of her paddle into the sand and stopped her forward progress. She held her breath.

She saw no one around.

Quietly she pulled herself back until the kayak was invisible from the bridge. She hoped. She hid behind a veil of willow, listening and waiting.

A man appeared on the house side of the bridge. He was maybe in his fifties, but tall and wiry in shapeless farmer's pants tucked into tall rubber boots that shone with water from fording the snye. He wore a faded shirt with the sleeves rolled up, revealing formidable forearms. His nose was hooked, under a craggy forehead, bristling with a healthy mat of gray eyebrows. His hair was thin, a gray sheen over the sun-dried dome of his skull. He had his hands in his pockets, and he was looking around, as if he had heard something.

With her hand grasping a thin branch of willow, Mimi inched her way back farther still, wishing the damn kayak wasn't so damn bright.

Then suddenly there was a rustling in the thick bush beside her, and from out of nowhere a dog appeared and started barking at her like crazy, its whole body shaking with excitement.

"Clooney?" shouted the old man. "What is it, girl?"

And Clooney, a hound of some kind, took those words as command enough to splash through the stream to Mimi's side, barking even louder.

Leaning away from the dog, Mimi lost hold of the

branch and then of her balance, and before she knew it, the kayak flipped. She screamed and went under.

"Come!" shouted the man, who was splashing toward her, right down the middle of the snye. "Come here, girl!"

Clooney obediently abandoned her catch and bounded through the water toward her master, while Mimi struggled to get her legs out of the kayak.

"Jesus H. Christ!" she shouted.

"Lordy, Lordy, what have we here?" said the man as he reached down to offer her a hand. She clambered to her feet without him, soaked and swearing a blue streak, which only made the dog bark all the louder and dance around on the shore.

"Lordy, Lordy," said the man again. There was a hint of laughter in his voice, which only made Mimi angrier.

"What the fuck are you doing here!" she shouted. Then she slipped on a rock and ended up once more in the drink.

"Whoa, hold on, lass, hold on," the old fellow said, reaching out again to give her a hand. She slapped his hand away and was content, for the minute, to just sit there up to her chest in the snye.

His hand was huge and gnarled and strong. He wouldn't budge, so she took it, reluctantly. Soon enough she was on her feet, sopping, undamaged, but seething mad.

She had swallowed some water and started coughing. The man, who was still holding her arm for support, now smacked her on the back, until she was able to free herself from him and stumble a few feet away to the bank.

Meanwhile, the man had grabbed the dog by the collar. Clooney was wagging her tail and looked anything but dangerous. She was a hunting dog, Mimi suspected, the color of a kindergarten kid's paint palette, muddy gray-brown, and with splotches that looked like they had been finger-painted onto her pelt.

Clooney barked at her.

"I'm not a duck!" shouted Mimi.

Clooney barked again.

"You all right?" said the man. His voice reminded Mimi of a gate that needed greasing.

"I'm fine," she snapped. She was rooting around in the snye for her running shoes. She had taken them off and they had fallen into the water, which was so stirred up she couldn't see a thing.

"Clooney has a habit of sneaking up on her quarry," said the man. "Don't you, girl?"

Clooney barked and licked his face.

If this genial display was meant to endear the dog to Mimi, it failed. She had found her shoes, which she chucked into the long grass on the bank. She struggled out of her flotation device.

There.

She sniffed and wiped her hair back off her face, rubbed the water out of her eyes, and tried to stand up straight. When she looked at the stranger, he was ogling her chest. She crossed her arms, shivering from the chill.

"What do you want?" she demanded.

"The name's Peters," he said. "Stooley Peters, from up the road. Just came by to see the lad. Got him my bill for the snowplowing."

"Snowplowing?"

The man nodded. "From last winter, eh? I done his drive for him."

Right. Peters, the keeper of Paradise. What a laugh! She'd noticed the name on his mailbox when she was out jogging.

"I'm not much at the paperwork side of things," he said. "Takes me a good long while, you know, to get around to it. What with the seeding and chores and such."

"Jay's on his way," she said. "He should be here pretty soon."

He nodded. "Good, then we can just wait and get to know one another."

She couldn't help but laugh. "I don't think so," she said. "Why don't you just leave your bill in the mailbox."

He scratched his chin. "If that's the way you want it," he said.

She maneuvered her way around the kayak, grabbing the towline in her fist, and splashed toward the bridge.

"Your shoes," he said. He was behind her now and held her sopping running shoes in one meaty hand.

She reached out to get them and he handed them to her, though he didn't let go right away, so that she had to tug to release them from his grip. *Having a good old time*, she thought.

Peters stepped onto the bank, dragging the dog with him. Clooney barked.

"And *you*," said Mimi to the dog, "can just shut up."

"Boy," said Peters, wagging his head. "You're quite the snappish thing, aren't you?"

She turned to him, pushing back a wing of hair from her eyes. "I'm a regular sweetheart, Mr. Peters, unless someone and his dog scare the shit out of me."

"Well, we're sure sorry about that, aren't we, Clooney?"

Clooney wiggled and whimpered and jumped up to lick her master's face again.

"Yeah, well, you're not as sorry as me," said Mimi. She had been keeping ahead of Peters, not wanting him staring at her breasts, which is what he seemed determined to do, as he kept pace with her along the bank.

Her headache was back with a vengeance. She felt like a fool. A wet fool.

"Around these parts," said Stooley Peters, "we put a fair amount of stock in neighborliness. Maybe where you come from it ain't the same."

Mimi nodded. "Damn right. Where I come from, we shoot neighbors," she said. It turned out to be a good mood breaker.

Peters slapped his knee and laughed, a dry, barely audible laugh. "But, honest now," he said. "We look out for one another. It's pretty far off the beaten path and all, being as the Upper Valentine don't go nowhere no more."

"What with the bridge out and all," Mimi muttered under her breath, aping his thick accent.

"What was that?"

"Nothing."

"Yeah, well, nothing's pretty well what I thought I heard," he said.

Mimi hauled the kayak up onto the shore on the opposite bank from him. "Look," she said. "I didn't mean to be rude just now. I'm having a really bad day. Okay?"

"Happens," he said, nodding his head vigorously. "Seen a few of 'em myself."

Quite a few, she thought. But his face didn't seem so malevolent, now that there was a stream between them. There was a bit of a twinkle in his dark eyes. And the dog seemed to like him.

"You can let her go," Mimi said. "I'm not afraid of dogs. Just don't like it when they attack."

Peters let go of the dog, which immediately tore off toward the road. For some reason, Mimi felt more vulnerable now that there was just the two of them. She wrapped her arms more tightly about her.

"I'll leave you to get yourself sorted out," he said. "You know where I am if you need anything."

"Paradise," she said.

"Right." He laughed. Then he tipped an imaginary hat and turned to walk back to his truck, bending to grab at a stalk of grass as he walked.

"Mr. Peters," she called.

He turned. "Call me Stooley," he shouted back to her across the little stream.

"Stooley," she said. "Have you seen anyone poking around here?"

"Poking around?"

"Yeah," she said. "You know, just hanging around the snye."

He scratched his head. "Well, there's the Page boy, of course."

"Not him. Someone else."

"What kind of someone?"

Mimi shrugged. This was getting nowhere. "Some-one's been kind of . . ." What was she supposed to say? "You know, messing with stuff."

"You have anything stole?"

"Yeah."

He pursed his lips. "Well, if it's big stuff, I'd say call the police. But maybe it's just a prank, eh? Kids, you know."

Right. Kids.

She realized, too late, that it had been a mistake to ask him a question. He had taken it as an invitation and was heading back toward her, about to cross the snye.

"Well, thanks, anyway," she said. "I've got to be going now."

He stopped, up to his ankles in the stream. "If I see anything, I'll be sure to let you know." He tapped his brow with his finger. "I'll keep an eye out," he said.

But she could tell well enough what he was keeping an eye out for.

≥ CHAPTER NINETEEN ⩽

THE IDEA CAME TO CRAMER at the computer store, as he was tearing the hard drive out of an old PC. He abandoned the job, the electronic guts spread out all over his workplace, and went online to the Mac site, where he surfed for a few minutes. Then he sat back down at his desk, deep in thought.

"You okay, Cramer?"

It was Hank. He had just come into the back room with a handful of invoices.

"Oh, yeah. I was just daydreaming."

Hank chuckled. "Well, it's good to see you *not* doing something for a change."

"Sorry."

Hank waved off the apology, a good-natured expression on his face. "Are you sure you're going to be okay holding down the fort next week?"

"Absolutely," said Cramer. "Really, I was just—"

"Just taking a wee break," said Hank. "People *do* take breaks, young man."

"Thanks," said Cramer, returning his attention to the job in front of him. But not all of his attention.

Working day and night didn't leave much room in Cramer's life for more than daydreaming. But, finally, Saturday came and he had the day before him, although he had to be at the plant by eight. When he woke up around noon, Mavis was out. He was glad. He didn't want any confrontations, not today. He made his way down Butchard's Creek and out onto the Eden, enjoying more than ever the freedom of the moment and filled with anticipation of what lay ahead. As much as he longed to see Mimi, he was almost hoping she wouldn't be there. The sooner he had a chance to get into her house, the better. He was going to get the ball rolling. It was time to make a move.

There were curtains up. They hadn't been there last time. Yellow curtains, open for the day. There also seemed to be a party going on. A white Toyota Camry was parked behind Mimi's car, and loud music was coming from the place.

He circled the house by cover of the brush. But after a while he ventured nearer, drawn by the music, the laughter, until he was crouching under the kitchen window.

There were only three people, as far as he could tell: Jay, Mimi, and another female. They were in the front room. He peeked over the sill. The table was littered with dishes. Then a girl wandered into the kitchen, heading toward the bathroom.

Cramer ducked out of sight and slid down the wall to a crouching position. *Iris Xu.* Did that mean she and Jay were still together?

Somebody whooped with laughter. Cramer swatted at a mosquito. They were thicker near the ground, in the shadows. Then he heard voices entering the kitchen, and he skedaddled to the brush behind the shed. Taking a wide berth, he made his way back toward the snye. He was almost at the stream when he heard the back door opening and he hid behind a tree.

It was Mimi. She was in the yellow sundress she'd been wearing in the documentary on her JVC. One of the thin straps hung across her arm. Her feet were bare, her arms heavy with colorful bangles. She was alone. And Cramer allowed himself to believe she had known he was there. She had sensed his presence, sensed the power of his attraction to her. He had wished her outside and she had come. It was a sign. His luck was turning.

She walked away from the house, down the lawn — down toward him — punching in a number on her cell phone. Cramer held his breath, pressed himself against the trunk of the tree.

"I got your message," she said, so near, it was almost as

if she were talking to him, as if she knew he was the one who had scribbled his sentiments on the dewy windshield of her car.

"Yes, *all* the messages," she said, her voice testy.

He hoped it wasn't him she was talking to, not like that.

"No . . . No, *you* listen to me for a change."

But the person on the other end of the line didn't seem to want to listen. Cramer dared to look. She was three or four meters away, hunched over her phone, her free hand covering her other ear, the better to concentrate. Her hair concealed her face.

"Yes," she said. "I hear you. I *hear* you *loud and clear*!"

She grumbled. "So? So? You were worried. Fine. You wanted to know I'd arrived safely. Fine. I get it. Thanks. But you know what, Lazar? That might have been *genuinely* touching if you had phoned just the *once* and left a message. But you phoned twenty times, and you know what occurred to me? I'll tell you. It occurred to me that you weren't phoning to see if *I* was okay, Lazar. You were phoning because *you* were *not* okay. Because—"

But she didn't get any further. And as Cramer watched, her body stiffened.

"There is no way," she said. She laughed but there wasn't any humor in it. "There is no *fucking* way!"

Cramer pressed his head against the rough bark. He could imagine a voice at the other end of the line pleading with her, desperate.

"Listen, I'll tell you why I haven't phoned, if you want to know."

But, apparently, Lazar didn't want to know. And when Cramer looked again, Mimi was holding the phone away from her face, staring at it with her mouth hanging open. Then she brought the receiver back to her ear.

"Enough, already!" she shouted, stamping her foot on the sandy ground. "You *say* you can't get over me. But that's not it at all. What you can't get over is *yourself*."

There was silence then. The music at the house stopped pounding, the snye stopped gurgling, the birds stopped singing, the insects stopped buzzing. All Cramer could hear was the pulse in his head. Peering out again from his hiding place, he saw Mimi shake her head back and forth. When she finally spoke again, there was no passion left in her voice, only what sounded to Cramer like resignation.

"I tried to do it right," she said. "I really tried."

She listened, rolled her eyes, sighed, and then nodded. "Okay," she said. "Yes. Yes." There was another pause and then she said "yes" one last time before closing the phone without a good-bye.

She stood, her shoulders drooping, staring down toward the snye. She looked so little and so weary. Cramer was west of her, downwind, and he could almost—*almost*—smell her. He wanted so much to walk over to her now and take her in his arms. He wouldn't have to say anything—he wouldn't need any clever speech. He would hold her, and she would realize that he meant her no harm, that he would look after her, that she was loved. The idea took hold of him. It was as if this was meant to happen, he told himself. He was a neighbor, after all. He could pretend he had just arrived there and seen her in distress. Was it so farfetched?

But then he heard the back door open and shut, and Iris appeared and headed down the lawn toward Mimi, who turned to greet her, though she said nothing.

"Nice dodge on doing the dishes," said Iris.

Mimi laughed. "Yeah, well, I'd rather have been doing dishes."

Iris touched her arm. "Did you do the deed?"

Mimi shrugged. "Sort of. He says he needs closure. So I said why don't you closure yourself in a mine somewhere."

"Really?"

"No." Mimi sniffed. "I said he could call again."

"Ah." Iris looked disappointed. "So it's not quite over."

Then Mimi smiled devilishly. "I said he could call again. However, I'm getting a new SIM card *today*."

"You are so bad, girl."

Mimi nodded, but her smile slipped. "I needed to know, Iris. Where he was at. Whether he was dealing with this."

"And he isn't?"

Mimi shook her head. "I don't know how I never saw it, but the man is a total wack job." Her voice broke a little as she spoke.

And Iris took Mimi in her arms and rocked her back and forth. "You still want to come with us?"

"Uh-huh," said Mimi, pulling away from the embrace at last. "How soon can we go? Like how about an hour ago?"

"Fine with me. It looks to me like you need a megadose of lying on a raft, soaking up the sun."

Mimi laughed. "Well, a megadose of something."

She laughed and the two of them headed back toward the house.

Twenty minutes later, they left, the three of them. Mimi was carrying a backpack. It looked to Cramer as if they were going to be gone for quite a while. They drove off in the Camry, and as soon as the car was out of sight, Cramer headed toward the house. He hadn't gone but a few feet when he heard a loud snap behind him. He spun around and looked toward the snye. His eyes scanned the underbrush. Someone was there. He walked slowly down to the stream, his ears peeled. Nothing. A deer maybe. A rotten branch falling? He waited a full ten minutes before he headed up to the house.

CHAPTER TWENTY

THEY HAD GONE to Iris's cottage on Saturday. Mimi had tried to beg off initially, but Iris had insisted.

"Are you sure?" Mimi looked from one to the other, but her gaze ended up on Jay. He could tell she wanted his blessing—he could see it in her eyes. He nodded and was quick about it. She was sharp and any delay would give him away. She would think he didn't want her along and she'd be wrong.

"Hey, if I want you to buzz off, I'll give you a quarter," he said.

"It'll cost more than that, bud."

The bantering didn't quite fool him, and soon enough she changed her mind. "You know, on second thought, I'm really on a roll with this new scene I'm writing. I think I'll pass."

So Jay got down on his knees and wrapped his long arms around her legs and pleaded until she just about fell over and agreed to come. Everyone was laughing. The happy trio. But she looked at him funny, all the same, as if she knew there was something up. She was right, but he wasn't sure himself what was up. He and Iris didn't desperately need to be alone. They wouldn't be, anyway, at her parents' cottage. It was Mimi alone that he was worried about. The house at the snye was secure; he had to believe that. It was Mimi he was worried about. She had been alone a lot lately. Maybe too much.

Jay had seen a movie about the composer Gustav Mahler. The opening shot was of a lake in the mountains somewhere: a dock, a boathouse, and early morning mist swirling on the water. Quiet. The camera dollied in on the boathouse, and suddenly the whole place exploded. He found himself thinking about that as he and Mimi waded back across the snye bright and early Monday morning. They'd had a good time, but halfway through the weekend, he had started worrying about the house. The girls had called him on it.

"First you want me to come along because you're worried about leaving me alone," said Mimi. "Then you wish you'd left me there because you're worried about the house."

"Jackson is just a worrier," said Iris.

"Yeah, well, worry about this," said Mimi, and handed

him her fishing rod, which was all snarled. They had been sitting in the middle of the lake with fishing rods as an excuse for doing nothing. So he had picked away at the knots and tangles and kept his worrying to himself for the rest of the weekend.

They'd left Iris at the lawyer's office in Ladybank where she had a summer job. Jay was driving the Camry. He was going to drop Mimi off and make sure everything was okay before heading back into town. And everything did look okay. Pretty as a picture, with the tall grass and wildflowers nodding in a light breeze. But Jay watched the house carefully, waiting for the whole thing to blow up.

Mimi babbled on about a scene she was going to rewrite, but he hardly heard her. They had arrived at the shed by then, and he stopped in his tracks.

"What?" she said.

He pointed.

The back door was ajar.

Jay ran for the stairs, Mimi to her desk. "Oh, thank you, God, thank you, thank you," he heard her say as he charged upstairs, two steps at a time. Presumably her computer was still there. His computer was still there, too, and he breathed a long sigh of relief, leaning on his knees to catch his breath. Mimi joined him and gasped.

He looked up, and his gaze, so narrowly fixed when he first got there, now saw what he had missed. Two of his guitar stands were empty.

The cops took almost an hour. By then Jay and Mimi had discovered that the back door had not been forced but opened from inside; the window in Mimi's bedroom had been smashed. Glass lay everywhere on her bed, in her open suitcase—everywhere!

But that wasn't the last of the surprises. Jay had gone down to the snye to lay a two-by-ten plank across the broken bridge for the cops, figuring they wouldn't want to wade over, when suddenly Mimi came running down to him. "The camcorder's gone," she said.

"Oh, crap," said Jay.

"And that's not all. My computer beeped at me."

Jay stared at her. "Huh?"

"It's never done that before," she said. He laid the planks down and then followed her back up to the house. She had left the laptop partially open. Jay crouched and peered inside, then slowly raised the lid. The screen was black. He pushed the power button. Nothing.

"It beeped when I opened it," she said.

So Jay closed the lid. Then pressed the button to open it.

Beep, beep, beep.

He jumped back. They both did. "Like that," said Mimi. "Three beeps."

"And it never happened before?" She gave him an exasperated look.

Constable Roach came alone. They were short-staffed, and Jay got the unmistakable impression that a breaking and entering was no big deal. Like maybe people got burgled every day. Roach took down the story.

"So that's a wine-red thirty-gigabyte JVC HDD?"

"Right. And it's worth?"

"About six hundred, American."

Then he turned to Jay. "And two guitars plus cases?" he said, reading his notes. "A Gibson ES-175 with a sunburst finish and a powder-blue Fender Stratocaster?"

"Baby blue," said Jay.

Roach made the change. "And their value, roughly?"

Jay shoved his hands in his pockets, shrugged. "Somewhere around three or four grand," he said.

While Roach wrote this in his notes, Jay swallowed hard and risked the question he had been afraid to ask. "Any chance I'm going to see the guitars again?"

Roach grimaced. "Depends on whether you got robbed by crooks or musicians," he said. "I'm guessing these are pretty high-end instruments?"

Jay nodded again, a sick feeling coming over him. The loss was beginning to sink in.

"If your thief was some budding rock star, you probably won't see either of them again unless it's in a club somewhere. And if you think you do, do *not* attempt to do anything. Come to us. But from what you tell me— the troubles you've been having—I suspect your visitor finally decided to step up his game, make a move."

Jay swallowed hard. Mimi took his arm.

"We'll alert the music stores in Ottawa and Kingston, the pawnshops," said Roach. "You don't by any chance have serial numbers or anything like that?"

Jay nodded, though he had forgotten until then. "They're back at the house—my mom's house. I'll phone them in."

"You do that." Roach looked impressed. "You'd be surprised how few people bother." He glanced at Mimi.

"Don't even ask," she said. "I'm one of those people you're talking about."

"How long will it take?" said Jay, turning back to the policeman. "Getting in touch with the music stores and all that?"

"Oh, I'll do it right away. Soon as I get out to the cruiser."

Jay must have looked hopeful, because Roach sighed. "But you're not optimistic?"

Roach rubbed the side of his nose with the end of his pencil. "Depends," he said. "If they broke in Sunday, they might not have been able to dump them yet."

And Jay could guess the rest. They'd been gone since early Saturday afternoon.

It was only as Roach was about to leave that Mimi mentioned about her computer.

"It beeped at you?" said Roach.

"Yeah, I know. It sounds pretty lame," she said. "But it is a pretty weird coincidence that my computer goes down when this perp comes around."

Roach smiled in a patronizing way, which made Mimi furious, from the look on her face. And Jay jumped in to defend her. "It's not as crazy as you think, sir," he said. "The guy who's been breaking in did some weird stuff to my computer, too. Left little messages, whatever."

Roach nodded. But then he shrugged and turned to Mimi. "I didn't mean to take what you said lightly. It's just that I don't know what to tell you. The item is still here."

"Yeah, and beeping at me!" said Mimi. "God, I'd like to . . ."

"Like I said, miss, you come to *us* if you find anything. Anything at all."

"Like if we find any clues?" said Jay. Roach nodded.

"The fucked-up computer *is* a clue," said Mimi, glaring at the officer. He smiled at her again, and Jay wanted to warn him that he was walking on thin ice. But Mimi wasn't finished. "Think about it," she said. "This guy has been sneaking in here for months, and he's never done anything like break windows or steal things—well, not big things. There's something screwy about this."

Roach flipped back through his notes. "You said you locked the storm door out back, which you figured was how he had been getting in?" Jay nodded. Roach shrugged. "So, he comes back, sees you've taken precautions, and it bugs him. Bugs the heck out of him. So he decides to make you pay."

Jay nodded again. But when he looked at Mimi, she was still fuming.

"Miss," said Roach. "I understand you're angry. You have every right to be. And we'll do what we can. But I gotta tell you, this was a pretty hit-and-miss burglary. They left two computers, an iPod—I don't think we're dealing with professionals here. It's not the modus operandi of a typical rural B and E. See, out here, your specialists back a van up to the door, knock, and if anyone answers, pretend they're lost. If no one answers, they take as much as they can and split. Now, you've got that broken bridge, which would likely be enough of a deterrence to any kind of ring—not worth the bother to cart stuff back and forth across the stream." He paused, looked around. "What I see is someone on foot, who took just as much as he could carry. And what's easier to carry than a couple of guitar cases and a camera. I'd guess it might be local kids."

"Which doesn't explain leaving the iPod," said Mimi, and all Roach could do was shrug. But then Mimi's eyes lit up. "Somebody nearby, you think?"

The officer considered the idea. "Could be," he said.

"Because it's weird," said Mimi, "but somebody nearby said the same thing you just said a few days ago."

"What do you mean?"

Mimi turned to Jay. "Remember when I told you about my run-in with Stooley Peters?" He nodded. "I told him we were having problems, and he said it could be kids. Which really bugs me because kids always get blamed." Then she turned back to the officer, her eyes big. "And that might explain leaving the iPod. I mean, a kid wouldn't leave it, but an old geezer might."

It was a good point. Roach pursed his lips.

"Who's this Peters fellow?"

Mimi told him where Peters lived. The policeman said he would look into it.

"Good," said Mimi. "Thanks."

"I'm not promising anything."

"Yeah, I know, but it'll piss him off, anyway, which is fine by me."

"Do you think Peters screwed around with your computer?" said Jay.

Mimi shrugged. "Maybe he was going to steal it and then he dropped it, which is why it's beeping. I don't know."

"We'll be sure to get in touch with Mr. Peters," said Roach, closing his notebook. "But, like I said, you get any ideas—you come to us. You hear me?" The warning was clear.

Mimi nodded but she didn't look any too happy.

They headed down the lawn with Roach. "Can you answer me one more question?" Mimi asked.

"What's that?" the cop asked.

"Do they have the death penalty up here?"

Roach chuckled and, shaking his head, went on his way.

"Bet he doesn't talk to Peters."

"He said he was going to."

Mimi snorted. "Yeah, right, he was one step away from patting me on the head and saying, 'There, there, little lady.' What an asshole."

Jay went to give her a hug, but she sloughed it off.

"Hey," he said. "In case you forgot, I also got ripped off." He had no idea if the stuff was covered by his mother's home insurance. She'd said something about it once, but he hadn't paid much attention.

Back at the house, Mimi went straight to her desk. She sat down, leaning on her elbows, staring at her laptop. "I'm sorry, Jay," she said. "I just feel violated. And why is it that cops make you feel like you're to blame?"

Jay rested his hand on her shoulder but sensed somehow that she didn't want to be mollified, so he pulled away. But he didn't go away. And after a bit, he leaned his backside on her desk so that they would be facing each other if and when she decided to look up.

"Maybe we should get out of here," he said.

"What do you mean?"

"Pack up and leave."

She looked furious. "Hell no," she said. "That's what this guy wanted all along."

"And we ignored him so he gets tough, and now I'm out two very expensive instruments and you're out a camcorder. We stay and what's he going to do for encores?"

Mimi's eyes flashed. "Get his balls shot off," she said.

Jay smiled. "Guns aren't easy to score up here."

"We'll see about that," she said.

He looked at her hard. She was kidding—had to be.

"You've sure got a lot of moxie," he said.

"I don't know about that. Hey, I don't even know what moxie is, come to think of it. But this whole thing sucks, Jay. Whoever was leaving you bluebirds and snake skins, and figured out how to get in here without ever leaving a trace is *not* the same person who smashed in my window. Think about it."

Jay nodded. But he was thinking that the guy who filmed Mimi at the window with her own camera might just want it back to see his handiwork. It was all pretty ugly.

He couldn't tell if Mimi had thought about what purpose the thief might have for the camera. She seemed angrier than anything. She didn't just want her stuff back—she wanted to get even. There was bravery in her he didn't feel himself. If she wanted to stay, then he'd tough it out. But he could feel his strength slipping away. He could feel a darkness seeping into him. It wasn't just the guitars; it was bigger than that. He doubted Mimi would understand. Rage kept such feelings at bay. Rage burned up sorrow.

She stood up and put her arms around him. He held her tightly, trembling. Finally they pulled apart. She pushed the hair back from his forehead. "You looked as if you were floating away on me," she said.

He nodded.

"I'm sorry about your guitars," she said. "That is totally shit."

"And I'm sorry about your pretty red camcorder and the beeping computer," he said. "But there's this place in town. PDQ Electronics. The owner knows Macs."

≋ CHAPTER TWENTY-ONE ≋

PDQ ELECTRONICS WAS TUCKED behind an office-supply store down an alley off Forster. Without Jay's instructions, Mimi doubted she would ever have found the place. Computer repairs were obviously not a Main Street business in these parts.

A buzzer sounded as she entered, but no one appeared at the counter. Mimi contented herself with looking around. She picked up a packet of recordable discs and a new ink jet for her printer, assuming—hoping—she'd be able to use her printer again.

Still no service, although she thought she heard someone in the back room. She cleared her throat. Nothing.

"Hello? Anybody home?"

And now a man appeared, wiping his hands on a white cloth, stopping in the doorway with a startled look on his face.

"Are you open?" said Mimi.

He recovered and smiled shyly. "Yeah," he said. "Sorry, I was listening to something on my iPod." He looked down, bashfully, but when he raised his head, he looked straight into her eyes and his own eyes were on high beam. They were deep blue—as blue as the logo on the Epson ink cartridge in her hand. Ink-cartridge blue. Amazing.

"Well, there's no law against that," she said.

He frowned. "Pardon?" he said.

"Against listening to your iPod," said Mimi, heading toward the counter—drawn toward it, more like. "Unless you're listening to Whitesnake," she said. "I think there may be a law against that."

Again with the awkward grin. Not a bad face. His nose was on the large size but noble, she decided. And there was a leftover smattering of acne on his neck. But what a neck—like steel cables. He was in his early twenties, she guessed. Thick through the shoulders, sculpted biceps. And all of it on display since he was wearing nothing but a T-shirt tucked into jeans with a big rodeo-type belt buckle. He shrugged.

"I'm not much on Whitesnake," he said. "I was listening to this band out of Montreal. Arcade Fire?"

Now it was her turn to look surprised. "Get out of town," she said. "Really?"

"Yeah. There isn't a law against them, is there?"

She laughed. "No, it's just . . . well, so sick," she said.

"Pardon?"

"I mean *sick* like 'That is so *sick*, man. Like *good* sick. Oh, never mind."

She stopped herself—faked zipping up her lips. And he just stared at her, his mouth a little open, tempting her to zip his lips closed as well. But no, touching his lips would not be a good idea. There was something disturbing about him. Not bad disturbing. *You're here on business, Mimi,* she told herself, and hoisted her computer case onto the counter.

"You got some kind of problem?" he asked.

"Yeah," she said. "Big-time. But a friend of mine said you're the man to see."

She pulled out her laptop and laid it before him on the counter.

"A PowerBook," he said. "Mr. Pretty's the Mac guy."

"And he's . . ."

"Uh, well, he's on vacation this week."

"Right," said Mimi, and tapped a little tattoo on the counter with her fingernails. Then she smiled sweetly. "So I'm stuck with you?" she said, and hoped it didn't sound too flirtatious. What had come over her, for God's sake?

"I could like maybe, you know . . . take a look?"

"That would be very nice of you."

"What's up with it?"

"It beeps at me," she said.

"Beeps?"

"Yeah. BEEP, BEEP, BEEP. Like that. Scary."

He stared at the computer. He leaned lightly against

the counter, his fingers splayed, taking his weight. She watched the muscles in his forearms flex, the veins pop. But he was gentle as he unlatched the top. And the computer beeped, just as she had said it would.

"Hmmm," he said, scratching his head. Then he turned to the store's computer mounted on the counter and started tapping away at the keys. "I'll go to the Mac website," he muttered, not taking his eyes off the screen. "See what they say."

"You're so kind. Thanks." *And I'll continue to ogle your delicious arms,* thought Mimi, but decided that she should at least try to seem more interested in his research. She couldn't see the screen and ended up looking at the man. There was something odd with his right eye, as if the pupil had bled into the cornea. A blue seeping.

"Huh," he said, after a moment. "It seems to be the code for a motherboard problem."

Mimi winced. "Is that as bad as it sounds?"

He shrugged. "Let's take a look."

"I always have problems with mothers," she said.

He glanced at her, his eyes humorless.

"A joke," she said.

"Oh. Right." Then his eyes let her go, and he gently turned the laptop upside down. He went into the back room. The cloth with which he had been cleaning his hands now hung from his back pocket, drawing attention to his butt. *I have been in the wilderness too long,* thought Mimi.

He returned with a little yellow screwdriver and

proceeded to remove a panel from the back of her Power-Book. He took a flashlight and looked into the exposed opening. She craned to see what was inside, then realized she was crowding him, blocking his light.

"Sorry," she said, pulling back. He smelled of after-shave and fruit gum.

He had a stern look on his face as if this was major surgery and she shouldn't be there without a mask and gown. She stepped obediently away from the counter. The surgeon went back to his investigation. He reached into the cavity and, after wiggling something a bit, pulled out a two-inch-long piece of high-tech equipment with gold teeth and all kinds of software patches.

"This is a memory module," he said. He peered into the cavity again. "You have ports for two of them in case you want to boost your memory."

"I just want to get back the memory I already had," said Mimi.

He held the module up to the light and squinted at it. "Weird," he said after a bit.

"What?" she said.

"There's some kind of smear of something . . ." He looked at her with a perplexed expression on his face. "I don't know for sure, but it looks like someone took a col-ored marker to the contact points."

He held the module close to her eyes, and she could see on the gold teeth the slightest blush of red, here and there.

"That *is* weird," she said. Then she looked closer still and sniffed. Sniffed again. "It smells like . . . like lipstick," she said.

He sniffed it, too. "I wouldn't know."

"Could that be the problem?" she said. Then added, "Duh!"

He shrugged, but she dared to think that he looked a little bit more keyed up than he had before. A little *hopeful*, maybe?

"The contact has to be one hundred percent," he said. "Even a film of ink or lipstick like that and the contact would be, you know, broken." He looked at her quizzically.

"Believe me," she said, resting her hand on her chest. "I do not open up my computer and doodle on it." She took the memory module from him and peered at it again. "Anyway, it's not a shade I'd ever wear."

He managed a tightly packaged little smile, which she returned to him opened. Then, distractedly, he reexamined the gold head of the module. "Just a second," he said. And again he walked back into his work area, returning a moment later with a tiny paintbrush and a bottle of foul-smelling liquid. Mimi scrunched up her nose.

"Nail polish remover?"

"Acetone," he said. "Same thing, I guess." He delicately wiped the top of the module until every trace of the red was gone. Then he waved the module in the air, gently.

When it was dry, he carefully replaced it and screwed

the panel back on. He turned the computer over and opened the lid.

"No beeps!" said Mimi.

"So far, so good." Then he turned the computer to face her.

"You want to give 'er a go?" he asked.

"Is it going to blow?"

"I don't think so."

She grinned, pushed the power button. And now her computer sang out a proud note to let her know it was leaping into action.

"I don't believe it," she said, as she watched her familiar desktop swim into place before her eyes. There was Harpo Marx, grinning his gorgeous face off! It gave her such a jolt of happy relief. Her world was still intact! She clasped her hands together with glee. "I don't believe it."

The repairman leaned around the edge of the laptop, and she turned it so that he could see the magic, too. "Your boyfriend?" he asked.

"My dream boyfriend," she said, but she was giggling now. She double-clicked on one of the files and it sprang to life. "Oh, wow!" she said. "You did it! You did it . . . What's your name?"

"Cramer," he said.

"Cramer!" she said, and gave him a high five. "Here you are taking my computer apart and saving my life, and we haven't even been introduced. I'm Mimi," she said, offering him her hand across the counter. "Mimi Shapiro."

He took her hand and squeezed it, only very carefully, she thought, because had he wanted to, he could have probably crushed it.

"I can't thank you enough," she said. He bobbed his head around self-consciously. "No, seriously. I was expecting to have to go into Ottawa or maybe Seattle, but my friend said I should try here first. Wow!" She took a deep breath and waved her hand in front of her face.

"How much do I owe you?"

He held up his hands as if he had no idea.

"Oh, come on, Cramer," she said, reaching into her purse. "You have rescued me from a fate worse than death. What do you charge for saving damsels in distress?"

Now he truly blushed. He looked down, held up his hand in protestation. "No charge," he said. "It was just a lucky guess."

She placed her hand on her throat. "Then I won't try to bribe you with money anymore. Thank you. Thank you very much. But, oh! I'll buy stuff," she said, and placed the discs and ink jet on the counter.

"Okay," he said, and started to write out a receipt. He looked up and smiled gravely, a little ill at ease. "This friend," he said.

"Who, Harpo?"

"The one who said you should try here."

"Oh, right."

"Could she have done this?"

For a moment she didn't understand what he was

getting at. Then his eyes strayed from her face to the computer she was packing away in its case.

"Oh," she said. "No. No. Believe me, it wasn't him."

"Okay," he said, nodding. "But the thing is somebody did it."

Mimi hung the case from her shoulder, held it close to her side. "I know." There was an awkward silence, but she really didn't want to start trying to explain about the situation. It sounded too spooky, too perverse.

"Maybe you should keep it locked up?"

"Funny you should mention that," she said with a laugh stripped of any amusement.

"Why is it funny?" he said.

Mimi looked at him, standing there all earnest with concern. It made her a little uncomfortable. "We had a break-in," she said.

"Bummer," he said. "And was your place like all locked up and that?"

"Yeah, but locks don't seem to work on this . . . Well, let's just say we've had more than one break-in."

Now Cramer's brow creased with concern. "Is it some old boyfriend, maybe, who's still got a key?"

Mimi hugged her computer case. Was this computer knight with the disquieting pecs going to offer his services as a bodyguard? She grinned to herself and then sobered up and shook her head. "Uh, that's unlikely," she said.

He looked apprehensive, almost hurt. Then she noticed, with relief, that the receipt was finished, and she busied herself taking out her wallet.

"I really don't know how to thank you, Cramer," she said as he swiped her card. He looked at her and bobbed his head, and she wondered if he was going to say "Aw, shucks" or something like that. Then she noticed a little stand that held a stack of business cards. "I should take a card," she said. "In case of emergency."

"Uh, that's my boss's card," said Cramer.

"Hank Pretty," she read out loud. "Oh, I get it, 'PDQ— Pretty Damn Quick.' That's cute."

Cramer bobbed his head again. "Here," he said, and he took the card from her, picked up a pen, and printed his name and number on the back of it.

"This is my home number, eh?" he said, handing her the card. "I usually only work here a couple days a week."

She grinned as she took it from him. "Cramer"; no last name. She shoved it in her pocket. "I usually have to work a lot harder to get a guy's phone number," she said, and enjoyed watching him blush again. Enjoyed it a bit more than was entirely healthy. *Time to get out of here,* she thought. And so, with a little neutral kind of wave, she turned toward the door. She was almost at the door before he spoke.

"I hope I see you again," he said.

She turned and smiled. "Me, too," she said. "Thanks so much."

Then she left, and when she glanced back through the

door to wave one last time, he was still staring at her, his hands in his pockets. His mouth was open, and she had the odd, exhilarating feeling that he was trying hard to catch his breath.

≽| CHAPTER TWENTY-TWO |≼

THEY HAD MET. They had shaken hands. He had held her hand, so cool and smooth. His plan had worked. He wasn't used to that. He wasn't used to wanting something and it actually coming true. He had never believed in luck because then he would have had to face the fact that he didn't have any. But maybe—just maybe—things were changing.

And he hadn't blown it. He didn't think he had sounded too stupid. He didn't always get what she was saying, but he'd made her laugh—well, once anyway. It hadn't been so hard. It would be easier next time. He wasn't exactly sure how this amazing thing called "next time" was going to come around. He'd have to think about that.

He walked through the rest of his workday in a kind of a daze. All he could think of was Mimi. Face-to-face, she was more beautiful than ever. Her eyes—the way she had looked at him! She seemed to like him, but it was more than that, and for one terrible moment he had thought she recognized him. But there was no way she could have seen him. No way. And now they'd met. And they would meet again. Somehow, though he couldn't quite see how. What else could he break and then fix? He laughed out loud, alone in the store. But he was only kidding. He would never break anything of hers again.

For that one week Cramer was holding down two full-time jobs. He had to be at PDQ by 10:00 AM to open up and stay there right through until closing time. Because he was working the night shift at the plant, it didn't make much sense to go home—took too much time and too much wear and tear on the car. But when he suggested that to Mavis, she had a shit fit.

"You're going to strand me out here?"

"Well, what am I supposed to do?"

"It is *my* car, for Christ's sake!"

He wanted to tell her that it wasn't really her car anymore. It wasn't just that he paid the insurance and the license and kept it topped up with gas. In the six years he'd been driving the Taurus, he'd replaced just about every damn part in the thing.

"So you'll drive me into town in the morning?" he said. She didn't answer. She wandered away, rubbing her hands together, and stared out the window.

"I could get to the plant if I'm in town. One of the guys on my crew could give me a lift, I guess."

Still she didn't answer. He had no idea what he would do about getting home from the plant at four in the morning if she took him up on his offer. Hell, maybe he'd just sleep in the back room at PDQ.

"Mom?"

She turned and gave him a sour look. "Do whatever you like," she said, and went outside. Somehow he was the bad guy. But, then, what else was new?

They ended up coming to a compromise. If she needed the car, she'd drive him in and pick him up at five. Then he'd take her home and go to work. It was a lot of driving and a lot of wasted time, but she had things to do, she said. Things to do.

She had pretty well abandoned her art. And she had abandoned asking about the money. He was doing what he could, but he wasn't going to keep saying to her every goddamned day how he would get her the money. She had to believe in him, the way he believed in her. And until the money was in his hands, he wasn't going to make any promises he couldn't keep. He owed her that much. Sometimes it seemed to Cramer that his mother's life was a promise she couldn't keep. Somebody had to do it for her.

He allowed himself to think that she was looking for work. Maybe that's why she needed the car. He fantasized about coming home one day and her surprising him with the news. He fantasized about quitting one of his jobs.

He fantasized about having a life! He'd never questioned his life, really. This was it—the one you got. You did the work. You looked after things. You picked up where you left off yesterday. End of story. But now—*now!*—he wanted something. He wanted something big-time. He wanted a new life. And he had done a bad thing to get that new life started. He hated himself for it. Hated the foolish games he had been playing lately and what it had brought him to. But then again those foolish games had brought him to Mimi.

When Mimi told him about the break-in, the look on her face was like a hard fist plowing into his stomach. He was dead afraid he was going to confess, right there, right then. He imagined the words spilling out of him, and it felt as if it took every muscle in his body not to break down and tell her. He couldn't bear the thought of making her unhappy. But what he couldn't bear even more was the thought of her being angry with him. He'd heard her talk to that guy on the phone. Seen her temper flare up, and he didn't want that temper aimed his way. He would never give her a reason to turn on him like that. Never. So there would have to be this secret between them, and that was too bad, but it couldn't be helped. He would just have to live with it. One more burden.

It was Wednesday morning that he got the call he'd been waiting for. It also just happened to be the first day of August and he noticed that—noticed that Day One of his new life was starting on the first day of the month.

He had to go right away. He locked up the store and put the little sign up on the door. BACK IN A FLASH, the sign read. And Cramer had to laugh. Back in a flash with the cash.

He called Mavis and told her to be home for dinner. He said he'd bring something. What did she want, KFC or a pizza? Chinese—whatever!

"What are you talking about?"

"It doesn't matter," he said. "Just choose."

"What are we celebrating?"

"The first of the month."

"Cramer, are you stoned?"

He was almost offended, but he thought he could hear just the tiniest bit of excitement in her voice, as if she had caught some of his own excitement.

"You have a fantastic day," he said. It was something Hank Pretty said to customers, and it sounded like the exactly right thing to say. Then laughing, he hung up. He expected her to phone back, but she didn't. So he got a deluxe pizza with pineapple and ham, because he knew that was her favorite.

She was there when he arrived, waiting at the door. He smiled and hoisted the extra-large-size pizza box high for her to see. She was standing just inside the screen door, and she didn't open it even when he was standing right on the step. She looked odd—frightened.

"Mom? You okay?"

"I'm fine," she said, staring at the box in his hands. "What's going on, Cramer?"

He had hoped she might have set the table in anticipation of him bringing home takeout. Especially since he had to head off to the plant in an hour or so. He'd imagined on the way home that she might even pick some flowers and put them on the table the way she used to do sometimes when there was something to celebrate—any old thing. But the table was cluttered with mail and half-finished cups of coffee and a plate with toast crumbs on it that had been there for days.

Still, she seemed pleased with the pizza. So he set the table around the mess, and when they were finally sitting across from each other with their plates filled, he reached into his pocket and handed her a folded envelope.

"Here," he said.

She took it from him gingerly, glancing suspiciously at the offering.

"What is this?"

"Open it," he said.

She did, reluctantly, and he just about wanted to scream, he was that excited. But he held it in and watched as she took out five crisp, new one-hundred-dollar bills.

She stared down at the money, and Cramer waited breathlessly for her to respond. He wondered, after a bit, if she was crying, but when she finally raised her head, her eyes were dry and cold and hard.

"Where'd you get this?"

He had rehearsed this moment all day, and it sure hadn't been like this.

"What do you mean, where did I get it?" he said.

"Hank's away, isn't he? Did you take this from the till?" Her eyes were large, troubled.

"Do you think I'd steal from Hank?"

"I don't know what you'd do."

"Jesus! What do you even *care* where I got it!" He was immediately angry at himself—at the irritation in his voice.

Her eyes skittered away from him. She looked haggard. He wondered suddenly if she was ill or something.

"Mom," he said, his voice soft. "I got a bank loan, okay?"

She looked at him with surprise. "You did what?"

"I got a bank loan. Hank cosigned for me." She looked down at the money sitting on the open palm of her right hand. He reached across the table and closed her hand around the money. She stared at her fist. "There's a pretty good chance I'm going to get hired on full-time at the plant," he said quietly, as if he was talking to a sick person. "That'll mean a raise and benefits and all that kind of stuff. And so I thought, why wait? You need the money now and you've got it."

She didn't look up, and since the aroma of the pizza was driving him crazy, he launched in, with one eye on her waiting for the smile, the thank-you. He had no idea what was going on in her head. No idea whether she believed him or not, and he didn't even really care at this point. She had managed to siphon just about every drop of joy out of the moment. It hadn't been easy to lay his hands on that kind of money. He didn't want much in return. But damn it all, she could at least acknowledge it.

And then she did in a most unexpected way. She started laughing. He looked at her and saw the smile on her face and started laughing as well. This was more like it. But he stopped laughing eventually and was well into his second slice of pizza before she stopped. And by then, he was really seriously beginning to wonder whether his mother was losing her mind.

CHAPTER TWENTY-THREE

A WEEK PASSED with no word from the cops on the missing guitars or the JVC. Roach did phone back to say he had talked to Peters. The old man had been at a farm auction all the way down in South Mountain on the Saturday, or so he said. He'd bought a new UTV—had the dated receipt to prove it. When Roach told him what he was looking for, Peters invited him in, without a search warrant. Let him search his truck and his car as well.

"He could have hidden them anywhere," said Mimi when Jay reported the call to her. "He's got a pile of outbuildings up there in Paradise."

"Roach admitted that, but he doubts Peters is the culprit. Apparently, he only just made it back from the auction, hauling the UTV because of car trouble. When the cop was there, the car was up on blocks with the motor stripped down."

"What about his truck?"

"The license plates are from 1976. He's not supposed to take it on the road."

"Yeah, but he does."

"Only out here. He'd get pulled over for sure if he took it on any main roads."

"So the car-on-blocks thing is a trick."

Jay looked hard at her. "Do you really think Peters is that smart?"

No, she didn't, but the police investigation sounded pretty dumb.

"Phone them back," said Mimi a few days later. Jay threw up his hands. So she contacted Constable Roach herself, who filled her in on the latest details.

"We've expanded the search to Toronto and Montreal," he said. "Plus we're checking eBay. We're still looking. The items are on all kinds of databanks now. The serial numbers are a big help." *Thanks for reminding me*, thought Mimi, but she didn't say anything. "Sometimes stolen goods turn up months later. There's a big bust and when we sort through the goodies—voilà!"

"And what about Stooley Peters?" Mimi asked.

But he had nothing on Peters. The man had no record. And he had been forthcoming with the police. "I went back a second time," said Roach, which surprised Mimi. "I have to say that Peters seems like a dead end."

Mimi didn't argue. It seemed like a pretty good description of the old fart.

Jay was fatalistic. "Maybe it's the gods of music telling me to get serious."

"What are you talking about?"

He shrugged. "I want to be a composer, not a pop star. I want to be taken seriously. The electric guitar is . . . it's adolescent."

"It sounded great to me."

"Thanks, but that's not the point. I've been thinking a lot about this, and the only valid way you could incorporate a guitar solo into a piece of serious music is ironically."

Mimi looked perplexed. "Or how about because it sounded good?"

He threw up his hands. He was doing a lot of that lately. "You don't understand," he said. "It's not that simple."

And Mimi was about to remind him that the name of his new piece was *Simple*, but he wandered off. She had wanted to add that the real point was someone owed him a few thousand bucks. And she had also wanted to say that what were the gods of cinema trying to tell her by letting her movie camera get stolen?

"And then he crawled off somewhere to be morose" was how Mimi described the scene to Iris. The two of them had stumbled on a craft fair down by the basin in the heart of Ladybank. It was a hot and sunny summer afternoon, with just enough breeze off the water to convince Iris that a craft fair was a better option than the air-conditioned coffeehouse by the park. It was more of a rummage sale and pretty chintzy, but Mimi loved it and only wished she had her camcorder with her.

"Jay likes to make people happy," said Iris.

"What do you mean?"

"He likes to give people what he thinks they want, especially teachers. He compartmentalizes. You've got your rock and roll here and your serious music here. And these people listen to this, and those people listen to that."

"But that's garbage," said Mimi. "What about passion? What about your 'inner music,' or whatever?"

"That would be good," said Iris. And Mimi wondered if she was blowing her off, but actually she had spotted an enormous red sun hat.

"What do you think?" she said.

"It looks like a UFO," said Mimi. Iris bought it anyway and put it on. It dwarfed her but cast a beautiful woven shadow over her face.

"It's ten degrees cooler under here," she said.

"And you *look* ten degrees cooler," said Mimi. Then she spotted the worst baseball cap she had ever seen. It had fishermen's excuses written all over it and badly drawn cartoons. "I have so got to get this for my friend Rodney," she said.

"Does he like to fish?"

"Only for compliments."

At the next booth Iris found a game of Mouse Trap, all set up. "The cheese is missing," said the lady behind the table. "But that way you can supply your own."

"You think it would work with Asiago?" Mimi asked.

The woman nodded. "Or Limburger, if you can stand the smell."

"I like that," said Mimi, but what she really liked was the woman's pitch. She bought the game, and the woman said she'd pack it up for them while they continued shopping.

"Shopping," said Mimi with a sigh. "That's what's been missing from my life." At another booth she found a knitted EpiPen holder that you could attach to your belt. She bought it and put her canister of mace in it.

"You look like a cowboy," said Iris.

"The fastest draw in the East," said Mimi practicing a few times. And then her eyes strayed to a table of bobble heads, and she gasped with delight.

"A bobble-head Mountie," she cried. "I promised Jamila a Mountie." She couldn't believe her luck and immediately text-messaged her friend to let her know the good news. Then she followed Iris to a display of carved duck decoys, which is where she was standing, wondering about the whole idea of making something beautiful like a decoy in order to trick ducks so you could blow them to bits, when Jamila texted her back.

ran into l.c. asked where u were.

"Uh-oh," said Iris.

Mimi was furious. There was no way Lazar accidentally

~236~

"ran into her." She fled the fair and made her way to a quiet spot down by the water. Iris, wisely, stayed behind. Mimi could barely talk she was so angry. She had bought a new SIM card, but she was going to have to let Lazar know her new number, anyway. He did not answer, so she left a message. "Phone me," she said. *"And stay the fuck away from my friends!"*

The others were going out that night, but Mimi opted to stay home. There had been no further disturbances at the house, which might have been because they seldom left it unattended. In any case, she was not afraid. Part of her believed that Constable Roach was right, that the perp had toyed with them for a while and then made a hit and was gone. If he was a local, maybe he saw the cop car there and got cold feet. Good. But part of Mimi still dreamed of a confrontation, of whipping out her mace canister and, when the bastard was stumbling around blind, hitting him senseless with a chair or something.

She was watching *When Harry Met Sally* and missing New York when Lazar phoned her back.

"What are you doing stalking my friends?"

"Mimi, calm down."

"Do not tell me to calm down. This is not about me. *You* are a pervert. Do you realize that?"

"That is not the case. And I was not, as you say, stalking your friend."

"Lazar," she said. Then paused to take a weary breath.

On the screen Meg Ryan had her finger raised at Billy Crystal, about to give him a lecture. Then the image dissolved into a screen saver of a rain forest. Behind Lazar she heard urban sounds, an echoey loudspeaker voice—the subway, maybe?

"I want to come up there," he said.

"You don't even know where 'there' is," she said.

"Actually, I do."

Mimi sat up a little straighter. "What's that supposed to mean?"

"It means what it means."

"So help me, Lazar, I am this close to calling the NYPD."

"I was not stalking your friend, all right? Why won't you believe me?"

Mimi was breathing hard, a little frantic. "All Jamila knows is that I'm in Canada. News flash, Lazar, Canada is a BIG PLACE."

"You're right, of course," he said. "But she did mention that there was this house where you are staying that your father owns. So I took the liberty of calling him."

Mimi froze.

"Meem? Are you still there?"

"You what?"

"I talked to him, and he was kind enough to give me your address."

Mimi thought her head was going to explode. Blood pounded against her skull like a tsunami against some fragile island wharf.

"Meem?"

"He did *not* tell you where I am," she said in a voice only just above a whisper.

"Meem—"

"Stop calling me that!"

"Mimi," he said, "things have changed. Big things. Sophia has gone to see her parents in Chicago."

"What does that have to do with anything?"

"She and I are separating. I have told her about you."

It was like a nightmare. Every sentence seemed more improbable than the last.

"I am coming," he said.

"No! You are not. And if you do, you won't find me here."

Her face felt like it might burst spontaneously into flames. She could barely breathe, and into the blood-pounding silence came a noise. A noise that was not in the subway or some shopping concourse in Manhattan but nearby. Outside the house. It sounded like a struggle of some kind. Was that a shout? She peered through the curtains.

"We will talk, face-to-face," he said. "It will be different."

She heard a voice cry out.

"Lazar, I've got to go."

She was on her feet now and moving toward the kitchen.

"You wait and see," said Lazar, his voice buoyant,

filled with easy good humor. "It will be good between us. As good as it was."

Through the kitchen window, Mimi could see a shadowy flurry of activity just beyond the illumination from the kitchen light.

"Lazar—"

"I understand, Mimi," he said, interrupting her. And he went on talking, but she wasn't listening anymore. She only heard him dimly, a background noise to the struggle in the bushes. She pressed her face against the glass.

Then she gasped.

"What is it?" the voice on the phone demanded, but she hung up. All her attention was on the figure lying facedown in the long grass just past the shed, his old head poking out of the shadows into the light.

Stooley Peters. By the time Mimi had grabbed a flashlight and her mace, he was on his knees, groaning. He looked like some mangy animal.

"Mr. Peters?"

He groaned again. Groggily, he clamped his hand over his head. In the flashlight beam, she could see blood. His skull was bleeding!

For a moment she didn't know what to do. She was afraid to relinquish her hold on her mace canister and certainly not on the flashlight. Nervously, she aimed it at the bushes, seeing nothing but foliage in every direction. But foliage by flashlight had never been the same since *The Blair Witch Project.* She swung around, as if maybe the old man's assailant had sneaked up behind her. But there was nothing—only the shed with its own jumble of shadows lit by the light pouring out of the kitchen door.

Peters groaned again and mumbled something.

"Shhh!" she said, because she had heard another sound. Yes. The sound of something or someone crashing through the bush, quite far away now. She listened to the sound recede until it was gone. It could have been an animal, spooked by all the noise. She didn't think so. Summoning up her courage, she holstered her mace and knelt on one knee beside the old man.

"Are you okay?" she said.

"Hell, no!" he said. "Give me a hand?"

He weighed a ton. And he stank. She wondered if he had pissed himself.

It took all her effort to get him to an upright position. She had to shove the flashlight in the waist of her jeans, and it shone up at them, underlighting his bony old face like some ghoul. He was as dizzy as a drunk, though she couldn't smell alcohol on him. Only fear and hot anger and the disagreeable odor of someone who didn't wash any too often. She scrunched her nose shut as she placed his arm over her shoulder and staggered back toward the house. But he couldn't be too injured, she realized. It was not by chance that his limp hand brushed against her breast. At least it wasn't chance the second time it happened.

When she had deposited him, as quickly as she could, in a chair at the kitchen table, she found a facecloth and doused it in cold water to clean the wound on the back of the old man's head.

He was bent over the table, his head on his arms. But the moment the facecloth touched his scalp, his head flew up and Mimi jumped back, his nobbly skull just missing her jaw. The man reached up and took her hand in an iron grip and wrestled the cloth from her. She pulled away, rubbing her hands on her jeans.

"What happened?" she said.

He stared at her, his eyes unfocused. "What do you think happened?" he said. "I got my head stoved in is what happened."

"By who?"

Peters didn't answer her. He took the cloth, now smeared with blood, and staggered to the sink.

"Let me do that," said Mimi. But the old man paid her no attention. He turned on the tap, and bending his long frame forward, he splashed his face with cold water, getting a great deal of it on the linoleum floor while he was at it. Mimi leaned on the other end of the counter, still trying to catch her breath. After a few moments, the old man stood up straight and turned off the tap. Mimi handed him a towel. He took it from her with shaking hands, muttering the whole time, and began to dry himself off. There was a lot of blood on the facecloth and towel, but the wound on Peters's head did not look too deep, as far as she could tell.

He walked by her and examined his head in the mirror in the bathroom—seemed to know his way there, she thought, but then the door was open so maybe she was wrong. She watched him from the doorway. His crowlike eyes were darting back and forth in the mirror as he felt the welt on his head with his gnarled fingers.

"Hit me with a two-by-four," said the old man after a while.

"You saw him?"

"No," he snapped. "Saw *it*, though. Just as it come at me—the two-by-four—out of the corner of my eye. The bastard."

Now that he was on his feet again, he was feisty, ready for a fight. His face scowled at her from the mirror as if she was somehow responsible for what had happened.

"That's the one who's been stealing from you," he said. "Not me!" He poked himself hard in the chest, and the cold expression on his face left no doubt he was referring to the visit he'd had from the cops.

"Would you like a drink or something?" she asked.

He turned from his ministrations and looked her up and down as if she had propositioned him. She stepped back, wishing now she had left him outside. He was tall and farm-hardened. His forearms were leathery and strong.

"I don't suppose you've got a dram of rye," he said.

She shook her head. There was wine and a can or two of light beer, but she didn't want him to get any ideas. He shambled out of the bathroom, across the kitchen to the window, where he pulled back the curtain and scanned the darkened yard.

"He'll be long gone," he said.

"Who?"

"That right son of a bitch who crowned me." He shook his head and winced. Then he turned to look at her. "Maybe if I had a little lie-down," he said. "I'm feeling a bit woozy is all."

Mimi moved away from him until she bumped up against the counter.

"How about I call 911?" she said.

He grinned. "With this?" he said. He reached down and picked up her phone, but he didn't hold it out to her. His eyes said, *Come and get it.*

"Mr. Peters," she said. "You'd better get home."

"And how am I going to do that?" he said, leaning hard on the table as if any minute he was going to faint. It was a feeble performance. "Maybe you could drive me?"

"I'll tell you what," she said. "Jay's phone is just upstairs. How about I go and phone the cops, and they can drive you home?"

He glared at her. "You'd like that, wouldn't you?" he said. "You like siccing the cops on your neighbors."

"That's not how it was," she said.

"Oh? So how was it?" he said.

"Mr. Peters—"

But he cut her off. He poked himself in the chest again.

"You owe me, girl," he said, and mingled with the hostility in his eyes was a strong dash of lechery.

Mimi saw it clearly, and any misgivings she had vanished.

"He's been watching you," he said, pointing his thumb back over his shoulder. "That critter, whoever he is."

"Really?" she said.

He nodded. Made himself tall, tucked in the tails of his pewter-colored work shirt, with its worn and oil-stained cuffs.

"So let me get this straight," she said. "This *guy* was watching me, but it was *you* who got hit over the head from behind."

He stopped tucking in his shirt and glowered at her from under steel-gray eyebrows. "I was passing by on the road, when I seen someone."

"Really?"

"Damn right. Some shadowy figure messing around that pipsqueak car of yours. I stopped, see. Come back to take a look."

"Lucky me," she said, and she made no attempt to hide her contempt.

He took a step toward her, and her hand immediately went to her hip. She slid out her trusty mace and held it where he could see it. His eyes swayed from the canister to her face. And she wondered if he could read in her eyes just how ready she was to use it.

"You sure got yourself a heap of attitude," he said.

"I'm not in the market for a Peeping Tom, Mr. Peters."

He glared at her but didn't say another word. He sniffed and headed past her to the door. With every bit of courage she could muster, she stayed put. Just let him so much as touch her and she'd fill his lecherous eyes with something *really* hot!

He stopped at the doorway, turned, and pointed a finger at her.

"A word of advice," he said. "You keep parading around with next to nothing on, you're going to have more than you bargained for. You hear me? More action than a feral cat in heat."

Mimi stepped toward him with the canister aimed and watched him flinch, throwing up his arm to guard his face. "What I wear *parading around* in my own house with the curtains drawn is *my* fucking business. Now get out of here and don't come back. Ever."

He left, muttering darkly. She slammed the door after him and locked it. And as soon as he was good and gone—as soon as she heard the engine of his truck roaring—she gave in to gravity. She slid down the face of the door all the way to the floor and burst into tears.

≽❘ CHAPTER TWENTY-FOUR ❘≼

Harry NEVER DID ACTUALLY get together with Sally. Not that night. Mimi was already in bed when she realized she had left the two of them frozen there on the screen. She crawled into the front room, to her desk, and shut down the computer. Then she crawled back.

"Why am I crawling?" she wondered out loud.

So as not to be a silhouette on the curtains, that's why.

She lay in bed, reliving the scene over and over.

She had no doubt that Stooley Peters would have tried something if she hadn't stood up to him. But what about the other person? There had been someone else there. Peters didn't strike himself on the back of the head with a two-by-four. And she had heard someone fleeing. So who was watching whom? And why, suddenly, was she the attention of sneaks and creeps? She had run away from New York to escape the increasingly alarming focus of an ex-lover. But it seemed as if her safe house in the pretty forest was anything but! And that made her think a disturbing thought. Watching Hitchcock's *Psycho*, she had come to the morbid conclusion that the Bates Motel was what the Janet Leigh character deserved for her crime. She'd only robbed a bank, but, still, the Bates Motel became her own personal hell. Was that what Mimi was getting? Shit. And why did she have to start thinking about *Psycho*!

Blame Lazar. And only then, in replay, did she realize what she had not recognized while talking to him. She sat bolt upright in bed. The empty echoey sound behind him on the phone had been an airport.

He was on his way.

She turned her lamp back on and checked her watch. Somehow two hours had passed. It was 1:30 in the morning. What could she do? The trip from New York probably wasn't much over an hour if he got a direct flight. If he rented a car, he could be here any minute!

She jumped out of bed, but with no idea what to do. She could look up flight schedules on the computer—wait, no she couldn't: no Internet connection. She combed her fingers through her hair and walked in circles, swearing bloody murder.

She flicked off the lamp and padded to the front window. Carefully, she pinched back the curtain. There had been a full moon on July 30, and half of it still shone in a clear sky. The world outside was bright with lively shadows. She would see anyone approaching from the snye. And she would hear a car arrive, wouldn't she?

She watched for a full moment, shivering a little, turning the shadows into a stealthy crew of intruders. Her heart was beating out of control. This was ridiculous! She stamped her foot and swore at her father for his utter uselessness—no, it was worse than that, his betrayal! That's what this was. He was not only the world's worst father— he was a traitor! He was also potentially the accomplice to a murder.

She had the advantage over Lazar, she figured. She had never been so outraged in her life. Was this what they called a bloodlust? Because she wanted blood, a lot more blood than she'd seen trickling down the kitchen drain from the head of an old pervert. She wanted revenge. And she wanted it now. She checked her watch again. Almost 2:00. She followed the LED to her cell phone charging on the desk. She sat and dialed her father.

"Did I wake you?" she asked.

"No," he said, sounding perfectly awake. "Mimi?"

"Yes. I thought I'd better phone and say my good-byes before the psycho arrives here to kill me."

There was only the slightest of pauses before he chuckled. "Ah," he said. "Mr. Cosic, I presume."

"Yes, Mr. Cosic. So, it is true? You told him where I was?"

"In a manner of speaking," he said.

"Father, do you know what you did? That man is mentally unstable. I am truly frightened."

"Don't be," he said.

"That's easy for you to say. You're safe in your loft in the middle of safe old Manhattan. I'm in the middle of nowhere with a maniac on his way here because of you."

"Right, the middle of nowhere. And you've met your half-brother, I hear."

"Don't even get me started on that."

"You aren't getting along?"

"Marc! I swear I am going to scream. Yes, I am getting along with Jackson. He's wonderful. You should meet him sometime. But that is *not* what I'm talking about." There was a pause at the other end. *You should meet him sometime:* that had been a low blow. Well, hell; it was as much as he deserved. "Dad," she said, trying to rein herself in. "Lazar Cosic is the reason I'm here. How could you tell him where I was?"

"Mimi, do you want to hear the whole story?"

She was about to let loose a string of invective the likes of which this man had never heard from his worse critics. But something snagged her up. The *whole* story?

"What did you say?"

"I said that I think you should hear what happened. I think you might find it amusing. And by the way, hi, how are you?"

He was playing with her. Testing her. He had something up his sleeve. "Fine. Thanks for asking. Now talk."

And so her father told her about Lazar phoning him. How he had told Marc that Mimi was up for a teaching assistanceship in the fall semester and the school needed to get a contract to her pronto.

"You know it's all a big fat lie," she said.

"I wasn't born yesterday," said Marc. "I humored him. 'Couldn't they e-mail her the contract?' I said. But he was ready for me—a smooth operator. 'No. Not in the case of a contract. Had to be on letterhead. Had to be the real thing.' He was good, Mimi."

"And it's all crap," she said.

"I know. I remembered seeing him with you at Caprice."

Mimi was taken aback. "Really?"

"Of course. And after you were gone, I looked for the gentleman's name in the gallery guest book. It was right after yours. That's how I knew who he was when he called."

Mimi leaned into her desk, hugging the phone to her ear. He had noticed Lazar that day at the gallery. He had noticed her. But it wasn't just that; she actually found something like comfort in her father's casual manner, his seeming indifference, after the theatrics—and geriatrics—of the evening. She only hoped that he was not so detached as to have actually given Lazar what he wanted.

"So even though you knew he was lying—"

"Oh, surely it was just prevarication," said her father. "Maybe they do want you to TA at NYU?"

"Knock it off. They don't hire sophomores. And this is serious. Did you or didn't you give him my address?"

"I did," he said. And Mimi went cold all over. But before she could say anything, her father continued. "I told him about the old family cottage on the South Shore of Nova Scotia where you were holed up."

"What?"

"You remember, don't you? Oh, wait. You weren't there. It was just your mother and me. Lovely place. About two hours out of Halifax. Down near Liverpool. Sandy beach, quiet bay, wonderful privacy. I gave him very precise directions."

Something welled up in Mimi. Something horrified mixed with something warm. She wanted to scream and laugh — she could hardly hold it in.

"You didn't," she said.

"I did."

"Oh, my God."

"So, I presume that that is where he is heading. He struck me as precipitous enough to fly off with nothing more to go on than that."

Mimi couldn't speak. What was it she heard in her father's voice? Behind the affected world-weariness and the complete lack of proper fatherly disdain at the mess she had got herself into. "You are wicked," she said. "Did you know that?"

"I am and I did."

"You knew he was going to come after me."

Her father sighed. "I gathered," he said, and the humor in his voice slipped a notch. She heard a glass clink. Heard him take a sip of something. Wine, she assumed. Maybe Scotch at this late an hour. "I was also able to deduce that this Mr. Cosic—Professor Cosic?—"

"Associate professor."

"—Was, as you say, the reason you had bolted in the first place."

"Yes," she said timidly, for her father did sound like a father now, and she was unaccustomed to it.

He sipped from his drink again. "Are you all right up there?" he asked. "You and Jackson hitting it off?"

Was this his way of getting back at her for sniping at him? No. Her father just didn't get such things. "We are," she said. "He's really nice. I like knowing him." It was no use saying more. Not at this time of night.

"Well, good."

This might have been the place that a real father would have chided her about not getting in contact, not even letting him know she had arrived safely. But Marc wouldn't do that. She was a tiny bit glad; she didn't need chiding right now, considering everything else that was going on.

"You still there, Mimi?"

"I was thinking," she said. Could she tell him what was going on? No. She was too strung out, too tired. "I'm okay," she said.

"When you didn't call, I guessed you must be."

She swallowed. She had been too angry with him to

call—to even let him know she had arrived. "I'm sorry I didn't let you know I was here."

"Lou called. I suppose she told you. And your mother had the courtesy to e-mail me with an update. I wasn't worried."

And she knew that much was true. Her father hadn't developed the parental skill of worrying about his children. He'd missed all of that. Wasn't it, strangely, part of her attraction to him? Or it had been when she first started to visit him. Now she wasn't sure.

"So, it has been good for you?" he asked, to fill the silence of all that she was not saying.

"It's been . . . educational," she said. "And thanks for what you did."

"Hmmm," he said. As if thanks from an offspring was new to him and he was uncertain what to think of it. He drank something. She heard ice cubes, so it was Scotch. She imagined him in his studio. Alone? Yes, she suspected he was, somehow, or he wouldn't have talked to her for so long. And she suddenly realized that Marc would probably end up alone, which was sad, even if it was as much as he deserved.

"I imagine we'll both be hearing from the professor," he said.

"What if this backfires? Aren't you afraid he'll kick your ass?"

Her father laughed. "If he's smart, he'll thank me. But I'm not holding out for it."

Mimi yawned, tried to stifle it, but her father heard.

"Get some sleep," he said. "Call me sometime."

"I will," she said. "Thank you, Daddy."

There was a pause, a low chuckle, then he hung up. No "Love you, sweetie." As if. But she was glad she had called him Daddy.

And Mimi walked back to her bed on the floor over the trapdoor and fell into something like sleep. Though at some point in the night she dreamed of earthquakes, a low rumbling coming from deep beneath the quiet, little moon-drenched house.

≫I CHAPTER TWENTY-FIVE I≪

THURSDAY MORNING MIMI SAT at her desk staring at the phone numbers of people her father had known before he was even her father. When he was Jay's father. No, that wasn't right, either. He had left before Jay was born. How many of these people laced together by elaborate doodles had known of Marc Soto's departure? It was sudden, she guessed. Had he packed, left a note, sent flowers?

Through the window she watched Jay glide into view, the yellow of his kayak almost blinding in the green veil. She saw him lie back flat as he disappeared through the arch of the bridge and then reappear on her side. Peeka-boo. She smiled. Seeing him was a tonic. And there was a lot to talk about, although she had already given him a blow-by-blow description of Wednesday Night Fever. He had phoned from Montreal, of all places. One thing had led to another, and he and Iris had ended up driving down to see a new band, the Bell Orchestre. A rock band with French horns. Fabulous. Brilliant. They had stayed over at a friend's apartment.

"Everything okay where you are?" he had asked.

"Funny you should ask," Mimi had said. He had been worried, but she assured him she was okay and not to hurry back on her account.

But he was here now, and she would have him all to herself for a bit. There was still this strange pleasure of a boy you got to have all to yourself sometimes without any fuss or muss. It was confusing, when your heart wasn't quite sure where it wanted to be. Sometimes when she was alone with him, her heart was in her throat. She had the feeling he felt the same way about her. She was glad that Iris was in his life. And hers, too, for that matter.

And, as it turned out, it was Iris she was going to get to hang with that day, if only for an hour or so. It was clear pretty well from the moment Jay arrived that his mind was elsewhere. He was excited about writing something. And, reluctantly, she was glad. He had become so quiet lately, as if, apart from the guitars, the robber had taken his voice. But he was bubbling over today. He did ask whether Lazar had phoned back yet.

"No."

"Weird."

She agreed. "Maybe he threw himself in the ocean. No, he'd never do anything that convenient."

She expected—wanted—Jay's righteous indignation to flare up again and make her feel less guilty about Lazar's fateful journey to the east coast. But he was itching to get to work, to start something new—a new composition.

"That is so good."

He nodded, a little nervously. "The Bell Orchestre really inspired me," he said.

"But?"

"What do you mean, 'but'?"

"Well, you look as if you've got a big *but* just waiting to pop out of you."

He smiled. "I'm nervous," he said. "I'm always like this when I start something. Like I won't remember how."

"Oh, that kind of nervous," she said.

"The first thing I'm going to do is erase *Simple*."

"Really? Isn't that a bit excessive?"

He shook his head vehemently. His jaw was clenched. "Got to. Got to move on."

And he wanted the place to himself. Apparently, Iris was free for lunch, at twelve, if she was interested. The invitation was pretty transparent. But Mimi wasn't put out. He had been so glum lately; it was good to see him excited again.

She showered and put on a flippy skirt and a loose cotton lavender-colored top and headed into town. She was supposed to meet Iris at a place called the Hungry Planet and went looking for it early, figuring she'd check her e-mail at the coffee shop first. But as she approached the place, a figure appeared before her, stepping out of a grotty-looking Ford and gathering some things from the backseat before slamming the door.

"Hey there, stranger," she said.

Cramer turned to see her and got this flustered look on his face. "Hi," he said, recovering somewhat. He wiped his head as if to push the hair out of his eyes had there been any hair. His other arm was full of electronic doodads, which he cradled against his chest.

"Heading to work?"

He nodded. "Any trouble with the computer?" he asked, bobbing his head at the case swinging from her shoulder.

"Have you ever heard of this theater game where you can only talk in questions?"

"Pardon?"

She laughed. "Forget it. Hey, do you have time for a coffee?" It was clearly the right thing to say. Mimi experienced the rare delight of watching his whole face seem to open up before her very eyes.

"I would really like that," he said.

"Cool."

"I'll just put this stuff back in the car?"

"Or you can bring it along," she said. She tugged at a cable hanging from one of the doodads. "You know, in case we can't think of anything to talk about."

He grinned. "We'd have to be pretty bored," he said. And she laughed, which made his smile widen even more.

His teeth weren't great, but you can't have everything.

As he put the electronic stuff in the car, she chatted away at him, and the next thing she knew, he wasn't smiling anymore. "If you're like meeting someone for lunch, I don't want to horn in, eh?"

"Oh, boo," she said. "You're breaking my heart."

He looked down, scuffed his shoe on the pavement. She had mentioned Iris's name. Was that what had spooked him? "Do you know Iris?" she asked.

"It's not that," he said. "I guess I was just, you know . . ."

She did know. He has been hoping that it would be just the two of them. So she was right; he did like her. She checked the time on her cell phone. "Hey," she said. "We've got twenty minutes all to ourselves."

He gazed at her. "Maybe we could just walk?" he said. He nodded toward the end of the block. "Down to the park?"

"Sure."

So they set off down the street, crossed the road into McGinty Park, and made their way to the river.

"You play hockey?" she asked.

He looked surprised. "Not much anymore. Why?"

"You look like a hockey player. All those muscles. Not that I know any hockey players."

Cramer pointed at a little scar above his ear. "I got that playing hockey," he said. "And that ain't the only one, either."

"Rough game," said Mimi.

"Stupid game," he said.

And Mimi laughed.

They sat on a bench right beside a wide pond. The water was high, well up over the bank. There were toddlers on the other side toddling under the watchful gaze of a small clutch of mothers, most of whom looked to be no older than Mimi.

"This is nice," said Cramer.

She looked at him. "Oh, yeah? So why are you frowning?"

He looked surprised. "Was I?"

"Uh-huh."

"Sorry." He shrugged, looked out at the pond.

She poked him in the arm. "Come on, tell me. Wazzup?"

He leaned forward, resting his arms on his knees. He looked down, saw a stone, and picked it up. Chucked into the pond. One of the toddlers on the other side was drawn to the ripples and started walking toward the water only to be corralled by its mother and given a good hugging.

Mimi laughed. "That was close," she said. But from the look on Cramer's face, he hadn't noticed the little drama.

"Hey," said Mimi. "Talk to me, former hockey-player person. What's eating you?"

He looked at her, and she looked back into his crazy blue eyes, knowing, somehow, he was getting up the courage to say something important, maybe even something intimate. Then he looked away, seemed to change gears.

"It's my mother," he said.

"Is she sick or something?"

"I don't know. Maybe. I'm beginning to wonder. But it's not *sick* sick, like," he said. And he tapped his head. "She's an artist. A painter."

"Really?"

"Yeah," he said.

"So she's not '*sick* sick' just arty?"

He rolled his eyes. "Some days," he said. "Some days, it's . . ." He paused. "She has good days and bad days."

"And today was a bad one?"

He nodded. "Oh, yeah. Really bad."

"That's really a coincidence because—"

But Cramer interrupted her. "She's like on this creative journey?" he said. "She's got this book called *The Artist's Path*?"

"Oh," said Mimi. "I know it."

He looked stunned. "You're kidding me."

"No," she said. "Honest." She had been about to tell him her father was an artist, too, but she was glad she hadn't. *The Artist's Path*, as far as she could tell, was a book for dilettantes and dabblers.

"Wow," he said, shaking his head, his mouth hanging open a little. "I never met no one—anyone—who ever heard of it or like that."

She nodded again. "Well, now you have."

"Yeah," he said. "Now I have. So, you know what they

can be like, eh? Artists?"

"Oh, yeah," she said. "Big-time."

"Like it can be kind of, you know . . ." He waggled his hand in the air, palm down.

She did the same with her hand, and they both laughed.

"Wow," he said again, and rubbed his head.

His hand was so large, so strong. Mimi looked away. She was feeling just the slightest bit short of breath. Then she noticed her cell phone, still in her hand, and saw that it was nearly noon.

"Listen," she said. "I've got to meet Iris."

"Oh, yeah. Right." He seemed flustered again and immediately jumped to his feet.

"Are you sure you don't want to join us?"

He thought about it, looked pained, she thought, but shook his head. "Hank'll be waiting for me," he said, but he didn't fool her.

"Let's do this again, Cramer, okay?"

He smiled. "Okay," he said.

"Cool."

They walked back to where his car was parked, and he gathered his electronics from the backseat again.

"It was good seeing you," he said. "It was good to talk to you like that."

"Same for me," said Mimi, and reached out to shake his hand. He took it and almost lost the equipment he was cradling.

"Oops!" she said, grabbing some kind of a measuring device before it slipped out of his grasp entirely.

"Thanks, eh," he said. "And about the coffee—"

"A rain check," she said.

"Pardon? Oh, right. Yeah. Right." He chuckled. "They say there's going to be some rain. Like soon."

Mimi grinned. "Good," she said.

"Yeah," he said. "Like it's a sign?" She nodded. And he looked as if he wanted to say more but couldn't think of a thing. Then, with his head bobbing, he started off. He turned and waved. "Thanks," he said.

"You're welcome."

Then he stopped and came back. "Hey, you still got my number, right?"

"You betcha," she said, giving him a little salute.

"Well, just phone if you need any help."

"I will."

He nodded seriously. "I hope you don't," he said. Then he looked horrified. "That's not what I meant to say. I meant I hope you don't run into any—"

She cut him off with a laugh. His confusion was endearing. "I knew what you meant, Cramer," she said. "And I won't hesitate to call if I need you . . . uh, need to. Thanks so much."

He took a deep breath, as if this interchange was burning a great deal of calories and he'd soon have to skate back to the bench to recuperate.

His face got serious again. "And no one's been

bothering you up there?" he said.

"No," she said. "We seem to be out of the woods." Then she laughed at the unintended pun.

"All right," he said. "Good one!" And he gave her a thumbs-up.

She returned the gesture.

And then with a tip of his head, he left, swiveling to look at her again, a few paces down the path. He flashed her a smile.

She sighed. Nice smile, bad teeth or not.

"Hey."

She turned and there was Iris approaching from up Forster. "Hey, yourself."

"Who's the muffin?" said Iris, shielding her eyes to catch the last glimpse of Cramer as he ducked down the alley to PDQ Electronics.

"Mr. Cute Butt," said Mimi. "A little short on the snappy repartee but nice. Very nice in a hockey-player kind of way."

"Charm enough for your charm bracelet?" said Iris, and Mimi laughed out loud, a little raucously.

"Who is he?" said Iris.

"Cramer. He's the one who fixed my computer. I don't know his last name."

"I thought Hank Pretty fixed your computer."

Mimi shook her head, holding open the door to the restaurant for Iris. "Maybe Cramer's a Pretty, too," she said.

"There are lots of them around these parts," said Iris, and then stopped in her tracks. "Cramer, Cramer. Why does that ring a bell?"

"Because of Jerry Seinfeld?"

Iris shook her head. Then she snapped her fingers. "Cramer Lee," she said, and turned to Mimi with her dark eyes sparkling.

"What about him?"

Iris dropped her voice. "Cramer Lee was the kid who used to follow Jay around in high school."

Mimi looked at her in disbelief. "Get out. The one you were talking about? He sounded like a nerdy kind of kid — a twerp."

"He was," said Iris. She turned as if to make sure Cramer wasn't still around. "*That* was Cramer Lee we were leering at?"

"I guess."

Iris made a wry face. "He certainly bulked up."

"Oh, yeah," said Mimi, as they took a table. "Pecs, traps — the works." She picked up her menu and fanned herself vigorously. "Is it hot in here or what?" she said.

⇒| CHAPTER TWENTY-SIX |⇐

HE WANTED TO ASK HER OUT. He had a couple more days off. They could do something. He wasn't sure what. Just go for a walk maybe. Go for that coffee—cash in his rain check. But how? She had his number, but he didn't have hers. Could he just show up at her place? How about if he ran into her? He could go out running along the Upper Valentine around the time she did. It would be this big coincidence. But would it appear like too much of a coincidence? That's what he was afraid of. What was far stronger than his fear, however, was his desire to see her.

Friday bloomed an August day of rare perfection. Cramer worked out hard but slow, took his time, enjoyed every curl and crunch. He felt every muscle fiber in his body stretch and contract. He had sculpted himself into something. She had noticed. He had been someone no one noticed, but Mimi had noticed. He'd seen how she looked at him. It was worth every chin-up and dead lift.

He showered and changed and made himself a few sandwiches. He wouldn't come home at all that day. Mavis wasn't around. He had offered to drive her into Ottawa for art supplies, but she had said she'd go alone. He wasn't sure when she was planning on doing that, but he didn't care anymore. He had gotten her the money she wanted. It had not been easy. And that was it. He was done. The rest was up to her.

From a tree he watched Mimi sitting by the snye in white jeans and a peach-colored halter top, her hair tied up in a rose-colored scarf. She just sat, her feet bare, occasionally reaching out a toe to stir the water gurgling by or leaning back on her elbows until her face was full of dappled sunlight.

How he would have liked to sit there beside her. Not talking—not doing anything. Not so much as touching her. He had never felt like that before. Someone he just wanted to be with.

He would take her out in Bunny. He could imagine her leaning back against the thwart—except he'd take pillows along for her to lean on. She could drag her fingers in the water, like in some old movie or like that. They would have a picnic—he knew just where. He'd buy wine. He'd ask her to choose. She could teach him about things like that: wine and fancy stuff and conversation.

He suddenly felt this huge sense of shame about what he had done to them. To Jay as well as Mimi. It was envy, jealousy. It had coursed through his veins as thick as sludge. But that had all changed. Kind of like open-heart surgery.

Mimi got up and walked back to the house. She came out a few minutes later in a bikini, with her flotation device on. She took the kayak and made her way down the snye to the river. He followed her on foot, along the bank, a safe distance back, quiet as a ghost. He watched her from the shore. He imagined her overturning and him swimming out to save her. He imagined giving her mouth-to-mouth, watching her chest rise and fall as life flowed back into her lungs. Then, as her eyes opened and she saw who it was that had saved her, she would take the hand resting on her chest and she would hold it against her breast.

At a little after six, Iris showed up at the snye in the white Camry in a turquoise blouse and black skirt and slingbacks, with her hair tied back in a yellow ribbon. She had just come from work, he guessed. She was carrying a bag from the liquor store. Jay, all dressed in white, met her at the bridge, and they kissed for a long time, before they made their way across the bridge, balancing with their arms out on a plank someone had placed there.

There was a perfect breeze on this perfect day, so the mosquitoes stayed away. The three friends moved a table out onto the grass and placed a white tablecloth on it and set it with plates and silverware. Soon they were sitting there eating some kind of salad and drinking wine.

The summer evening closed in around the dinner party on the lawn. It wasn't completely dark, but they brought out tea candles. Cramer shimmied down his tree and moved silently closer. They would not hear him. Jay had his acoustic guitar, and they were singing. They drank and sang and laughed. Then one or the other of them would drift into the house and come back with something else to eat or another bottle of wine. And Cramer imagined walking out of the gathering night right up to the table.

"Cramer!" Mimi would say, and throw her arms around him. "I was just thinking about you." Then he would drift into the house and return with a chair of his own. He would watch and listen. That would be enough. He would smile at the right moment, be careful not to drink too fast or too much. He would be attentive—he was good at that. He would leap up to get more fruit or whatever.

"No, let me," he would say. And Mimi would touch his hand. And then . . .

And then what?

The mosquitoes didn't move in until 9:05, and the dinner party broke up only to reassemble inside. Slapping at bugs, Cramer waited most of another hour, drawing as close to the house as he dared, hoping for one more glimpse of her.

Bats escaped from the eaves of the little house and swooshed around him, gorging on the mosquitoes and not making a dent in the population. Still he stayed on, steadfast. It was what he knew how to do. And there was another reason for staying. That old bastard Stooley Peters. Mimi wasn't alone tonight, but Cramer would stay as long as he could, keeping guard. He would be her guardian if he couldn't be anything else. This would be the good secret to offset the bad secret. This would be the decent thing he did to compensate for all the wrongness.

It was the next day, Saturday, when tragedy struck. The sun was just going down when she came outside, and to his shock he saw that she was crying. What could have happened? He had been close enough to hear her cell phone go off—that old song by Queen. Was it the man with the foreign-sounding name that made her cry? The one she had dumped? What had he done now, because Mimi was weeping—holding herself and weeping. Cramer wanted to swing down out of his roost and take her in his arms. The sky was still light enough to see her face, and although it was disfigured with tears, it was as lovely as ever. Even more beautiful because it was filled with need. He wanted to kiss her tears away, hold her tight. And it was in that rush of yearning that his foot slipped. He didn't fall but he swung out for one tense moment, and in grabbing for a handhold, a branch snapped off in his grasp, cracking loudly.

It was all over in a moment. She had not seen him; he was sure of it. But she was aware of his presence. Through the thick foliage of the maple, he saw her looking around. She stopped crying. She was staring up into the trees, sniffing, wiping her eyes on her sleeve. He didn't dare breathe.

When she spoke, she didn't raise her voice. She didn't sound frightened or even angry, but her words were like knives.

"You are a sick person," she said. "Do you know that? You are really sick." She walked down toward the snye until she was almost beneath him. "What have we done to make you hate us so much?"

No, not hate.

"You robbed us blind. Wasn't that enough?"

What was she talking about?

"What is it you want?" She paused, then she let out a long shuddery breath. "Just go away. Please. Leave us alone."

She didn't yell. It was exactly as if she were talking to him, except that what she said hurt more than he could bear. Then she sniffed, rubbed her nose, and went back in the house. He didn't hear the door slam.

Cramer slithered from his branch and stood at the base of the tree breathing hard. What was she talking about? He started toward the house. What the hell was she talking about? He stopped, walked back toward the snye, slammed his fist hard against a tree.

Robbed them blind?

That isn't what you said about a rock taken from a windowsill. It wasn't even what you said about a picture in a silver frame. What did she mean? Something else.

Something big. And then it came to him and he went cold all over. *Stooley Peters.*

He'd caught the bugger sneaking around, figured him for a Peeping Tom. Maybe he'd done more. Could he tell Mimi that? Yes. He would walk up to her door right now. But he couldn't. She'd know he was the one in the tree and she'd hate him.

He took a deep shaky breath. He would deal with this himself—find a way.

He slunk away through the glade, and when he was out of earshot, he ran, whipped and slapped and slashed at by the underbrush, until he arrived at last at the cove where he kept Bunny hidden under a blanket of cedar boughs.

He was bleeding. The back of his hand, his cheek, his left ankle. Angrily he tore off the tendrils of undergrowth still clinging to him. Then he cleared Bunny of her cover, and, grabbing the gunwales, he launched himself out onto the darkening water. He dug his paddle down deep, right into the muck of the Eden, almost spilling himself in his desperate need to escape that horrible place where a girl had said that to him.

You are a sick person. Do you know that? You are really sick.

Not just any girl—the most beautiful girl who had ever talked to him. He thrust his paddle into the water and with all the strength in his shaking body propelled Bunny out into the river. He was crying now. Crying in great sobs. Crying in rage.

"It isn't fair! It isn't fucking fair!"

And he was so wrapped up with the unfairness of everything that he didn't notice what was happening to him.

He was going down.

The boat was filling up with water. From holes all along its keel, the river poured into Bunny, and with every stroke he only drove her farther down into the water. He stopped, midstream, and sat there, sinking.

⇉| CHAPTER TWENTY-SEVEN |⇇

LAZAR CALLED SATURDAY from the Lord Nelson Hotel in Halifax, Nova Scotia. It was pricey, he said, but in for a penny in for a pound. *What does that mean?* Mimi wondered but didn't ask. He sounded almost cheery, as if the terrible joke Mimi's father had played on him had snapped him out of his stupor. He was in the process of raiding the hospitality fridge in his room for tiny bottles of booze. He had rented a car and driven down the coast to where she wasn't. And then he had driven back to Halifax.

"A very big lesson," he said. "A very expensive lesson."

Mimi kept her lips zipped. She was not going to apologize for what her father had done. But it seemed Lazar wasn't looking for an apology.

He made Mimi laugh with his running commentary of what the hospitality fridge had to offer in the way of alcoholic diversion. It reminded her of when they first started seeing each other. How he was always explaining how things worked: how subways ran on the energy created by people on treadmills in gyms all over the city; how smog was necessary to hide the hooks that held up the skyscrapers. He would take her to obscure dives he had discovered, where the waiters knew him and treated him like a king and her, like the king's consort. She could hear that same sense of wound-too-tight fun in his voice tonight. Then he sighed and she expected the worst. But he surprised her. Well, he had always been surprising.

"I have been crazy," he said. "I thought crazy in love but perhaps, really, just crazy. No?"

She had a lump in her throat. Was this a setup?

"Are you still there?" he asked, his voice gentle. But she couldn't speak. "If you have hung up," he said, "I will just keep talking anyway and then tell myself we had this discussion and it's, as you would say, all good."

"I'm still here," she said.

"Good, because I would rather talk to you than to myself, but I wouldn't blame you for hanging up."

Mimi swallowed hard. Was this a trap? "I'm sorry," she said. "I . . ." But she wasn't sure what she could add. She was sorry in a way and she wasn't really sorry in another way, but she was confused and wary.

"You have no reason to be sorry," he said. "This wild-goose chase was not your idea. And even if it was, I gave you no options." He sighed. "Sophia has left me," he said.

"You told me."

"But I only told you half a truth," he said. "It wasn't because of you, Meem. It was because of me. I have been unfaithful for so long. I thought it was different with you. You know? Different. Ah, of course you know. Well, now I know, too. Crazy, hey?" She heard the sound of another cap being snapped open on another tiny bottle. "A slow learner," he said, and chuckled sadly.

"Lazar," she said. "It was fun—at first, I mean."

He laughed again, a little drunkenly. "At first, yes," he said, but not unkindly.

"I didn't want to run away, but I couldn't think of . . . You were so . . ."

"No, don't remind me!" he said. "It is painful to think of the last couple of months. You were clever to go. You are a clever girl. A talented girl."

Mimi could feel the tears coming, welling up in her. Relief and release from all that anger. And sadness, too. Sadness at the part she had played in this.

"You will not have to worry about me being a pest anymore."

"Lazar, I—"

"No. It's true. I have been a pest. But I have come to my senses, okay? And I am leaving NYU."

Mimi was on her guard again. "What do you mean?"

"I mean what I say. There were rumors in the department. My reputation was . . . how can I put this delicately?" He laughed. "I *cannot* put it delicately. Let's just say, my reputation was catching up to me. So, to save myself the mortification of being dismissed, I have offered my resignation."

"Lazar, I never said anything—"

"To the dean? Of course, you didn't. You didn't need to. I have no one to blame but myself. But all is not lost. I have found work."

"You have?"

"I'm going to Baylor."

"Where's that?"

Lazar laughed. "A good question," he said. "It's in Waco, Texas. I have to learn how to say that. It's *Way-co*, yes? I did not know this at first."

"You're moving to Texas?" Mimi tried to imagine Lazar in a cowboy hat.

"It's the largest Baptist university in the world," he said. "Me teaching in a Baptist university. Communication studies. I tell you, my world is . . . how shall I say this? Changing?" he said. "Yes, that puts a good spin on it. Changing."

Mimi was shaking with relief. He was moving thousands of miles away. And she refused to feel guilty, and yet—

"You will be happy?" he asked. She wasn't sure, but there did not seem to be any malice in what he was saying. "Because it is important to me, after everything, that you are happy. Well, a little bit sad. Yes?"

"Okay," she said meekly. "But—"

"No *buts*, Meem. You be happy. That is good. And

before I get too ridiculous, let me just say thank you for the good times and say good-bye, you delightful creature."

And it was over.

Quietly he hung up. And she knew he would not call again. Which is when she started to really cry. She cried so much she thought she would drown the little house, and so she went outside. And then she heard the sound of a branch cracking.

When she spoke to him—the man in the trees, wherever he was—she felt as if she was in some bizarre off-off-Broadway play. The girl who talks to trees. She spoke without fear because, quite frankly, she had nothing left in her. She was emotionally exhausted. And if this monster dropped out of the tree with Jason's mask on his face and a gleaming meat cleaver in his hand, she would have only laughed in his face.

She went inside and took her little vial of poisonous spray to bed with her. To sleep, perchance to scream.

Her mind drifted in and out of the elevator in the many-floored House of Sorrow. *Ding!* Regret. *Ding!* Denial. *Ding!* Outrage. But finally she dozed off, only to wake suddenly with the words "up there" clanging in her head like a fire alarm.

Up there?

She had heard someone say it. She could almost hear someone saying those two words in her head. "Up there." For a moment or two she couldn't figure out why the words seemed so jarring. Then it came to her.

Cramer Lee on the street outside the Hungry Planet, his eyes filled with concern.

No one's been bothering you up there.

That's what he had said. But there was a problem with that. A big problem.

She had never told him where she lived.

Was she crazy? Well, there was one way to find out. She flipped on her lamp and looked at her watch. Not even eleven. She crawled across the mattress to the chair where she hung her purse and looked through it until she found the business card with his phone number scrawled on the back. Then she flipped on the lights in the front room and sat at her desk. With the card in front of her, she punched in Cramer's numbers. Then she leaned on the desk, her eyes staring straight ahead, willing it to be him who answered. It wasn't. "Hello," said a sleepy woman's voice.

And Mimi pushed END. But it wasn't because she had woken up Mrs. Lee, if that's who it was. She terminated the call because of something very odd she saw before her on the wall. One of her father's telephone numbers. A number he had etched over more than once and drawn an elaborate frame around. Beside it were the initials M.L. The number was the same one she had just called.

❧ PART THREE ❧

๑ Sometimes the pain was too much.

He wanted to scream but he couldn't scream. His mouth felt as if it were wired shut, and so the scream smashed around in his head like some enraged, caged, wild thing, shaking every bone of his skull, exhausting him.

He dreamed.

He was in the tunnel again, a small bag clutched in his teeth. Then he was in the room under where she lay. He took the bag from his mouth and laid it in the corner of the room of dirt, like a good dog returning something to his master. Then he stood, though he could not stand up all the way. He listened, his ear pressed against the roof that was her floor. In his dream he could hear her breathing; resting his palms on the trapdoor, he could almost feel her. It was as if he was holding her up. There was a noise in the room. She was stirring, awake—if he could only reach her. He had to try to explain. He knew what he would say—he'd had a lot of time to think about it. Could he change the past? No. But he could change that small piece of the past that was him—that was still him. He would say something like that. He couldn't think beyond that. Couldn't think what she would say, couldn't reach her, couldn't—

"Cramer? It's all right," she said, her voice urgent but so quiet, speaking just to him. "Shhh, calm down already."

He felt—imagined—no, felt her hand on his chest, just lying there. "Shhh. Listen . . ."

⇒∣ CHAPTER TWENTY-EIGHT ∣⇐

CRAMER WOKE UP in the middle of the night to the sound of a drive shaft torquing too high. His eyes snapped open. There were headlights out in the yard. *The cops,* he thought, almost relieved, as if getting arrested would give his misery some real shape. But by then the screaming motor had crested the steep driveway and was clunking on bad suspension across the yard, and he knew no cop would drive a vehicle in that bad condition.

He slipped out of bed, stepped over the sopping clothes strewn across his floor, and stared out the window. Waylin Pitney's ghostly panel truck was pulling into its usual place behind the drive shed on the lip of the hill, pulling as far forward as the space allowed to hide the truck from anyone passing by on the road.

Lights were on downstairs. And as soon as the engine was cut, Cramer heard the screen door slam. Mavis stepped out into the yellow light seeping from the front window. She was in a sleeveless summer dress. There wasn't much back to the dress, from what he could see. Her hair was all done up. This wasn't a surprise visit. Not to her, at least.

From around the corner of the drive shed, Waylin appeared, the yard light revealing a white tee, jeans, and cowboy boots. His long shadow was behind him and then it passed him, as if in a hurry to get to Mavis. But only his shadow hurried.

"Hi ya, doll," he shouted.

"Hi yourself," she said. She had her hands clasped behind her back, and she was swiveling left and right from the waist like some teasing schoolgirl. Waylin stopped halfway across the yard to look back, apparently to make sure the vehicle was out of sight. And Cramer could hear through his open window his mother swear. But not out of anger, he thought. She had sworn because she couldn't wait one more second. Then she was running in her bare feet across the yard to Waylin, and he was twirling her in the air.

Cramer made his way back to bed and pulled the covers up over his head, hoping the party wouldn't get too loud. Hoping it wouldn't end in a fight.

The next thing he knew it was morning. Exhaustion had grabbed him by the scruff of his neck and dragged him down into oblivion. Not even his mother's midnight cowboy could keep him awake.

When Cramer thumped downstairs, Mavis was making

something from a cookbook, still wearing the little floral number with no back she'd had on the night before.

"There's flapjacks," she said in a cheery voice. But the flapjacks were cold. Cramer wandered over to the window. The Taurus was gone.

"How am I supposed to get to work tonight?"

"Since when do you work on Sunday?" said his mother, without looking up from the cookbook.

Cramer stared at her, astonished. "I work an eight-night shift and then have a four-day break," he said. "It's been that way for three years. It has nothing to do with what day of the week it is. I thought you knew that."

She glanced back at him, but the resentment in his voice had not registered. "Oh, didn't I tell you?" she said. "Merv phoned."

"My shift manager?"

"I don't know any other Mervs, honey," she said. "Anyway, he said to tell you you're laid off. Just temporary-like. He was nice about it."

Cramer stared at her in disbelief. Then he went to the phone and made the call. It was true. Nothing to do with Cramer. A bit of a work slowdown. Only be a few days.

"I thought you were going to make me full-time," said Cramer.

"And I am, Cramer. You can count on it. Just not right now. Relax. You take a bit of a vacation, okay? God knows you deserve one."

And that was that.

Mavis turned toward him, holding out her arms. "And since when do you come downstairs of a morning without saying, 'Good morning, Mama'?"

But he didn't go to her. He felt cut adrift. It was as if someone had drilled a row of holes in Cramer himself and he was sinking.

"Ah, come on," said Mavis. "It's not so bad, is it?"

Something happened to her when Waylin was around. She started talking like someone from another time— another planet. She reverted to some fifties idea of Mrs. Good Wife—a southern variety, about to serve up catfish and collard greens.

"Actually, it is bad," he said. "I've got this bank loan, just to name one thing."

That seemed to jog her out of her playacting. He glanced toward the porch that was her studio. Her abandoned studio. There was still no sign of newly stretched canvases, new jars of paint. He wanted to ask her what she had done with the money, but all he had to do was look at her to get his answer. The dress was new. She lowered her eyes, then turned back to the cookbook.

Cramer strolled outside in his boxers and torn T-shirt to have a look at the day. He picked his way barefoot to the edge of the hill and looked down the bank to where Bunny should have been.

He swallowed hard, clenched his fists, and closed his eyes tight with the effort to keep the obscenities inside him. He knew who was responsible for this. Peters. It had to be. Well, Peters would pay. But first of all, he had to recover Bunny.

You can't sink a canoe.

She'd be floating somewhere, up to her gunnels, but still afloat. He held a wet finger up. There wasn't a whisper of wind. Good. There would be just the current to carry her, and the current in the stretch of the river where he had lost her was not strong. Carrying the weight of a full cargo of water, she wasn't going to be moving any too fast.

He'd take the old canoe from the drive shed and a length of rope and something to stop up the holes temporarily. He'd get her to shore, empty her, and then drag her home. He'd fix her. She'd be as good as new. And hell, he had all day. Day and days!

He picked his way to the drive shed, his bare feet finding every sharp stone the yard had to offer. He wondered how drunk or high his mother must have been last night to sail across here to her man without feeling anything.

He opened the door and looked inside the drive shed. The old canoe wasn't there. It had been straddling a couple of sawhorses last time he looked. Was he wrong? Maybe it was in the old barn? But it wasn't there, either.

It felt like a plot.

He had dared to think his luck was changing, and it was, but it was only getting a whole lot worse! He smashed the flats of his fists against his temples. He had to get a grip. Deal with one loss at a time. The battered aluminum canoe was not the kind of thing anyone would steal. No one in his right mind. Or hers.

He looked toward the house. As if he had summoned her, Mavis appeared at the kitchen door with a dustpan, the contents of which she threw onto the path. Her eyes scanned the yard. He ducked back into the shadow of the barn door. Then, when she had gone back inside, he made his way down the hill to the creek and walked along it from his own landing place up past the outbuildings to a little glade of trees. And there it was. She had hidden the old canoe there, not wanting him to know she was using it. Why?

Back in the house, Cramer changed and made himself a few sandwiches. Mrs. Good Wife was in her room. Cramer didn't bother to say good-bye.

CHAPTER TWENTY-NINE

WE CALL THE COPS!"

They were in the front room, Jay leaning on the desk, Mimi seated at it, and Iris leaning against the wall.

"This is what Roach meant when he said 'if anything happens,'" said Jay. "Something has happened."

"Not really," said Mimi.

"No, I mean we have a clue. There is a connection."

"It's circumstantial," said Iris.

"Cripes, you've been working for a lawyer for a couple of weeks and suddenly you're an expert?" Iris glowered at Jay. "No, seriously," he said, "this is the guy who you say used to follow me around in high school, right? Suddenly it turns out his telephone number is on the wall of this house. That may be a coincidence, but it's a hell of a big one."

"You're right," said Mimi. "And so we need to find out what the connection is between"—she looked at the wall—"M.L. and this house."

"Presumably the L stands for Lee," said Iris. "And the woman you talked to must be the M. Didn't you say Cramer was talking about his mother? Maybe it's her?"

"Possibly," said Mimi. "She sounded about the right kind of age."

"Hold it, you two," said Jay. "Stop with the detective games right now." His face was red; Mimi had never seen him so steamed up. He pulled out his cell phone. "Maybe you're forgetting I got robbed, big-time."

"I'm not forgetting," said Mimi. "So did I."

Jay was busily scrolling through his phone list. Then he swore. "I didn't input Roach's number," he said. Then he looked at Mimi. "Did I give you his card?" She nodded and he held out his hand.

"Jay, I'll give it to you, but will you just let me try to talk this through? Please?"

He rolled his eyes and pocketed his cell phone.

"Jay," said Iris. "Just listen to what she has to say."

Jay sat back down on the edge of the desk. "Okay," he said without looking up. "Shoot." His hands were in his lap, the fingers woven together so tightly, the knuckles were red.

Mimi leaned back in her chair, scrubbed her face with her hands. What was she doing? Why was she so reluctant to call the cops? She kind of knew.

"First of all," she said, "the thing that tipped me off in the first place was him saying 'up there' as if he knew where I lived." The others nodded. "Now that struck me as bizarre, since I know I never told him. But if—and this is just a 'for instance'—*if* he happened to live around here, then he might have seen me drive by. Ms. Cooper is pretty distinctive in these parts, right? Or he might have seen me out running."

"So why didn't he say anything about it?" said Jay.

"I didn't ask. And like I said, he's shy."

She glanced at Jay, and he bobbed his head slightly. Not exactly a ringing endorsement. "I'll buy that, but it doesn't explain the number on the wall."

Mimi crossed her arms. "I know. That I can't figure out. My dad must have known whoever M. Lee is. And that is very freaky, I admit. But it isn't really criminal."

Jay just looked exasperated. "So we're back to *feelings*. Is that all you've got?"

Mimi didn't want to admit it, but feelings were exactly what she had. And she might as well express them. "Cramer Lee is just this boy—"

Jay groaned. "He must be around my age if we were in school together, for Christ's sake."

"Okay, he's this *guy*. But he's like a boy. He's not ironic. He's not wily or crafty. He's shy—kind of a bumbler—but he's really sweet."

Jay frowned. "As in really hot?"

"No," said Mimi, throwing up her hands. "I mean yes,

he's okay, but that is totally *not* what I'm saying. There is something about him that is . . . I don't know. I keep feeling there's something there—"

"Oh, come on," said Jay. "You've talked to him twice. Twice!"

"I realize that. And all I'm saying is that I'd like to talk to him again before we sic the cops on him. If his goofiness around me is a put-on, then he's, like, this brilliant actor. And I don't think that's possible. Not him."

"So he's infatuated?" said Iris.

"Maybe. But . . . Well, there is something about him. And *seriously*, I am not talking about his bod. Give me credit, okay? There is just this magnetic thing . . ."

Jay was staring at the floor so intently, she followed his gaze as if maybe there was a clue down there no one had noticed yet. Then he looked at her.

"Are you interested in him?"

Mimi sighed. "I don't think so."

Jay shook his head. "Because your track record with regards to boyfriends isn't exactly great, is it?"

Mimi bit her lip.

"That was totally harsh," said Iris.

"I'm sorry," said Jay, his voice sullen.

Mimi glanced at him. "Yeah, well, I guess I had that coming. For all you know, I'm this total loser when it comes to men. Maybe I'm into abuse. Masochism."

Jay let out a long sigh. "I said I was sorry. It was a dumb thing to say."

Iris left her post at the wall and came over to Jay. She slipped an arm around his waist. "Take a chill pill, okay?"

Jay dropped his forehead to her shoulder. Mimi got up from her chair and walked over to the window to look out at the day, a dull one, motionless, waiting. Was she crazy? More to the point, was she completely wrong about Cramer? Jay was right; this was serious. Cramer knew where she lived. That didn't mean he'd been breaking in. She tried to think of him hauling off the guitars. No. The movie camera? That was another thing. If he was infatuated . . . But none of it fit together in her head.

"Mimi?" Mimi looked at Iris, who was sitting beside Jay on the desk now. She had come straight from the office and was still in her work clothes. She looked so mature and smart. "There's something that troubles me," Iris said, her voice cautious, tactful. "When you took your laptop into the store. Cramer knew exactly how to fix it."

"He looked it up on a Mac website."

"I know, but you have to admit, it was pretty astonishing. All things considered. And he didn't want to charge you, right?"

Mimi nodded reluctantly. She had thought of this already and couldn't summon up the image of Cramer standing in *this* room wielding a tube of lipstick, his hand in the guts of her computer. It was just too difficult to imagine.

Then Jay came over to her. She folded her arms, looked down. She was still hurt by what he had said. But when she looked at him, his own anger had seeped out of his eyes and he had the hangdog look he slipped into so easily. "You said you spoke to that guy in the tree the other night. You told him he was sick. That what he was doing was sick. Hiding, watching. That's what you said, right?" She nodded. "And you honestly can't think that this character — Cramer, I mean — is capable of that kind of thing?" She shook her head. Jay raised his eyebrows, then leaned on the windowsill and looked outside. "So what do you propose we do?" he said.

She touched his arm, not quite able to believe he was going to give her a chance to do this her way. She looked over at Iris, who was holding up her hands in surprise.

"Thanks," she said to Iris. "Thanks," she said to Jay, and squeezed his arm.

"Tell me your plan," he said. "I haven't agreed to anything yet."

Mimi hadn't really gotten that far in her thinking. But it came to her out of the blue. "I'd like to write him a letter."

"And send it where?" said Jay. "To PDQ?"

"I guess. Maybe I could drop it off to speed things up, when he wasn't there."

Jay rolled his eyes. "This is beginning to sound like middle school."

"Hey, wait!" said Iris, snapping her fingers. "Is there a phone book here?" There was, a very old one, and in a moment Iris found what she was looking for. Out of the sixteen "Lees" in Ladybank, there was one "Lee, M." and it was particularly notable:

Lee M 1436 UpperValentineRd

"Whoa," said Jay. "We're twelve thirty-seven."

"So it's just up the road?" said Mimi. He nodded. "And he might have seen me out jogging, like I said?"

Jay nodded again. "You want to take a look?"

Her eyes brightened. "Okay," she said, "but why don't I write a letter, and we'll decide whether we're going to leave it when we see the place."

Hey, Cramer:

A strange thing happened. Quite a few strange things, really. First, like I told you, we've had these break-ins at our place. The last time, the window was broken and some valuables were stolen. Not nice. That was the time someone messed with my computer, which you fixed. Thanks. But then the other day when I saw you in town and we had such a good talk, you asked me how things were doing "up there," and although "up there" could mean a lot of things, it struck me as odd when I thought about it later because I had never told you where I lived. Now it turns out you live on the same road. Your telephone number is on the wall of this house. And there are other things, too. Apparently, you used to follow Jackson Page around back in high school. If you've read this far, you're probably wondering what I'm getting at. I kind of wonder myself. It sounds like I'm accusing you of something, and I don't want to do that. I'm sure there is some kind of explanation for all these strange things. And I want to know what it is. I want to talk to you. Would you do that? I have to know what's going on. I want you to be straight with me. My cell phone number is at the bottom of the page, if you want to call. If you'd rather talk face-to-face, call first. I don't want any more surprises.

Mimi

She added the phone number at the bottom.

"What do you think?" she asked.

Jay scratched his head. "You've invited him over. What if he is a nutcase?"

"I like to think I can spot the nutcases," said Mimi. "Like I know when to cross the street. I know when to curl my car keys into my fist with the meanest, sharpest one sticking out like a blade between my fingers. You know what I mean?"

The look Jay gave her wasn't hard to read.

"Okay, so I blew it with Lazar."

Jay read the letter again. "Do we really want this guy coming around?" he asked.

Iris looked at Mimi. "He's right, you know. Maybe this was all a ploy to get your attention. A creepy kind of courtship."

Mimi shook her head. "It started before I was here, remember? But I don't think he's dangerous. And, anyway, I've got my handy firearm," she said. And she patted her mace canister in its woven holster.

So they piled into Iris's Toyota and took off up the road, passing only two other driveways, one overgrown and clearly abandoned, before coming at last to 1436.

The driveway was steep and deeply rutted. The mailbox was rusty and sitting on a cedar pole that was leaning drunkenly toward the road. You could only catch a glimpse of the house behind a thick growth of sumac. It didn't look like much.

"Do we go up?" Jay asked.

The others shook their heads. There was no sign of any life, no car that they could see from the road. They sat silently in the Toyota, taking it all in.

"How old was that phone book?" asked Mimi. And Jay knew what she was saying: did anyone really live here? He opened his door and stepped out. The door of the mailbox squeaked noisily as he opened it, and Mimi's eyes darted to the crest of the driveway, expecting Cramer to appear, or M.—whoever she was. But no one came.

Jay held up the contents of the mailbox for their

inspection: circulars mostly, addressed to "Occupant," except for a bill from Hydro Energy addressed to Mavis Lee. The bill was an overdue notice.

He shoved Mimi's letter in with the other mail. As Iris put the car in gear, Jay turned to look at Mimi sitting in the backseat. "I hope we're doing the right thing," he said.

≋ CHAPTER THIRTY ≋

It was dark before Cramer made it home, so he had to find his way up the creek by feel, like a blind man with a paddle for a white cane. Bunny lay across the thwarts of the old aluminum canoe. The holes drilled into her keel had been too wide to fill up with what he'd taken with him.

More than once he thought, with a shock, he was late for work. Then he remembered he had no job right now. No job, a girl he was crazy about who hated him, and a mother who was just plain crazy. Why pretend anymore that she wasn't? Why care? It didn't get you anywhere. He was down to one friend in the whole world, and she was filled with holes.

There were six holes in all, and Stooley Peters had been clever. Even in the light, Cramer might not have seen the damage when he first got to the canoe, because the holes were drilled on the other side of the keel to his approach. By daylight he would have probably noticed the holes as soon as he climbed aboard, but in the dark, it was only the cold water he noticed as it crept up around his knees.

Now Bunny lay, like the carcass of a dead animal, across the old canoe. But she was not dead. He would fix her. And he would get his revenge.

Waylin Pitney was noisy when he was happy and he was noisy when he was mad, and you had to stop and listen to figure out which was which. From the bottom of the hill, Cramer could hear him and this time the man was mad. Very mad.

A few weeks ago, Cramer might have charged up that hill, his fists ready to take him on. It was the opportunity he'd been waiting for, the moment he had been preparing for. If that man so much as laid a finger on Mavis in anger, he was going to show him what he was made of. That's what he would have done. But he wasn't going to burst through the door fists flying right now. He'd grown up in more ways than one.

He approached the house in a wide circle, rolling his shoulders, working out the tiredness of rowing upstream with an awkward cargo, eighty pounds, dry weight—more like ninety after a night marinating in the Eden. He didn't hear any screams. Mavis was shouting, but she sounded as if she was giving as good as she got. He'd still defend her, if it came to that. Habit was stronger than emotion. He would defend her out of habit.

Something had died in him, he realized. It was as if some nerve had been sliced clear through. He could feel his heart pumping hard, feel the fuel injection of adrenaline, but his anger toward this intruder—because that's all Waylin was—had transformed. He realized something, suddenly, that stopped him in his tracks. It wasn't just Waylin he hated right at this moment; it was her, too, the woman in there screeching like a banshee.

The idea made him dizzy. But when the dizziness left him, he was hit by something else. Why was he even there anymore? So he approached the house a different man than the one who had left it earlier that day.

The shouting had stopped by the time Cramer reached the house. He stood outside the screen door and peered inside. Mavis was alone, sitting at the table with her fist around a beer bottle. Cramer had heard Waylin head upstairs. He could hear him now, crashing around up there. He could see his mother wince and glance upward from time to time at a particularly loud noise, a look on her face as if she expected the ceiling to fall in. Beyond that, her expression was one of sullen rage.

She was wearing a red blouse he had never seen before, frilly and low cut. Another chunk out of the money he'd got for her. She was slumped in her chair, fuming. She had a cigarette on the go. She took a long drag on it and blew out smoke until her face disappeared. She was gone. Just like that.

Something crashed to the floor above her.

"Jesus!" She looked at the cigarette and dropped it in her beer bottle.

A door slammed, and cowboy boots strode along the hall above and came thudding down the stairs.

Waylin took a bottle from the case on the table and twisted off the top. He kicked a chair around until it was facing him and dropped into it.

"I'd love one, thanks so much," said Mavis.

Waylin kicked the leg of the table. "What did that little ass-wipe do with it?"

Now Cramer was listening.

"*If* he took it," said Mavis. "You sure you didn't lose it?"

"It's not the kind of thing you lose," he said. "So where the hell is he?"

"Damned if I know." But there was something about the way she said it that made Cramer prick up his ears. It seemed to have the same effect on Waylin.

"You do know," he said.

"I don't," said Mavis. Her voice was slurred from drink and rough from yelling.

Waylin stared at her, and she stared back as she helped herself to another beer. "Why do I get the feeling you think this is funny?" he said. "Because it isn't funny, Mavis. It isn't one bit funny. It's a gun, Mavis. You got that? An M-1911A1C."

"Sounds like a lottery number."

"It isn't a lottery number, believe me."

"No, it's an *automatic weapon*. I got you the first three hundred times."

Waylin chugged down his beer. "I am going to find him, Mavis. And when I do, I'm going to drown the little bastard, which is what you should have done in the first place the minute he was born."

"Ah, shut up," she said. But it surprised Cramer how little energy she put into it. Waylin might have been talking about taking out the garbage, the way his mother reacted.

"How 'bout I drown him for you, Mavis?" said Waylin, just to hear himself talk.

And Mavis took a long swig of her own beer and said nothing.

Then suddenly Waylin kicked out at the table so hard, a couple of empties clattered to the floor. Next thing he was on his feet and grabbing his jacket from the back of the chair. Cramer slid into the shadows around the side of the house.

"Where you going?" shouted Mavis.

"Out!" said Waylin.

The screen door flew open, and he marched across the yard toward the Taurus.

Mavis appeared at the door. "You're in no condition to drive," she shouted.

"Oh, yeah?" he said, turning as he walked, stumbling backward, getting his balance again, then fishing out the car keys from his pants pocket. "Well, you're in no condition for nothing else," he said. "So I'll just have to find someone a bit more lively."

"How you gonna get lucky without your automatic weapon?" she shouted. Then she started laughing, cackling like a witch.

Cramer sank to the ground and leaned against the wall as the car engine roared and the headlights came on. The lights swept the front of the house as Waylin turned out of the yard and down the drive. There was a mighty thunking sound as he hit the road, and then he was gone, his fist pressed to the horn in a final noisy display of rage.

Cramer waited, barely breathing until he heard the screen door close. Then he waited some more, sitting in the dark as the sound of the car horn disappeared into the night. He waited until there was no sound left but the buzzing in his head.

When he entered the house, his mother was cleaning up, dropping empties back in the carton in a desultory way.

She turned to look at him. "Where you been?" she said, but she didn't sound angry, just weary.

"Out," he said.

"Out," she said, and chuckled. "Men," she said. "Always out."

On the counter Cramer found the remains of a casserole, which he picked at with a fork. There were a lot of remains; it was burnt, the contents dry as sawdust.

"You want to see something?" she said.

He turned. She was holding something shiny between her thumb and forefinger. He walked over and she handed it to him. It was a nugget of gold the size of a marble.

"It's real," she said. "Waylin gave it to me."

Her voice didn't sound tired anymore.

"Where'd he get it?"

"Where do you think?" she said, taking it back from him and holding it up to marvel at its luster. Then she bit on it. "That's how you can tell it's real," she said. "You bite it." She didn't bother to explain how that proved anything and Cramer didn't really care.

"He told me once the miners have to strip and get hosed down before they leave the mine each day," said Cramer.

"Uh-huh, I know."

"It's so the miners don't get to take home even any gold dust."

"I know, I know. What's your point, Cramer?"

"Well, the only way he could get this out of the mine is by shoving it up his ass."

Her fist closed around the nugget and she glared at him. "That is so gross," she said. "I really don't know what's happened to you."

He turned away and picked up the case of beer, now full of empties, and carried it over to the pile by the door.

"It may be gold, but it's not a wedding ring, Mom," he said.

She glared at him and there was a gleam in her eye that was just plain mean. "You been seeing your girl-friend?" she said.

"I don't have a girlfriend."

"Come on, Cramer, fess up."

He stared at her. There was something disturbing in her expression, as if she wasn't just playing with him.

"You got something to tell your mama?" she said.

Cramer shook his head. "No," he said. "I've got nothing to say to you anymore. So, if you don't mind, I think I'll just go drown myself in the creek, which is what you should have done the moment I was born."

Cramer waited only long enough to see it dawn on her face that he was quoting Waylin, then he turned and left.

She called to him from the door. "You were eavesdrop-ping. That isn't nice!"

He didn't look back.

"And it isn't funny, Cramer. Cramer?"

The yard light was on, but he walked right through its wide circle of illumination out past the drive shed to the lip of the hill and looked down over the creek.

"I know about *her*, Cramer," his mother shouted. "You think I don't know nothing, but you're wrong." Then she cackled again. "If you only knew," she said.

He didn't turn right away. When he did, she had gone back inside. He was tempted to go back and ask what she was talking about. Demand it. Shake it out of her. But he was afraid to go back, afraid that in his anger he might do something he would regret. So he stood there and dug deep inside, with what strength he had left after a day that had gone on for years, and found not one glimmering nugget of sympathy for her.

I know about her, Cramer.

He stood until even in the moonlessness he could make out the shape of the boulders and saplings that dotted the hill down to the creek. His mother must have followed him to the snye. That's what she meant. That's where she'd been going in the old canoe. It was the last straw. The very last straw.

He turned toward the panel truck. He tried the back doors. Locked. Good, that meant the cargo was still on board. She was low on her springs, heavy with contraband. What was it this time? He didn't care. He tried the driver's door. Unlocked. Good again.

Everything was suddenly going his way. What a change!

There were no keys, of course. But he didn't really need keys. He let out the emergency brake and put the truck in neutral. Then he climbed out and went to the back of the big truck. He put his shoulder to it. Nothing. Not at first, but Cramer was patient and Cramer was strong. Stronger than anything. You could move a mountain if you were patient and strong. It was all about getting the thing rocking. Once you had the thing rocking, gravity would do the work for you. And he was strong not just from free weights and chin-ups and endless push-ups, but from years of paddling upstream. That's what his life was, paddling upstream. He heaved and, despite his fatigue, soon enough the truck was moving and moving, and then, finally, it was out of his control.

Foolish of Waylin to park it like this on the lip of a hill, he thought. Cramer watched the truck smash down the slope, bouncing and swerving. He hoped no tree was big enough to stop it, hoped no boulder would catch a wheel and hold firm. What a noise it made, all its innards crashing around. And then finally—*splash!*

Gravity had finished his job for him, and the rest was up to the creek. It was sad, thought Cramer, that Butchard's was only four or five feet deep. Then he turned away. There were other important things to do now. This was just the beginning.

≫| CHAPTER THIRTY-ONE |≪

IT WAS UNLIKELY anyone at the Lee household would check the mailbox on Sunday, but Mimi wasn't the only one at the snye who made regular trips to the window to peer through the curtains out toward the bridge.

Monday dawned cool and overcast. There was a front moving in. Iris left for work before nine but promised to return that evening. Around noon Jay got a call from his mom. They had been trying to get high-speed Internet service at the Riverside Drive house now that there was finally a transmission tower in the area. Apparently, the man could do the hookup that afternoon sometime between two and five. Could he be there? Jay said he would. He wanted Mimi to come with him.

"Are you kidding?"

"No," said Jay. "Leave Cramer a note or something; tell him we'll be back this evening." He laughed and shook his head. "How ironic. Leaving a thief a note."

"We don't know he's a thief, but I don't want to have that conversation again," said Mimi. "I'm going to stay." Jay looked annoyed. "I'll be careful."

Jay sat down. "Fine, then I'll stay. But you can phone Lou and tell her why."

Mimi growled. "That's not fair. Trust me, will you, for God's sake? I know this guy. I swear. There's some kind of explanation. Go. Scoot!"

But Jay shook his head and looked away. "What I said yesterday about your choice of guys—that came out all wrong."

"I'm glad to hear it."

"All I meant was that when Lazar started acting out, getting scary, he caught you off-guard, right? You weren't expecting it?"

Mimi nodded slowly. "I'm naive; is that what you're saying?"

"Yes."

"And the implication is I'm being naive about Cramer. How am I doing so far?"

"You're right on the money."

"Okay, I hear you. But you have to believe me when I say it's not the same thing." Jay opened his mouth to argue, then snapped it closed. He stood up and headed toward the door. "Aw, don't go away angry," said Mimi.

"Just go away?" said Jay. Mimi grinned and nodded. He didn't look happy about it, but he had given in. He always did and she felt a bit guilty about it. He came over to her. "If anything happens to you, I'm going to be really pissed," he said.

"That is so affectionate," said Mimi, and went up on her toes to give him a kiss, right on the lips. It didn't last long—wasn't meant to. But it was still a bit unnerving. "I'll be extra specially careful," she said.

Because the weather looked so bad, he took her car. He hadn't been gone more than a few minutes when Mimi heard an unmistakable noise out on the driveway.

Stooley Peters had pulled up in his rackety old half-ton. With her own car gone, she thought about locking the doors and pretending not to be there. But considering how quickly he arrived, she figured he must have seen Jay drive away alone. So she bolted down toward the snye, not wanting him to get anywhere near the house, only taking the time to throw on a baggy sweatshirt, which nicely hid her mace canister in its holster.

They met at the snye, she on her side, hoping he'd stay on his. He looked as if he had dressed to go to town. He was in clean denim jeans, a denim jacket, and a mostly white shirt. His hair was slicked down. More like a Sunday-come-calling getup, she thought, which, she had to admit, was better than covered in blood, but not a cheering thought. He didn't have his dog with him. Mimi wasn't sure that was a good thing. But what was a good thing was that he was wearing shoes, not rubber boots. If he wanted to ford the snye, he'd have to take the bridge and she'd just pull the plank, if she had to.

"I come by yesterday," he said, from the other shore. "No one was home."

"What can I do for you, Mr. Peters?" she said in a businesslike way.

He rubbed his hand down the side of his jeans, as if he wasn't used to wearing clean clothes and they felt odd. "I got to thinking about last week when I was over here, eh?" he said. "I guess I got a little outta hand."

He paused but Mimi didn't respond. If he thought she was going to let him off the hook, he was dead wrong.

"Anyway," he said. "I thought I owed yous an apology."

"Apology accepted," she said.

"I figure it was probably the head injury, eh? Kinda made me . . . you know . . ."

"Randy?" she said.

"Yeah, well . . . uh . . ."

"Like I said, apology accepted."

He made a salute as if he were tipping the edge of a cap. He smiled—not a good move on his part, because his teeth were anything but inviting. Then he pulled a flat brown bottle from his jacket pocket and held it up for her inspection. It was a Mickey of something; she could guess what.

"Thought maybe we might have a little Canadian Club to celebrate," he said.

"To celebrate?"

"Hell, yeah," said Peters, and he was beaming now. "You see I know who's been messing around up here." He looked triumphant. "Your secret admirer."

This caught her off-guard, but she hoped it didn't show. "You do, huh," said Mimi, without a trace of happy surprise in her voice. Which seemed to tick Peters off.

He flung up his finger pointing west, up the road. "It's the Lee boy," he said, his voice less cheery by a few degrees. "Seen him with my own eyes."

Mimi tried to maintain her composure, but it was an effort. "Where'd you see him?" she asked.

"How 'bout I come over," he said.

"How 'bout you don't," she said, her voice sharp. "Just tell me where'd you see this . . . this person?" He looked put out. "What was he up to, Mr. Peters?"

"Well, I'll tell you. I seen him a couple times, you know, but the last place I seen him was up that tree," he said, pointing at a thick and many-branched maple right behind her. She didn't bother to look. She knew pretty well which tree the stranger had been in Saturday night. And as much as she didn't want to believe it had been Cramer, it was hard to refute the old codger.

"And what was he up to?" she asked.

"I didn't stay around to find out," said Peters, with a great deal of self-satisfaction. "As soon as he was up that tree, I took off to where he hides his boat."

"His boat?"

"His canoe. A nice one, or it used to be." There was no way of misinterpreting the mischief in his voice or the smugness in his expression. His crooked canines were on showy display. "I don't think you need to worry 'bout him no more."

"Mr. Peters," she said, her hands on her hips, "what are you saying?"

"I'm getting to it. Keep your shirt on." She bit her tongue. "Yes, ma'am," he said. "The lad was coming down here by way of the river, see. In his canoe. Down the Eden, then up the snye. But I got him. Got him good." Then his hand went into his jacket pocket, and he pulled something out and held it up for her to see.

"Know what this is?" he asked.

She peered at the thing gleaming in his hand. "Some kind of drill bit?"

"You got 'er. A nice big five-eighth-inch bit. I put half a dozen holes in his little red boat. Fixed his wagon, I guess you could say."

Jesus, thought Mimi. "You put holes in his boat?"

"Damn right. Scuppered him."

She nodded, not sure what to say, surprised to find herself worrying about Cramer. "And what happened?" she said.

But Peters was in no hurry to answer her question. "You see, I got a pasturage backs down onta the river. I was out in the tractor one afternoon a couple days back, and I seen him, the Lee boy, out on the Eden. Didn't make nothing of it at first. Seen him out there lots. Except, when I looked again, this here time, the other day, like, the boy was gone. That got me to thinking. So I tracked him down." Peters sniffed and stood up tall.

"So, did he sink? Did he drown?"

"Damned if I know. But I'm guessing he got the message, loud and clear."

Mimi felt very ill at ease. "So what if he comes around with a shotgun or something?"

"Oh, I wouldn't worry about that," said Peters, but it was clear to Mimi from the tone of his voice that he hadn't thought about it one bit. He hadn't thought beyond getting vengeance. That's what this was about. It must have been Cramer who cracked him one on the head. Peters hadn't done this for her. Or maybe he had, in a way.

"Sure you won't have a little snoot of this?" he said, holding up the bottle.

"No thank you," she said.

"Aw, come on," he said. "Let's let bygones be bygones." And now he did head toward the bridge, in surprisingly large steps, and by the time Mimi could get in motion, he was already on the plank that spanned the broken arch. But he stopped in his tracks.

The silence was shattered by the sound of the truck starting up.

The smile vanished on Peters's face. He spun around. "What the—"

But his words were drowned out by the sound of his

vehicle backing down the driveway. Peters turned and ran after it, and Mimi followed, rounding the bend in time to see the truck pull out onto the Upper Valentine, and then with a screeching of the gears and a roar of the engine take off west, with Peters in hot pursuit, yelling his head off and soon enough left in the dust.

≫ CHAPTER THIRTY-TWO ≪

CRAMER SAT ON THE BANK of the river catching his breath and watching Stooley Peters's old Plymouth long-bed go down. The river was deep here, and there was a roiling turbulence in this stretch, though not enough to suck the heavy old vehicle downstream. He'd left the windows open. She'd go down quick enough. He would enjoy every minute.

He was aware of the fact that this was the second vehicle he had sunk in less than twenty-four hours. *How about the Taurus as well?* he thought. *Maybe this is my calling, sinking things!* But no, it wasn't like that, really. In Peters's case, he was just paying the old man back, an eye for an eye. What he'd done to Waylin Pitney's truck filled with stolen merchandise was something more. It was like saying good-bye.

He hadn't been able to manhandle the barrier out of the way, so he'd had to back the Plymouth up and crash through it. There was just enough cracked and weed-choked macadam beyond the barrier for him to stop from going over and ending up in the drink. He hadn't counted on the brakes being so soft, the tires so bald. For one brain-numbing moment, he thought he was done for. But the old dame stopped with one front wheel over the lip of the crumbling hillside and Cramer jumped free. The rest was grunt work.

Peters was swearing enough to turn the air around him blue. Mimi worked hard at not smiling. She kept her distance from him, but, judging from the language, it was as if he didn't know she was there. He ran out of fuel and stopped cursing eventually. Then he got this strained look on his face as if he was thinking and it was hard work.

"You got that little phone on you?" he said, holding his hand up to his ear, with his pinkie extended for a mouthpiece, in case she didn't know what a phone was.

"It's back at the house," she said.

"Well, go get it," he said, and started marching back down the driveway. But she ran ahead of him and stopped in his path.

"I'll go make the call for you. You can wait right here."

He looked as if he might argue the point, but something, probably the determination on her face, made him change his mind.

"Call the cops," he said.

"Okay. Hey, and I can even tell them the license plate number."

"You remember it?"

She shook her head. "Not the number, exactly, but I did notice it was issued in 1976. That ought to make it easy to find."

She hadn't noticed much in the way of irony in Peters's conversation so far, but he picked up on hers quickly enough. And he raised his hand as if he wanted to give her the back of it, except that she was a good healthy ten feet ahead of him.

"Around here, missy, it's against the law to steal somebody's vehicle." Then he swiped the air with his large mitt of a hand, as if he'd said all he wanted to say to her, and stomped back out to the road and on toward Paradise.

But what Mimi was thinking was that the Upper Valentine ended in the direction that Cramer was heading. She had run there often enough to know. It was about three miles, she guessed. She could make it in under twenty minutes.

As she changed into her jogging gear, she wondered if it had been Cramer. They had not caught sight, through the dust the truck kicked up, of who was behind the wheel. But considering Peters had scuppered his canoe, as he put it, she had a feeling the old man was right. And if it was Cramer, there was no use waiting around here for him to show.

It was three o'clock when she hit the road, but it looked more like eight. The sky was low and black and heavy with rain. She was glad she'd put on long pants for the run; there was quite a wind. It was 3:25 when she got to the busted barrier.

She stared down the steep hill to the river. She could just make out the right front end of the truck, tilted upward like some black and rusty boulder just under the surface. Even as she watched, it sank from view. Then she looked east and west, her eyes scouring the hillside. The slope was steeper to the west, the brush more dense. If he was still here, that's where he'd be, she thought. There was no other way out of here.

"I'm not sure if you are here, Cramer," she shouted to the hillside. "But I'm going to pretend you are and hope maybe you'll come out of hiding and talk to me."

She looked around. Nothing. The wind was loud in the trees; the storm was close.

"Cramer?"

The sweat was drying on her, chilling her face and arms. She pushed the hair out of her eyes.

"I don't know if you got the letter we left at your place," she said. "We want to talk to you. *I* want to talk to you." Oh, this was ridiculous! For the second time in two days, she was talking to an invisible man. A man in the trees, a man up a hill. He had to be there. She could *feel* he was there.

"I'm not sure what you've been playing at," she said,

"but I want to hear your side of the story. Like maybe it was Stooley Peters who was poking around, and you were keeping an eye on him. Or maybe you were spying, but there was a reason. Cramer?"

She turned in a long slow circle.

"Do you like me, Cramer? Because I feel this connection. Do you feel it, Cramer? And I guess what I want to know is why you would steal Jay's guitars. Why? That's what I can't figure out. I can't see you doing that."

She stared at the steep hillside and then looked up because she had felt a drop of rain. And then suddenly she looked back down the road because a car was coming.

⋙ CHAPTER THIRTY-THREE ⋘

IT WAS PETERS IN A CAR of about the same vintage as his truck, but with a more recent license plate. Mimi watched with despair as he pulled up to within a few yards of where she stood. He got out and with only a nasty glance her way went to the edge of the precipice and looked down. He turned to her.

"Did you see anything?"

She nodded. "It's gone," she said.

He swore, looked around, and then looked back at her. "What about the boy?"

She shrugged. *A good question,* she thought. *What about the boy?* But then Peters turned to look up, through the rain, at the hillside with which she had been having her one-sided conversation or soliloquy or whatever it was.

"He up there?"

"Do I look like I know?"

Peters was standing near enough to her that she could smell whatever gunk he'd put in his hair when he'd come a-calling. But she wasn't frightened of him at all. His attention was on the hillside. He was chewing away at his lower lip, scanning the brush, as she had done, but, from the stormy expression on his face, it was pretty clear they did not have the same motives. And in the next moment, it became clearer still. He walked over to his car, opened the back door, and took out a rifle.

"You see this, Cramer Lee? You come out right now and I'll hold my fire. You stay hid and I start peppering the bush with this thing—see how you like that!"

He had been ready to go to her. He had been that close to standing up, making his way down the hill, and coming clean. He even knew near enough what he would say, or at least the first thing he would say. *I am not a thief,* he would declare to her, his hand on his heart. He would not be tongue-tied. There would be a lot of explaining to do, but everything depended on her believing that he had not stolen Jay's guitars, although he had a sinking feeling he knew who had. He would explain to her about who Jackson Page was to him and who he was to Jackson Page. That's how he would start.

And then—Cramer's luck being what it was—Peters arrived and he had a gun. A shotgun, twelve-gauge, by the look of it. And he might have started shooting, but the storm came instead, and it didn't take but a moment before there were sheets of rain pounding down on the road, and Peters was running for the shelter of his car. And it still might have worked out, because Mimi wouldn't accept the old man's offer of a ride. She backed away from him, yelling at him, though Cramer couldn't hear through the rain what it was she was saying. But then there was an almighty flash of lightning and a thunderclap, so loud and close that Cramer covered his head with his arms as if the whole roof of the sky was caving in. And when he looked up again, through the gray veils of rain, Peters was dragging Mimi to the car and pushing her in. And they drove off.

Jay stood on the screened-in porch looking out at the storm. The river looked like an ocean, wild with whitecaps. It was lucky he hadn't kayaked down from the snye or he would never get back. He checked his watch. Where was the Internet guy? He should never have done this. Never let Mimi talk him into letting her stay up there alone. How did she do it? She was four years younger than him, for Christ's sake! Chutzpah—that was it. Guts. He was gutless. That was what was wrong with him. It was what was wrong with his music. Who cared what was right, what was serious, what was befitting? He had gotten by so far on clever. He had gotten by so far on pitch-perfect. He had gotten by so far on following the rules. But what he hadn't done was anything remotely gutsy. If he wanted electric guitars in his goddamned piece, then he should just use electric guitars! Of course, he didn't *have* an electric guitar anymore. And he couldn't help thinking that it was his gutlessness that had led to this impasse.

Thunder crashed, not far away. He phoned Mimi again. He had tried a couple of times without any luck. He tried to tell himself the storm was responsible. He hoped she was okay. If anything happened to her . . .

"Hello?"

"Thank God!" he said. "Where are you?"

"Mr. Peters is driving me home," she said. "Aren't you, Mr. Peters?"

"From where?"

"It's a long story."

"What's going on?"

"I'm fine. But I can hardly hear you." She was shouting now. "I'll tell you all about it, when you get back out here."

"Okay," he said.

"But, Jay? Stay on the line, okay? Did you get that?"

"Yeah. Sure. What's up?"

"Just in case Mr. Peters accidentally forgets to stop and let me off."

"Is he kidnapping you?"

"No. But better safe than sorry, right?" Thunder boomed again, louder on the phone than outside Jay's place. The storm must be centered up that way. "Are you still there?" she asked.

"I'm still here," he said. "I won't leave."

"I know it," she said, and he marveled at her confidence in him.

"Ah, here we are, now. Hold on."

"I'm holding."

Jay listened, heard the sound of the car slowing down, muffled by the rain. Then the car door opened. After that he couldn't hear anything but the rain pelting down and the car door slamming shut.

"Home free!" Mimi shouted above the clamor into her phone. "Thanks, bro!"

And she hung up.

Cramer wanted to go straight to her, straight to the house on the snye. He didn't trust Peters, but it wasn't just that. He had held too much inside for too long. That was part of what had gotten him in this mess. Somewhere along the line, he had let holding himself together get confused with holding back anything that he might really want. Maybe he could even put that into words for Mimi. He had this crazy feeling that he could say anything to her, and the thought of it pushed him on through the storm. But there was something he had to do first, en route. And soon enough he saw ahead, the mailbox, hanging on its chains from the cedar pole, bouncing around in the wind like a piece of flotsam on choppy water.

He looked inside. There was no letter there. So he ran up the steep drive, the gulley down its middle churning with brown runoff, and across the windswept yard to the house. The screen door was flapping, slapping back against the wall with each gust. The inner door was wide open, the doorstep and linoleum floor sopping wet.

The house had been turned upside down. There wasn't a drawer that hadn't been opened, its guts spilled out on the floor. Every cupboard had been raided, the studio torn apart. Upstairs was the same.

Cramer hadn't known what he would find, but this mess did not fall outside of his expectations. He stood looking coolly around, realizing that this was something he could not clean up. This was the kind of disaster that would have happened ages ago if he hadn't been there to stop it from happening. Why was this only clear to him now?

There was nothing he wanted from here. Well, almost nothing. In the kitchen, he found a blue velveteen bag with a yellow string to close it. A bottle of Seagram's whiskey had arrived in that bag many years ago, but now all it held were a handful of silver spoons that had belonged to his grandmother. He chucked them out and went back up to his room to recover what it was he would take with him. He felt a sense of urgency, as if this house, like everything else around him, was on the verge of sinking. He found the stone and, under his mattress, the picture of Mimi. He wrapped it in a facecloth and placed the two objects in the little blue velveteen bag. Then he stepped back out into the storm.

≫| CHAPTER THIRTY-FOUR |≪

MIMI CHANGED INTO DRY CLOTHES and threw her sopping tracksuit into the bathtub. The rain clattered on the tin roof, and she wished that the fireplace worked. She brushed her hair in the bathroom. It was after five; Jay wouldn't be long now. Then the knock came at the kitchen door.

She stood stock-still, suddenly panic-stricken, although she had been hoping for him to come. Cramer. It had to be Cramer.

The knock came again, louder, more insistent.

She was sure she'd seen the last of Peters. When he had dropped her off, he had not so much as glanced at her. He had looked like what he was: an old man.

So, Cramer then. Had he been up there at the end of the road? Had he heard her little speech? Had he read her letter? Was she ready for this?

She opened the kitchen door and was shocked to see a woman there, not old, but hunched over as if she were, her elbows pressed tightly to her sides, her face bowed, as if she were still out in the slashing rain.

"Good grief," said Mimi. The woman looked at her, imploringly.

"Come in," said Mimi, taking her by the arm.

She was shaking violently, drenched, injured. Her hair was flattened against her skull by the rain. A pink stain, high on her cheek, proved to be blood seeping from a head wound. Her eyes bled mascara.

She was wearing a flimsy baby-doll, which, plastered to her skin, revealed a body that was shapely but too old to be dressed this way. And the finishing touch to this apparition was a large pale blue leatherette handbag slung over her shoulder, as if she'd been caught in a downpour while shopping at the mall.

Mimi helped her to the table. "I'll get a towel," she said. And she did, a big one, but it was ridiculously inadequate. The woman was soaking head to toe, shaking violently and sobbing by now. "Hold on," said Mimi, and dashed to her room. She came back with the comforter from her bed and wrapped the woman in it.

"Thank you," the woman mumbled.

"What happened?" said Mimi. "Did your car break down?"

It was hard to tell whether the woman was nodding or just shivering.

Mimi took the towel and started gently drying the woman's hair, careful of the head injury. Déjà vu. This place was turning into a hospital for head cases! The woman didn't wince. Perhaps she was too cold to notice. Mimi stopped and peered into her eyes. "Would you like something hot to drink?"

The woman nodded. Mimi dropped the towel on a chair and went to fill the kettle. She put it on the stove top and turned on the burner.

"There," she said, turning back to her guest. Her guest who was now holding a gun.

"Hello, Mimi," she said.

Mimi stepped backward, recoiling from the sight of the gun.

"Don't move," said the woman. Her voice was still shaky, but her hand, surprisingly, was not, and there was way too much resolve in her eyes to take any chances. Mimi slowly raised her hands.

"What are you doing? How do you know my name?"

The woman didn't speak right away. She seemed to convulse from the cold, but her aim didn't falter much. Her eyes were green but bloodshot. So bloodshot that Mimi wondered if there was internal bleeding.

"We're going to make a phone call," the woman said.

"A phone call?" said Mimi.

The woman nodded, then shuddered again, so hard Mimi hoped the gun would shake right out of her grasp. It didn't and Mimi found herself staring at it. She'd never seen one up close. The barrel didn't look more than four inches long. It was bluish black. The nose was snub and in its center was that darker blackness.

"I need dry clothes," the woman said, trembling.

"Okay," said Mimi. "I'll get something."

"Don't move!" the woman barked. "Didn't you hear me?"

"Yes," said Mimi. "Yes." The woman's face was distorted with anger. "Take it easy," said Mimi.

The woman stood, slowly, clutching the comforter closed at her throat with the same hand that held the handbag. She waved Mimi forward with the gun. "We'll go together."

Once in the bedroom, Mimi got to her knees and looked through her suitcase for something warm. A sweatshirt, cotton pajama bottoms. Meanwhile, she closed her hand over the knitted holster with the mace in it. She glanced at the woman, who looked around the room distractedly. Mimi managed to slip the canister into the pocket of her hoodie. Then she got to her feet and held out the clothes to the woman. She was standing just at the threshold of the bedroom door, and her eyes surveyed the room as if searching for hidden cameras or something. No, it wasn't that. There was an odd expression in her eyes and an eerie half smile on her face, as if there were pictures on the wall and the woman was delighting in the details. Then she seemed to remember where she was and returned her attention to Mimi. She waved the gun in a way that suggested she wanted Mimi to back up into the corner. And as Mimi backed away, the woman dropped the comforter and, leaning against the lintel of the doorway, began to slip on the pair of pants under her wet dress.

"I don't have anything valuable," said Mimi.

"Oh, yes, you do," said the woman. She was by now trying to tighten the drawstring of the pants but couldn't do it with only one shaky hand. She carefully lowered her gun hand, though not her eyes, and tried again to pull the drawstring tight with two hands, but she was trembling too much.

"Can I help?" said Mimi. She wasn't exactly sure why. Part of her said stay as far away from this madwoman as possible. But part of her said make nice. Make very nice. And what was it Pacino said in *The Godfather*? "Keep your friends close, but your enemies closer."

The woman stared at her, and Mimi had the feeling that she—this woman—was seeing her and not seeing her at the same time. As if Mimi was in some other dimension that the woman had to concentrate very hard to keep in view. She nodded and waved Mimi forward, until she was standing directly in front of her.

"No fooling around," said the woman, and placed the cold nose of the gun against Mimi's temple. Mimi closed her eyes. But her fingers found the ties and pulled them together, carefully into a knot. Then the woman pushed her away, and Mimi retreated to her corner.

Now the woman reached with her free hand behind

her back and undid the zipper of her dress, sloughed it off her shoulders, and let it fall to the floor. She picked up the sweatshirt and managed to slide into it, one arm at a time, only losing sight of Mimi for the split second that her head was lost in the neck hole. She smoothed the terry cloth against her wet skin.

"Are you . . . are you Sophia Cosic?" said Mimi.

"Who?"

"Nothing," said Mimi.

The woman looked derailed. Then she seemed to come back to her senses, what she had of them. "My name is Mavis. Mavis Lee. Ever heard of me?"

Mimi shook her head. She knew it must be Cramer's mother—the one who had lost her way on the Artist's Journey. But pleading ignorance seemed the best bet. "I didn't think you would've," said Mavis. "But your father has, all right."

"Pardon?"

"He might have forgotten me, but he sure won't ever forget again."

The look in the woman's eyes was triumphant and clearly fanatical. Mimi felt faint. She leaned against the wall for support. It was all coming clear to her. M.L.—the initials and phone number on the wall in the other room. Her father's lover and Cramer's mother. Which meant . . . No. No way!

Mavis must have seen something of what was going on in Mimi's head. She nodded. "Now you get it, don't you, honey? Huh?" Mimi didn't move a muscle. "He's all I have left of Marc," said Mavis. "That Page boy—oh, he's got the world on a string, hasn't he? And you—the same thing—everything money can buy. What'd my Cramer ever get? Nothing. Nothing! Marc Soto left us nothing."

"Mrs. Lee—"

"Don't call me *missus*. I'd be a *missus* if your father had done the right thing."

"Mavis, you're not the only person my father ever left."

"Is that supposed to make me feel better?"

"No. I just mean he left my mother as well."

The woman sniffed and wiped her nose with the back of her hand. "But he didn't leave *her* penniless, did he?"

"He didn't leave her a thing," said Mimi. But the news only surprised Mavis for a second or two, before she recovered whatever insane sense of purpose she had come here with. She had been hovering at the doorway; now she entered the room, the fingers of her left hand gliding along the wall as if the room was in darkness and she had to feel her way into it. Again she looked around, and now Mimi understood that she was lost in memory. But she snapped out of it pretty quickly as she drew nearer to Mimi. She leaned her shoulder against the wall, lowering the gun, but holding it in two hands in front of her.

"I saw you out running," she said. "Wondered who you were. Then I realized you were the same girl as in the picture Cramer had stuffed under his mattress." Her eyes glinted. "I sniffed it out. It was wrapped in a T-shirt that reeked of your perfume."

There was a low rumble of thunder. The storm was moving away. The rain went on unabated, but in the moment the thunder died, Mimi heard something. A car? Jay?

"What is it?" said Mavis.

"Nothing," said Mimi, too loud.

Silence filled the space between them. Maybe the noise had only been wishful thinking. But she suddenly realized that she needed to keep Mavis talking. "Cramer had a picture of me?"

"You and some other rich bitch. I decided I'd better do some snooping," said Mavis. "A mother likes to know what her boy's up to. It didn't take me long to find out. I've been here before." She looked at Mimi, nodding, waiting for her to respond. *Play dumb*, Mimi told herself. The woman glanced again at the corners of the room. "I was here often enough," she said.

"Mavis, I don't know—"

"Shut up!" Mavis wiped her nose again, this time with the back of her gun hand. She looked nervous, suddenly, and Mimi didn't think she wanted Mavis nervous.

"I'm sorry," she said.

"I couldn't quite figure out how he was getting in and out. Cramer, I mean. So, when the time was right, I found my own way in." She nodded her head toward the window. Jay had replaced the glass, but Mimi still found broken pieces of it now and then. "And that's when I found that movie camera of yours. Took it home to look it over. And there—there he was, older and losing his hair, but I recognized him, all right, even with the shades. Recognized the smile. The lying smile."

"Does Cramer know?"

"Who knows? The boy's not himself. I guess I've got you to thank for that."

"But does he know about him and me—about us being—"

"I said I wouldn't know what he knows," Mavis shouted. "He doesn't know his own mind anymore. Or who his mother is. Or what's right or wrong."

She stopped and made a face as if she'd just bitten into something bad.

"What about the guitars?" asked Mimi. "Was it you who took Jay's guitars?"

Mavis shrugged. "Distributing the wealth a little. Those guitars are long gone."

There was another noise. In the shed? Mavis didn't seem to notice. Mimi spoke up in any case, but not so loudly this time as to create suspicion. "Why are you telling me this? Why are you here? What is it you want from me?"

"We're going to make a phone call," said Mavis, as if it were going to be fun—a party game.

"You said that. But I don't understand."

"We're going to phone your daddy," she said. Then she

slid along the wall toward Mimi, stopping an arm's length away. "We're going to find out how much he thinks his pretty daughter is worth."

"What do you mean?"

"You know what I mean. You aren't stupid."

Mimi swallowed hard. Her right hand was in her pocket where she had been trying to work the canister of mace free from its holster without drawing attention to the activity. Now, with Mavis so close, it was a little easier, since the woman's field of vision was so much smaller. If there was somebody coming, she had to be ready for whatever happened. By now Mavis was face-to-face with her, staring directly into Mimi's eyes. "You got the same eyes as him. I wished in that film he hadn't had those dark glasses on. I'd have loved to see those eyes again."

She seemed to go off into a daydream, and while Mimi wasn't about to try anything rash, she managed to silently pop the top of the canister. Now it was just a matter of getting the thing out of her pocket. But Mavis had recovered from her reverie.

"What are you thinking?" she said.

"Nothing."

"Liar. You're thinking about getting away. But you can forget about it."

Keep her on task, thought Mimi.

"My father," said Mimi. "Marc. You want me to phone him?"

Mavis looked suspicious, as if this was somehow a different proposal than the one she had made. Slowly she nodded. Then she smiled expectantly. "Bet he'll be surprised."

"Yeah," said Mimi. She cleared her throat. "But my phone is in the kitchen."

Mavis shook her head. She backed away toward the bedroom doorway, tripping on the mattress, but righting herself too quickly for Mimi to do anything. At the doorway she picked up her handbag and reached inside. "Your little phone was just lying there on the kitchen table," she said. She pulled it out and crossed the room, stepping around the mattress this time. She handed the phone to Mimi.

Mimi stared at her. This was totally insane. Even if her father could pay whatever Mavis asked for, how did she expect to get her hands on the money or get away?

"Do it!" said the woman.

"Mavis, it's just that . . ."

"It's just that what?"

Better not try to explain, thought Mimi. So she punched in Marc's number. "What am I supposed to say?"

"Leave that to me," said Mavis. Her beat-up eyes glowed as she waited. But after a long moment, Mimi handed her the phone. It was an answering machine.

"You want to leave a message?"

Mavis glared at her. "Don't get smart with me," she said. She handed back the phone. She looked bewildered, as if her crazy plan had not included Marc being out. Mimi glanced at the phone's clock. *Where is Jay? Is he here?* If he was, he was being quiet, which meant he must have realized something was up. Her only hope was to keep talking and be ready to create some distraction. She quailed inside.

"Do you know what my boy did? My good boy?"

"What?"

Mavis moved closer to her, leveled the gun inches from Mimi's chest. "He destroyed merchandise worth thousands of dollars. Plasma televisions. Destroyed them."

"What are you talking about?"

"He made some people very, very unhappy. And do you know why? Do you know why he did it?"

Mimi heard a clunk. Surely Mavis must have heard it, too, but she seemed beyond hearing anymore. "I don't know why he did it," Mimi said. "Tell me why, Mavis."

Mavis poked her with the gun. "Shut up! What kind of game are you playing?"

"I'm not playing anything."

"You think I won't use this thing? You think I have anything left to lose?"

"No, no," said Mimi. "I mean . . . I don't know. It's just that I don't have any idea what you are talking about." There was another clunking sound, but Mavis only stared at her as if her anger was using up all her attention. As if whatever dimension Mimi was in was fading on her.

"Cramer went berserk," she said. "That's your doing."

"I don't understand."

"You drove him out of his mind," said Mavis, poking Mimi in the chest.

"Ow! Stop it!"

"I ought to just shoot you for what you did to him," said Mavis. And she brought the gun right up under Mimi's chin.

"That hurts!"

"You wanna know about hurt? Huh? Do you?"

"If you shoot me, you won't get anything out of Marc," said Mimi. She watched the woman try to piece together in her shattered mind what she was telling her. "He's got lots of money," said Mimi. "He'll probably pay anything you want. But not if I'm dead."

At first Mimi thought she had gotten through to Mavis. The woman's eyes seemed to clear. But as Mimi watched, the look on Mavis's face went well beyond anything rational. She looked sad—deeply sad—and Mimi had the feeling that Mavis was realizing the terrible lunacy of what she was doing.

"He'll never give me anything," she muttered. She lowered the gun but not far. "Why would I have thought Marc would ever give me anything?"

She seemed to actually be asking the question, and Mimi was about to answer her when she saw something out of the corner of her eye. Her foam mattress moved. She stared into Mavis's eyes, hoping the woman wouldn't see the hope in her own eyes.

"Let me try him again," she said. "He might have just been on another call."

Behind the woman with the gun, the trapdoor was opening slowly, silently. Mavis, oblivious, only shook her head. "Don't bother," she said. "Don't bother to call."

"Let me try," said Mimi, her voice a little shrill.

"No," said Mavis, her voice resigned. "I didn't think this through very well." Then she smiled, as if a new idea had come to her. "Wait a minute. Wait a minute. Maybe you *should* phone him. Yes. It isn't what Marc should give to me that matters," she said, her voice getting louder, more enthusiastic. "It's what I should give to him."

"Okay," said Mimi. "So I phone him again?"

"Yes," said Mavis, her eyes wide now, as if everything was suddenly becoming clear. "You phone him. And after you say hello, I talk to him, tell him where we are, the two of us. Tell him exactly where we are and that I've got a gun. And he starts talking about all the things he's going to give me so that I don't shoot you. And maybe I say, 'I've heard that before, Marc Soto.' I say that and then, with him right there on the other end of the line, I do it."

"Do what?"

"It. You. Shoot you."

The mattress erupted behind them as the trapdoor flew back on its chains, and in the same moment that Mavis spun around and Mimi drew the canister, Cramer emerged, head and shoulders, from the hidey-hole, his arm shooting out across the floor, grabbing Mavis by the ankles and pulling her off her feet.

She crashed to the ground, and her flailing arm knocked the canister right out of Mimi's hand. Mavis writhed on the floor, kicking out at Cramer's grasping hands.

"Run!" shouted Cramer.

Mimi pasted herself against the wall behind Mavis, inching toward the door, but Mavis, from where she lay, twisted around, so that the gun was aimed up at Mimi.

"Mimi!" Now Jay was at the bedroom door, and Mavis swung around to face him.

"Don't do it!" screamed Cramer, clawing at his mother's leg.

"You!" said Mavis, swinging her attention back to him. *"You!"*

Then the gun went off. The trapdoor shuddered with the impact of the shot, and Cramer, howling in pain, crumpled out of sight.

≽| CHAPTER THIRTY-FIVE |≼

THERE WAS A MAN STANDING on the bridge over the snye, squinting into the light of the Mini Cooper's headlights, holding up his hands to shade his eyes. His shoulders were hunched, pelted by the rain. It wasn't even six, but the storm clouds made it seem like twilight. Jay switched off the lights but not the ignition. The guy was his age but looked huge somehow, standing like that alone on the crumbling bridge, muscular, his head shaved, dressed only in a T-shirt and black jeans. Cramer.

He wiped his face with both hands, squinting from the rain. It was still coming down hard. He waved his arm urgently, then made his way toward the car. Instinctively, Jay locked the doors. What was going on? Where was Mimi? But now Cramer was at his window, his hands pressed against the glass, framing his face, and his face was filled with earnestness and fear. His mouth was moving.

He was saying something. Jay turned off the engine. "Mimi!" he said, pointing toward the house. "Hurry!" Jay nodded and Cramer stepped back to let him out. Jay opened the door.

"It's Mimi," said Cramer. "She's in trouble."

"What did you do to her?"

Cramer looked exhausted. He shook his head. "Have you got a cell phone?" Jay nodded. "Call the cops. And you'd better call for an ambulance, too."

"What the hell—"

"Just do it!" said Cramer, his voice urgent but not much above a whisper. Jay climbed back in the car, to make the call out of the rain. He punched in 911. Cramer was looking back toward the house, his fists coiled, his face filled with a gravity that frightened Jay. He made the connection, gave the directions.

"Tell them she's got a gun!"

"What?"

Cramer swore and grabbed the phone from Jay. "There's a crazy woman with a gun," he said. "Hurry!" Then he handed the phone back to Jay.

"You get that?" said Jay. The dispatcher did.

"Do not attempt a rescue," she said. He flipped the phone shut and jumped out of the vehicle, because Cramer was already hotfooting it back toward the bridge.

"They said not to try anything."

Cramer turned and cried out in a harsh whisper, "Don't slam the door!"

Jay caught the door in midflight and closed it quietly. Then he ran to catch up.

"They said not to try rescuing her," he said.

"Shhh," said Cramer. "Keep it down."

"But—"

Cramer turned to him, his face stern. "I heard you. I just don't know if we've got that option."

They had to cross the plank portion of the bridge single file, but as soon as they were on the other side, Jay caught up with Cramer. "For God's sake, tell me *something*!"

Cramer took Jay by the arm. "It's so fucked up."

"But—"

Cramer's hold on his arm tightened painfully. "Just stay with me," he said. "We can do this, right?" Then he was moving again, without waiting for an answer, moving in a crouch as if someone in the house might see them. There was a bag attached to his belt and banging against his hip. They moved swiftly up the wet lawn to the house and stopped, near the shed.

"What do we do?" whispered Jay.

Cramer was breathing hard. His face was filled with consternation, but his eyes were quick with possibility, and Jay stopped pressing him. Under the shed roof, the noise was deafening from the rain on the tin. "They're in the bedroom," he said. "I'm going to go in through the storm door—"

"You can't," said Jay. "I locked it."

Cramer shook his head. "I know," he said. "I can get

in." His eyes slid away from Jay's, embarrassed, but Jay didn't press it.

"So I'll go in the back door," said Jay. "The noise of the rain will cover any noise." Cramer nodded, then looked down.

"Take off your shoes," he said. "Get as close to the bedroom door as you can. I could see through a crack in the curtains; the bedroom door's open. Be ready, okay?"

"For what?"

"I don't know," said Cramer. "I don't the fuck know!" His eyes were filled with pain. He swallowed.

"So, be ready for anything," said Jay. "Any opportunity."

"Right," said Cramer. His eyes widened. He nodded. "Yeah."

So it was half a plan, but at least it was something. Then Cramer punched Jay on the arm—comrades—and disappeared around the shed.

It was like some nightmarish game. For all Jay knew, Cramer was nuts! But he didn't look nuts. He looked scared shitless. And, anyway, it was Cramer who'd suggested calling the cops.

As soon as he opened the kitchen door, he heard voices: Mimi's voice and the voice of another woman. There was an edge to her voice that confirmed the panic Jay had seen in Cramer's eyes. He crept through the kitchen in his stocking feet, turned left, and slid along the wall toward the open bedroom door.

The woman's voice grew louder, more strident, more threatening. They were talking about Marc, about a phone call. Jay hardly dared to breathe. He tried to place the figures in the room by the sound of their voices. Mimi was facing his direction; the stranger must have her back to the door. It would be safe to look, he thought, unless Mimi saw him and the woman noticed. But if she did—if she turned—maybe Mimi could hit her or something. No, it was too dangerous. And then suddenly nothing was as dangerous as what the woman was saying.

"Do what?"

"It. You. Shoot you."

Jay hurled himself into the room just as the trapdoor flew open, and Cramer exploded up out of the hole like a jack-in-the-box. The woman crashed to the floor. Her hand flew out as she fell and hit Mimi's hand, sending her mace canister flying.

"Run!" shouted Cramer.

"Mimi!" shouted Jay.

And then everything was happening too fast.

Jay dragged Mimi out of the room and there was a gunshot and Cramer howled with pain and the woman screamed.

"He's hit!" cried Mimi, and Jay clamped her hard around the waist to stop her from going back in there.

Then the gun went off again, and Mimi didn't need any urging to leave. They skittered through the kitchen and out the door into the shed.

"I called 911 fifteen minutes ago," he yelled into her ear. "The cops are on their way."

"He's hit!" yelled Mimi. "She killed him."

"They're sending an ambulance, too. Come on. There's nothing we can do!"

She was sobbing. She turned to him, looking lost and small, and he threw his arm around her, glancing over her shoulder, nervously, at the kitchen door, expecting to see the madwoman any minute. "Come," he said. "Quick."

They ran, hand in hand, down through the sopping grass toward the snye and were halfway there when they heard the third shot. They were far enough away now to stop and look back through the drifting veils of rain at the little house. And then they heard the sirens.

≥| CHAPTER THIRTY-SIX |≤

THE GUNSHOTS OF THAT NIGHT would stay with Mimi for a long time. It was as if the bullets had exploded inside her head and her bloodstream had carried the fragments to every cell in her body. She imagined minuscule shards of metal lodged in the mitochondria, or whatever subcellular organism it was that stored foreign bodies. So deep was the sense of those gunshots, Mimi wondered were she ever to have children whether the shots would be part of their memories, too.

The first bullet had ricocheted off the open trapdoor and smashed downward through Cramer's cheek, fracturing his upper jaw and jawbone and lodging in the anterior skull base. In an emergency craniotomy, his contused brain was cleared of damaged flesh and metal splinters, the fractured bone plugged with bone wax and mashed muscle taken from the fascia lata of Cramer's thigh. There were tubes to help him breathe and to keep down the orofacial swelling. There were cerebral decongestants being dripped into his head and antibiotics to fend off meningitis. There were anticonvulsants.

There were so many things that still might happen. Time would tell if there had been traumatic brain injury.

Mavis Lee was dead. That was the third shot. And Mimi found herself trying to imagine the madwoman's last few minutes. What happened between shooting her son and shooting herself? Did she look down into the hole where Cramer lay, half his face shattered, and realize who he was? Because Mimi was pretty sure it wasn't Cramer that Mavis thought she was firing at. "You," she said. *"You!"* There was so much in those words. Surprise mixed with some kind of weird delight in the first "you" and then utter, soul-wrenching fury in the second. Did she think it was Marc? Was it Marc's blue eyes she saw peering up at her from that face emerging as if from the grave? Is that who she intended to kill? And when she was alone, did she come to her senses long enough to realize that she had it all wrong?

The police dug the second bullet out of the wall above the desk in the front room. It was lodged in the plaster not a foot from where Mavis's initials and phone number were framed in pencil-crayon splendor. The irony was incidental and unintended. Mavis had been shooting at someone in the doorway—two someones—who were there one moment but gone by the time the gun went off. Jay had saved Mimi's life. And Cramer had saved her life, too, and might still lose his own.

He had been airlifted from Ladybank to the city, where he underwent a series of operations. Even when they moved him from intensive care, his head wrapped up like a mummy and with only his left eye and ear exposed, he was still unconscious. His one visible eye was closed, but Mimi watched it twitch, imagining he was trying to say something and trying to decipher this inarticulate language. She spoke to him, to his one open ear, imagining he could hear her—needing for him to hear her.

"We found the bag you left," she said softly, "with the picture in it and the stone." His eye twitched and she looked, hopefully, at Jay, who was sitting silently on a chair on the other side of the bed. He didn't believe the twitches were communication at all, but he was being indulgent about it. "Thank you, Cramer," she said. "It means a lot to us that you returned the things you took."

Mimi came often to the hospital. She had found a brother and then a second brother. It was the summer of discovering brothers, and she was going to do everything in her power not to lose either of them. All she could do right now, however, was be there, bear witness. At first, even the thought of Cramer's broken face made her feel sick. But she found herself drawn into his medical care, wanting to know about it in every detail. It became less gory the more she learned. The injury, the materials and methods required to reconstruct his face: she found that her repulsion eased as her interest grew. She asked questions— too many questions, Jay thought. She demanded to know how words were spelled so she could ask Dr. Lou what they meant or Google them herself. So "proptosis" was the displacement of the eyeball, and "pneumocephalus" was the presence of air in the brain cavity, and "hematoma" was the mass of clotted blood that formed in the tissues and body space as a result of broken blood vessels, and "debridement" meant the surgical removal of lacerated and contaminated tissue. She wrote these things down and wrestled them into the form of a report. In her clinical account of Cramer's suffering, she felt as if she was writing something that mattered. She had played at writing that summer. Writing fanciful scenes loosely based on her life. But this—this was hard and important. It was training, she thought, good training, she wasn't sure for what.

What she did know was that she was writing it for a very particular audience. She had told her father next to nothing so far about the extraordinary events of that summer. So she was going to write an account of meeting Jackson and Cramer and of what had happened in the end. The account, especially the last bit, would be in painful detail. Excruciating detail. Through the police, she was able to get a copy of the autopsy report of Mavis Lee. She was part of the story. Mimi would lay all this at her father's feet. She wanted him to know in a very itemized way what he had done when he promised Mavis Lee that he would marry her, what happened when you walk out on people.

"Isn't that a bit simplistic?" Jay asked. She nodded. She knew it was. "I mean, that's what Marc's going to say."

"I know," said Mimi. "He can say what he wants, he can deny what he wants, but he's going to hear about this."

"Do you think it will make any difference?"

She shook her head. "I doubt it."

"Maybe he never made such a promise to Mavis," said Dr. Lou. "This poor woman was clearly unstable. Maybe she built it up in her mind."

Mimi thought about that seriously, but it didn't change her mind. She had known Mavis Lee for something like half an hour—the longest half hour of her whole life—and she was clearly nuts. But as far as Mimi could tell, Marc had pledged something to that woman when he got her pregnant, whatever he might think, whatever he might say to the contrary.

"How do we know Cramer is really Marc's son?" said Jo.

"His eyes," said Mimi. And nobody questioned it.

"She may have been crazy even back then," said Mimi. "It doesn't matter. The truth is that my father is not a man who keeps promises."

She had a plan. Marc owed Cramer something, and she was going to see he got it.

"Sounds like emotional blackmail," said Jo.

"You bet. Big-time."

"He's twenty-two," said Jay. "He's not a kid."

"He might be too proud," said Lou. "Might not want to have anything to do with Marc."

"Maybe," said Mimi. "I wouldn't blame him. But I dropped in to see Hank Pretty, and he thinks Cramer has got what it takes to go to college. So I think Marc ought to do that for him at least."

Jay stared at her. "You went to see Pretty?"

"Somebody had to tell him what was happening. Anyway, if Cramer wants to go back to school, I'm going to make sure Marc pays up." She had decided that Cramer, whatever else he had done, had acted as her guardian. She just wanted to return the favor. All of this she would bring to her father's attention.

"Do you hate Marc?" Jay asked.

She shook her head. "It's not about love or hate; it's about right or wrong. I'm not going to let Marc off easy."

The cops arrested Waylin Pitney two hundred miles north of Ottawa on Highway 117, in the middle of La Verendrye Provincial Park, on his way back to Val-d'Or. The Taurus had broken down, and an officer with La Sûreté du Québec had stopped to help out, only to end up arresting him. In a surprising act of clarity, Mavis had phoned the police after the beating she had suffered at Pitney's hands. He had tried to kill her, she said, only she had held him off with his own gun before he had done too much damage. She told the police he had stolen her car and was traveling with several thousand dollars he had stolen from her and a valuable emerald necklace. She saved for last telling them about the panel truck filled with televisions that she had driven into Butchard's Creek.

Decisions had to be made. Cramer was holding stable now, and the worst was passed, but recovery would be a long and painful ordeal. There was the risk of meningitis, cerebrospinal fluid leakage, rhinorrhea, hydrocephalus, brain abscess. He would need medical attention when he left the hospital, and it would be awhile before he worked again. So Lou and Jo decided that, if Cramer wanted to, he could come and live with them.

"How do you feel about it?" Mimi asked Jay. They were driving to Ottawa again. It was late August. Soon she would have to go if she was returning to school. And she wanted to return to school, though she wasn't sure anymore about what she ultimately wanted to do.

"I'm good," said Jay, not looking her way. She waited. There was more and she wanted to give him the space to get it out. She was learning about that. "I mean I really hated him," said Jay. "I hated the guy who was breaking into my house, screwing with my head. But that wasn't the same guy I met the day . . . the day we . . ."

"I know which day you mean."

Jay swallowed hard and looked out the window at the dull scenery along Highway 7, on the outskirts of the city, the swampy land, the dead trees, the endless construction of new lanes. "I have this picture in my head of the way he looked when I got back to the house in that storm. He was standing on the bridge over the snye with the rain just pouring down on him. He was scary—intimidating. Like Frankenstein's monster. But when he talked to me, I could see that he was scared, too. Not just scared about what was happening in the house, not just scared about you. Scared at meeting me like that. Scared of me in a way. I guess he was going to try to do something on his own, then he saw the car and had to deal with me first so I didn't screw everything up."

"He needed you," said Mimi.

"Yeah," said Jay. "He did. He even said it. But it took me awhile to figure it out—later, I mean. At first I thought he was just coming to warn me, but he needed help."

"Of course he did. Shit, can you imagine? His own mother."

They were quiet for a while, both of them thinking about the scene in that little house in the middle of a storm in the middle of nowhere and how it all played out and how many other ways it might have gone down.

"Anyway," said Jay. "You asked how I felt about him living with Lou and Jo, and it's okay. It's better than okay. And it's not just something we *should* do, a duty. It's . . . I don't know exactly." He paused. "It's right," he said.

Mimi merged onto the 417. The hospital was twenty minutes away.

Jay laughed. "This sibling business is hell," he said.

"Who knew?" said Mimi, and grinned a little maniacally, as she flicked on her indicator light to pass a truck. "But, apparently, it's always like this."

"Oh, really?"

"Well, not quite like this. Jamila said something to me the other night when we were talking. She said when her younger brother was born, it really pissed her off. It was such an intrusion."

And they thought about that. About intrusions. How Mimi had burst into Jay's life two troubling months ago and how Cramer had been there already like something circling, planning to land, and then been born into their lives two weeks ago in a startling and bloody birth. Each of them had been unwelcome, uninvited. And yet they knew—Mimi and Jay did, anyway—that they were ready to spend the rest of their lives learning how to do this, how to welcome in the outsider and to become family. This most unlikely of families.

Had he heard the other shots when he lay in the bottom of the hidey-hole? Had Mavis spoken to him, apologized, cried over his battered body, said some final words? Or had he only overheard what had happened to her, while lying here in this dim room drifting in and out of consciousness? Had Mimi explained to him about his mother's death, or was it just her absence that let him know she was gone?

However it was that he knew, he had grieved alone in his darkness. He has missed her and ached for her and been furious at her for dying and finally, all on his own, come to a place of her being gone. The only question was how long she had been gone. It seemed like a long time now.

Mimi's hand was on his chest. She loosened the sheet that the nurse had just tightened. Jay was there, too, a little way off, as always. But his voice had sounded okay when he'd said hello. Like he wanted to be there.

"Do you know who I am?" Mimi asked, her voice soft and yet firm. "Do you know, Cramer, who I really am?" He wanted to nod. He wanted to take her hand and grip it tight and let her know. "How much did you hear before you opened the trapdoor?" she asked.

He had heard enough, enough to know who Mimi was. It changed everything and didn't change anything. He would have to try to explain that to her somehow. Find words to let her know that it was okay. Not to worry. There were so many words he was going to have to find. Words to apologize with, for one thing. He would somehow have to find a way to repay them for the harm he had brought upon them, the evil he had brought into their midst.

"We're here for you," said Mimi. "Right, Jay?"

"Right," said Jay. "But you're going to have to come out of hiding."

That made Mimi laugh. And maybe it was the sound of her gritty laughter or maybe it was hearing that they were there for him, but suddenly, as if he had been holding back, Cramer found the will to open his eyes—his one good eye. And it filled up with Mimi's face, and she was smiling. His sister.

ACKNOWLEDGMENTS

Chris Creighton brought the word *snye* into my life, and not just the word, either, but the actual place. She and her husband had bought a house on "the snye," and when I went to look at it, I was utterly enchanted. It was, as Mimi says, a magical place—a place where anything might happen. Thanks so much, Chris. I also want to thank Hadley Dyer, whose editing classes at Ryerson University looked at two early drafts of this story and provided some very useful advice. Fran van Oort helped with the guitar stuff; Jack Hurd helped me to program Jay's synth; John McFarlane gave me some good computer info; and Geoff Mason supplied all the canoe know-how a person could ask for. If I got any of it wrong, it was my fault, not theirs. Thank you, friends and neighbors. I have read excerpts from this story to my wonderful colleagues and the equally wonderful student body at the Vermont College of Fine Arts—the world's best audience. What would I do without you all? And finally, as always, endless thanks to Amanda Lewis, the person who suffers through those earliest drafts without complaining and then is gracious enough to be my first reader. And still, after thirty-four years, stays with me.

Otello: black, South America's top footballer.
Desmerelda: white, pop star daughter
of a right-wing politician.

Their sudden and controversial marriage propels them
centre stage where they burn under the media spotlight.
But celebrity attracts enemies, and some are very close to
home. When a young girl is found murdered, Paul Faustino
witnesses the power of the media in creating –
and breaking – lives.

**"Peet's thrillers, with their blend of sport and homicide,
are irresistible to teenage boys."** *The Telegraph*

**WINNER OF THE GUARDIAN CHILDREN'S
FICTION PRIZE**

MAL PEET

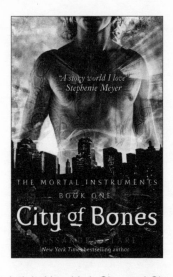

It's after dark in New York City, and Clary Fray is
seeing things. The best-looking guy in the nightclub just
stabbed a boy to death – but the victim has vanished
into thin air. Her mother has disappeared, and a hideous
monster is lurking in her apartment. With her life spiralling
into darkness, Clary realizes that she has stumbled into
an invisible war between ancient demonic forces and the
secretive Shadowhunters – a war in which she has a
fateful role to play…

**"The Mortal Instruments series is a story world
I love to live in."** *Stephenie Meyer*

During the long, hungry years of the Great Depression,
Harper Flute's family struggles to cope with life on the hot,
dusty land. Her younger brother Tin seeks refuge in the
contrast of an ancient subterranean world. A world that
nurtures but – as disturbing events in the community reveal
– can also kill. A world that is silent, yet absorbs secrets. A
world that has the power to change lives for ever.

**"A novel you can't leave alone while you are reading it,
and one that won't leave you afterwards."**
The Sunday Times

**WINNER OF THE GUARDIAN CHILDREN'S
FICTION PRIZE**